Don't get yourself noticed and you won't get yourself hanged.

PART murder mystery, part gothic fantasy, part steampunk adventure, *The Peculiar* is Stefan Bachmann's riveting, inventive, and unforgettable debut novel.

An Indie Next Top Ten Pick

"A book that, at times, recalls Dostoevsky's *Crime and Punishment*, Charles Dickens's *A Tale of Two Cities*, and more recent classics, such as J. K. Rowling's *Harry Potter* and Lemony Snicket's *A Series of Unfortunate Events*."
—*The Los Angeles Times*

"An absolute treat for readers of any age."
—*Publishers Weekly*

"Filled with healthy doses of suspense and action, this is a story young fantasy buffs are sure to enjoy."
—*The New York Times*

To listen to *Peculiar Pieces*, music written by Stefan Bachmann to accompany the book, please visit ThePeculiarBook.com.

THE PECULIAR

STEFAN BACHMANN

GREENWILLOW BOOKS

An Imprint of HarperCollins *Publishers*

The Peculiar
Copyright © 2012 by Stefan Bachmann
First published in 2012 in hardcover; first paperback edition, 2013.

The text of this book is set in 13-point Mrs. Eaves.
Book design by Paul Zakris

Library of Congress Cataloging-in-Publication Data

Bachmann, Stefan, 1993–
The Peculiar / by Stefan Bachmann.
pages cm.
"Greenwillow Books."
Summary: After humans win the faery wars in England, a half-human, half-faery child, scorned by both races, finds himself at the center of a web of intrigue and danger when he is stalked by a sinister faery.
ISBN 978-0-06-219518-0 (trade bdg.)
ISBN 978-0-06-224501-4 (intl. bdg.)
ISBN 978-0-06-219519-7 (pbk.)
[1. Fairies—Fiction. 2. Changelings—Fiction. 3. Magic—Fiction.
4. England—Fiction. 5. Fantasy. 6. Youths' writings.] I. Title.
PZ7.B132173Pe 2012 [Fic]—dc23 2012017914
13 14 15 16 17 CG/OPM 10 9 8 7 6 5 4 3 2 1
First Edition

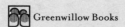
Greenwillow Books

To my mom and my sister,
who read it first
~

CONTENTS

Prologue

FEATHERS fell from the sky.

Like black snow, they drifted onto an old city called Bath. They whirled down the roofs, gathered in the corners of the alleys, and turned everything dark and silent, like a winter's day.

The townsfolk thought it odd. Some locked themselves in their cellars. Some hurried to church. Most opened umbrellas and went about their business. At four o'clock in the afternoon, a group of bird catchers set off on the road to Kentish Town, pulling their cages in a cart behind them. They were the last to see Bath as it had been, the last to leave it. Sometime in the night of the twenty-third of September, there was a tremendous noise like wings and voices, creaking branches and howling winds, and then, in the blink of an eye, Bath was gone, and all that remained were ruins, quiet and desolate under the stars.

There were no flames. No screams. Everyone within five leagues disappeared, so there was no one left to speak to the bailiff when he came riding up the next morning on his knock-kneed horse.

No one human.

A farmer found him hours later, standing in a trampled field. The bailiff's horse was gone and his boots were worn to nothing, as if he had been walking many days. "Cold," he said, with a faraway look. "Cold lips and cold hands and so peculiar."

That was when the rumors started. Monsters were crawling from the ruins of Bath, the whispers said, bone-thin fiends and giants as tall as the hills. On the nearby farms, people nailed herbs to their doorposts and tied their shutters closed with red ribbons. Three days after the city's destruction, a group of scientists came down from London to examine the place where Bath had been, and were next seen in the crown of a gnarled oak, their bodies white and bloodless, their jackets pierced through and through with twigs. After that, people locked their doors.

Weeks passed, and the rumors turned to worse things. Children disappeared from their beds. Dogs and sheep went suddenly lame. In Wales, folk went into the woods and never came out. In Swainswick, a fiddle was heard playing in the night, and all the women of the town went out in their bed-gowns and followed it. No one ever saw them again.

Thinking this might be the work of one of England's enemies, Parliament ordered a company of troops to Bath at once. The troops arrived, and though they found no rebels or Frenchmen among the tumbled stones, they did find a little battered notebook belonging to one of the scientists who had met his death in the oak. There were only a few pages of writing in it, badly splotched and very hurried, but it caused a sensation all over the country. It was published in pamphlets and newspapers, and limed up onto walls. Butchers read it, and silk weavers read it;

schoolchildren, lawyers, and dukes read it, and those who could not read had it read *to* them in taverns and town squares.

The first part was all charts and formulas, interspersed with sentimental scribblings about someone named Lizzy. But as the writing proceeded, the scientist's observations became more interesting. He wrote of the feathers that had fallen on Bath, how they were not the feathers of any bird. He wrote of mysterious footprints and strange scars in the earth. Finally he wrote of a long shadowy highway dissolving in a wisp of ash, and of creatures known only in tales. It was then that everyone knew for certain what they had been dreading all along: the Small Folk, the Hidden People, the Sidhe had passed from their place into ours. The faeries had come to England.

They came upon the troops in the night—goblins and satyrs, gnomes, sprytes, and the elegant, spindly white beings with their black, black eyes. The officer in command of the English, a well-starched man named Briggs, told them straightaway that they were suspected of great crimes and must go to London at once for interrogation, but it was a ridiculous thing, like telling the sea it must be judged for all the ships it had swallowed. The faeries had no intention of listening to these clumsy, red-clad men. They ran circles around them, hissing and teasing. A pale hand reached out to pluck at a red sleeve. A gun fired in the darkness. That was when the war started.

It was called the Smiling War because it left so many skulls, white and grinning, in the fields. There were few real battles. No great marches or heroic charges to write poems about later. Because the fay were not like men. They did not follow rules, or line up like tin soldiers.

The faeries called the birds out of the sky to peck the soldiers' eyes. They called the rain to wet their gunpowder, and asked the forests to pull up their roots and wander across the countryside to confuse English maps. But in the end the faeries' magic was no match for cannon and cavalry, and the rows of soldiers that marched among them in an endless red tide. On a great slope called Tar Hill, the British army converged on the fay and scattered them. Those that fled were shot down as they ran. The rest (and there were very many) were rounded up, counted, christened, and dragged away to the factories.

Bath became their home in this new country. It grew back a dark place, pressing up out of the rubble. The place where the highway had appeared, where everything had been utterly destroyed, became New Bath, a knot of houses and streets more than five hundred feet high, all blackened chimneys and spidery bridges wound into a ball of stinking, smoking dross.

As for the magic the faeries had brought with them, Parliament decided it was something of an affliction that must be hidden under bandages and ointments. A milkmaid in Trowbridge found that whenever a bell rang, all the enchantments around her would cease, and the hedgerows would stop their whispering, and the roads would lead only to where they had led to before, so a law was passed that commanded all the church bells in the country to toll every five minutes instead of every quarter hour. Iron had long been known as a sure protection against spells, and now little bits of it were put into everything from buttons to breadcrumbs. In the larger cities, fields were plowed up and trees chopped down because it was supposed that faeries could gather magic from the leaves and the dewdrops. Abraham Darby famously hypothesized in his dissertation *The Properties of Air* that clockwork acted as a sort of antidote to the unruly nature of the fay, and so professors and physicians and all the great minds turned their powers toward mechanics and industry. The Age of Smoke had begun.

And after a time the faeries were simply a part of England, an inseparable part, like the heather on the bleak gray moors, like the gallows on the hilltops. The goblins and gnomes and wilder faeries were quick to pick up English ways. They lived in English cities, coughed English smoke, and were soon no worse off than the thousands of human poor that toiled at their side. But the high faeries—the pale, silent Sidhe with their fine waistcoats and sly looks—they did not give in so easily. They could not forget that they had once been lords and ladies in great halls of their own. They could not forgive. The English might have won the Smiling War, but there were other ways to fight. A word could cause a riot, ink could spell a man's death, and the Sidhe knew those weapons like the backs of their hands. Oh yes, they knew.

CHAPTER I
The Most Prettiest Thing

BARTHOLOMEW Kettle saw her the moment she merged into the shadows of Old Crow Alley—a great lady dressed all in plum-colored velvets, striding up the muddy street with the bearing of a queen. He wondered if she would ever leave again. In the corpse man's barrow perhaps, or in a sack, but probably not on her own two feet.

Bartholomew closed the book he had been reading and pressed his nose against the grimy window, watching her progress down the alley. The faery slums of Bath were not kind to strangers. One moment you could be on a bustling thoroughfare, dodging tram wheels and dung piles, and trying not to be devoured by the wolves that pulled the carriages, and the next you could be hopelessly lost in a maze of narrow streets with nothing but gaunt old houses stooping overhead, blocking out the sky. If you had the ill luck to meet anyone, chances were it would be a thief. And not the dainty sort, like the thin-fingered chimney sprytes of London. Rather the sort with dirt under his nails and leaves in his hair, who, if he thought it worthwhile, would not hesitate to slit your throat.

This lady looked *very* worthwhile. Folks killed for less, Bartholomew knew. If the half-starved corpses he had seen dragged from the gutter were anything to go by, folks killed for much less.

She was so tall, so strange and foreign in her finery; she seemed to fill every nook of the murky passage. Long gloves the color of midnight covered her hands. Jewels glimmered at her throat. A little top hat with an enormous purple flower in it sat on her head. It was perched at an angle so that it cast a shadow over her eyes.

"Hettie," Bartholomew whispered, without turning from the window. "Hettie, come look."

Feet pattered in the depths of the room. A little girl appeared next to him. She was too thin, her face all sharp bones and pale skin, tinged blue from lack of sunlight. Ugly, like him. Her eyes were huge and round, black puddles collecting in the hollows of her skull. The tips of her ears were pointed. In a pinch Bartholomew might still pass as a human child, but not Hettie. There was no mistaking the faery blood in her veins. For where Bartholomew had a mess of chestnut hair growing out of his scalp, Hettie had the smooth, bare branches of a young tree.

She pushed a wayward twig out of her eyes and let out a little gasp.

"Oh, Barthy," she breathed, clutching at his hand. "It's the most prettiest thing I've seen in my whole *life*." He went onto his knees next to her, so that both their faces were just peeking over the worm-eaten wood of the sill.

Pretty indeed, but there was a wrongness about the lady outside. Something dark and unsettled. She carried no baggage or cloak, not even a parasol to shield herself from the heat of late summer. As if she had stepped from the shadowy hush of a drawing room directly into the heart of Bath's faery district. Her gait was stiff and jerking, as though she didn't exactly know how to work her appendages.

"What d'you suppose she's doing here?" Bartholomew asked. He began to gnaw slowly at his thumbnail.

Hettie frowned. "I dunno. She might be a lady thief. Mummy says they dress pretty. But isn't she far too splendid for a thief? Doesn't she look like . . ." Hettie glanced at him, and a flicker of fear passed behind her eyes. "Like she's looking for something?"

Bartholomew stopped chewing his nail. He peered at his sister. Then he squeezed her hand. "She's not looking for us, Het."

But even as he said it, he felt the uneasiness curl like a root in his stomach. She *was* looking for something. Or someone. Her eyes, half hidden in the shadow of her hat, were searching, studying the houses as she moved past them. When her gaze fell on the house they lived in, Bartholomew ducked down under the sill. Hettie was already there. *Don't get yourself noticed and you won't get yourself hanged.* It was perhaps the most important rule for changelings. It was a good rule.

The lady in the plum-colored dress walked the full length of the alley, all the way to the corner where it wormed into Black Candle Lane. Her skirts dragged over the cobbles, becoming heavy with the oily filth that covered everything, but she didn't seem to care. She simply turned slowly and made her way back down the alley, this time inspecting the houses on the other side.

She must have gone up and down Old Crow Alley six or seven times before coming to a halt in front of the house directly across the way from where Bartholomew and Hettie watched. It was an ancient, sharp-roofed house, with chimneys and doors that poked through the stone in odd places. Two larger houses stood on either side, pinching it in, and it was set a little farther back from the alley, behind a high stone wall. An archway was set into the wall in the middle. The twisted remains of a metal gate lay on the ground. The lady stepped over it and into the yard.

Bartholomew knew who lived in that house. A family of half-bloods, the mother a faery, the father a bellows worker at the cannon foundry on Leechcraft Street. The Buddelbinsters, he'd heard them called. Once they'd had seven changeling children, and Bartholomew had seen them playing in the windows and the doorways. But other people had seen them, too, and one night a crowd had come and dragged the children away. Now there was only one, a frail-looking boy with thistle-hair. Bartholomew and he were friends. At least Bartholomew liked to think they were. Some days, when Old Crow Alley was particularly quiet, the boy would steal out onto the cobbles and fight invisible highwaymen with a bit of stick. He would catch sight of Bartholomew staring at him from the window. The boy would wave. Bartholomew would wave back. It was utterly forbidden—waving at people through windows—but so wonderful to do that Bartholomew forgot sometimes.

The lady in the plum-colored dress stalked across

the rubble-strewn yard and rapped on the door nearest to the ground. Nothing happened for what felt like an age. Then the door was yanked open to the end of its chain, and a thin, sour-looking woman poked her head through the gap. It was the father's old-maid sister. She lived with the Buddelbinsters, minded their business for them. That included opening the doors when they were knocked on. Bartholomew watched her eyes grow round as saucers as she drank in the sight of the exquisite stranger. She opened her mouth to say something. Then she seemed to think better of it and slammed the door in the lady's face.

The lady in the plum-colored dress stood very still for a moment, as if she didn't quite understand what had happened. Then she knocked on the door again, so loudly it echoed out of the yard, all the way up Old Crow Alley. A few houses away, a curtain twitched.

Before Bartholomew and Hettie could see what would happen next, the stairs outside the door to the rooms they lived in began to creak noisily. Someone was hurrying up them. Next, a red-cheeked woman burst in, huffing and wiping her hands on her apron.

She was small and badly dressed and would have been lovely with enough to eat, but there was never enough to eat, so she looked somewhat wilted and bothered. When she saw the two of them on the floor she clapped her hands to her mouth and shrieked.

"Children, get away from the window!" In three steps she had crossed the room and was dragging them up by their arms. "Bartholomew, her branches were sticking right up over the sill. Do you want to get *seen*?"

She shooed them to the back of the room and bolted the door to the passage. Then she spun on them. Her eyes fell on the potbellied stove. Ash flitted out through the slats in its door.

"Oh, would you look at that," she said. "I asked you to empty it, Barthy. I asked you to watch out for your sister, and wind up the wash wringer. You've done nothing . . ."

In an instant Bartholomew had all but forgotten the lady in plum. "Mother, I'm sorry I forgot about Hettie's branches, but I found something out, and I had a very good idea, and I need to explain it to you."

"I don't want to hear it," his mother said wearily. "I want you to do as you're told."

"But that's just it, I won't have to!" He cleared his throat, drew himself up to his full height of three and a half feet, and said, "Mother, may I please, please, *please* summon a domesticated faery?"

"A what? What are you talking about, child? Who's that in the Buddelbinsters' yard?"

"A domesticated faery. It means it lives in houses. I want to invite a faery servant. I've read about it here and here, and here it explains how to do it." Bartholomew lifted a heap of old books from behind the stove and pushed them up under his mother's nose. "*Please*, Mother?"

"Larks and stage lights, would you look at that dress. Barthy, put those books down, I can't see properly."

"Mother, a faery! For houses!"

"Must be worth twenty pounds, and what does the silly goose do? Marches down here through all this muck. I do declare. Rusty cogs in that head and nothing but."

"And if I get a good one, and I'm nice to it, it would do all sorts of work for us and help pump the water and—"

His mother wasn't looking out the window anymore. Her eyes had gone stony-flat, and she was staring at Bartholomew.

"—wind up the wash wringer," he finished weakly.

"And what if you get a *bad* one." It wasn't a question. Her voice drove up between his ribs like a shard of nasty iron. "I'll tell you what, Bartholomew Kettle. I'll tell you! If we're lucky it'll sour the milk, empty our cupboards, and run off with every shiny thing it can get its fingers on. Otherwise it'll just throttle us in our sleep. No, child. No. Don't you *ever* be inviting faeries through that door. They're upstairs and downstairs and on the other side of the wall. They're all around us for miles and miles, but not in here. Not again, do you understand me?"

She looked so old all of a sudden. Her hands shook against her apron and tears shone at the corners of her eyes. Hettie, solemn and silent like a little ghost, retreated to her cupboard bed and climbed in, closing the door with the most accusing look. Bartholomew stared at his mother. She stared back. Then he turned and slammed through the door into the passageway.

He heard her cry out after him, but he didn't stop. *Don't get yourself noticed, don't let them see.* His bare feet were quiet on the floorboards as he fled up through the house, but he wished he could shout and stomp. He *wanted* a faery. More than anything else in the world.

He had already imagined exactly how it should happen. He would set up the invitation, and the next day there would be a petal-winged pisky clinging to the top of his bedpost. It would have a foolish grin on its face, and large ears, and it wouldn't notice at all that Bartholomew was small and ugly and different from everyone else.

But no. Mother had to ruin everything.

At the top of the house they lived in together with various thieves and murderers and faeries was a large and complicated attic. It ran this way and that under the sagging eaves, and when Bartholomew was little it had been filled with broken furniture and all sorts of interesting and exciting rubbish. Everything interesting and exciting had deserted it now, the rubbish having all been used as kindling during the bitter winter months or swapped for trinkets from the traveling faery peddlers. Sometimes the women crept up to hang their washing so that it could dry without being stolen, but otherwise the attic was left to the devices of the dust and the thrushes.

And to Bartholomew. There was one part where, if he was very careful, he could squeeze through a gap between a beam and the rough stone of a chimney. Then, with much wriggling and twisting, he would arrive in a forgotten little gable. It did not belong to anyone. There was no door, and only a child could even stand up in it. It was his now.

He had fixed it up with odds and ends that he had salvaged—a straw mat, some dry branches and strands of ivy, and a collection of broken bottles that he had strung together in a pitiful copy of a Yuletide garland he had read about. But his favorite part of the attic was the small round window, like the sort in a boat, that looked out onto Old Crow Alley and a sea of roofs. He never tired of looking through it. He could watch the whole world from there, high up and hidden away.

Bartholomew forced himself through the gap and lay panting on the floor. It was hot under the slates of the roof. The sun hammered down outside, turning everything brittle and sharp, and after that mad rush up seventy-nine uneven steps to the tip of the house, he felt like a little loaf under the pointed gable, baking.

As soon as he had caught his breath, he crawled to the window. He could see across the alley and the high wall, directly into the Buddelbinsters' yard. The lady was still there, a blot of purple amid the brown rooftops and scraggly, sunburnt weeds. The sour-looking woman had opened the door again. She appeared to be listening to the lady warily, her hands clamping and unclamping the gray braid that hung over her shoulder. Then the lady in plum was slipping her something. *A little purse?* He couldn't see it properly. The sour one retreated back into the house, all hunched up and greedy, like a rat that has found a scrap of meat and is determined not to share it with anyone.

The instant the door closed, the lady in plum became a whirl of activity. She dropped to the ground, skirts pooling around her, and plucked something from inside her top hat. A small bottle caught the sunlight and glinted in her hand. She bit off the seal, uncorked it, and began dribbling its contents in a circle around her.

Bartholomew leaned forward, squinting through the thick glass. It occurred to him that he was likely the only one who could see her now. Other eyes had been following her since the moment she stepped into the alley. He knew that. But now the lady was deep in the yard, and any other watchers in the alley would see nothing but the high and crumbling wall. The lady in plum had chosen the Buddelbinster house on purpose. She didn't *want* to be seen.

When the bottle was empty, she held it up and ground it between her fingers, letting the shards fall to the weeds. Then she rose abruptly and faced the house, looking as poised and elegant as ever.

Several minutes passed. The door opened again, a little uncertainly. This time a child stuck his head out. It was the boy, Bartholomew's friend. Like Hettie, his faery blood showed clear as the moon through his white, white skin. A thicket of red thistles grew from his head. His ears were long and pointed. Someone must have shoved him from behind because he came tumbling out of the door and onto the ground at the lady's feet. He stared up at her, eyes wide.

The lady's back was toward Bartholomew, but he knew she was talking to the boy by the way he kept shaking his head in a small, fearful way. The boy glanced timidly back at his house. The lady took a step toward him.

Then a great many things happened at once. Bartholomew, staring so intently, nodded forward a bit so that the tip of his nose brushed against the windowpane. And the moment it did, there was a quick, sharp movement in the yard below, and the lady reached behind her and jerked apart the coils of hair at the back of her head. Bartholomew's blood turned to smoke in his veins. There, staring directly up at him, was another face, a tiny, brown, ugly face like a twisted root, all wrinkles and sharp teeth.

With a muffled yelp, he scrabbled away from the window, splinters driving into his palms. *It didn't see me, it didn't see me. It couldn't ever have known I was here.*

But it had. Those wet black eyes had looked into his. For an instant they had been filled with a terrible anger. And then the creature's lips had curled back and it had smiled.

Bartholomew lay gasping on the floorboards, heart pounding inside his skull. *I'm dead now. So, so dead.* He didn't look very much like a half-blood, did he? From down in the yard he would look like a regular boy. He pinched his eyes closed. *A regular boy spying on her.*

Very slowly he brought his head back level with the window, this time keeping deep in the shadows. The lady in plum had moved a little ways distant from the boy in the yard. Her other, hideous face was gone, hidden under her hair. One long, velvet-gloved hand was extended, beckoning.

The boy looked at her, looked back again at his

house. For the shortest instant, Bartholomew thought he saw someone in one of the upper windows, a stooping shadow, hand raised against the pane in farewell. One blink later and it was gone, and the window was empty.

The boy in the yard shivered. He turned back to the lady. She nodded, and he moved toward her, taking her outstretched hand. She clasped him close. There was a burst of darkness, a storm of black wings flapping. It exploded up around them, screaming toward the sky. A ripple passed through the air. Then they were gone, and Old Crow Alley was sleeping once again.

CHAPTER II
A Privy Deception

ARTHUR Jelliby was a very nice young man, which was perhaps the reason why he had never made much of a politician. He was a member of Parliament not because he was particularly clever or good at anything, but because his mother was a Hessian princess very well connected and had gotten him the position while playing croquet with the Duke of Norfolk. So while the other officials were fairly bursting their silken waistcoats with ambition, plotting the downfall of their rivals over oyster dinners, or at the very least informing themselves on affairs of state, Mr. Jelliby was far more interested in spending long afternoons at his club in Mayfair, buying chocolates for his pretty wife, or simply sleeping until noon.

Which is what he did on a certain day in August, and which is why the urgent summons to a Privy Council in the Houses of Parliament caught him completely unprepared.

He stumbled down the stairs of his house on Belgrave Square, one hand trying to get the worst of the tangles out of his hair, the other struggling with the tiny buttons of his cherry-red waistcoat.

"Ophelia!" he called, trying to sound cheerful but not really succeeding.

His wife appeared in the doorway to the morning room, and he pointed an apologetic finger at the length of black silk that hung limply under his collar. "The valet's off, and Brahms doesn't know how, and I cannot *do* it on my own! Knot it up for me, darling, won't you, and spare us a smile?"

"Arthur, you must not sleep so long," Ophelia said sternly, coming forward to tie his cravat. Mr. Jelliby was a tall man, and broad-shouldered, and she rather small, so she had to stand on tiptoes to reach.

"Oh, but I need to set an example! Think of the headlines: 'War averted! Thousands of lives saved! The English Parliament slept through its session.' You'd find the world a far more pleasant place."

This did not sound nearly as witty as it had in his head, but Ophelia laughed anyway, and Mr. Jelliby, feeling very amusing, sallied forth into the noise of the city.

It was a fine day by London's standards. Which meant it was a day slightly less likely to suffocate you and poison your lungs. The black curtain of smoke from the city's million chimneys had been worn away by last night's rain. The air still tasted of coal, but shafts of light sprang down through the clouds. Government-issue automatons creaked through the streets on rusty joints, sweeping the mud in front of them and leaving puddles of oil behind them. A group of lamplighters was out feeding wasps and dragonflies to the little flame faeries that sat behind the glass in the streetlamps, dull and sulky until nightfall.

Mr. Jelliby turned into Chapel Street, hand raised

for a cab. High overhead, a great iron bridge arched, groaning and showering sparks as the steam trains rumbled across it. On normal days Mr. Jelliby would have been riding up there, head against the glass, gazing idly out over the city. Or perhaps he would have had Brahms, the footman, heave him onto his newfangled bicycle and give a good push to get him started across the cobbles. But today was not normal. Today he hadn't even breakfasted, and so everything felt spoiled and hurried.

The carriage that stopped for him was driven by a gnome, sharp-toothed and old, with gray-green skin like a slimy rock. The gnome drove his horses as if they were a pair of giant snails, and when Mr. Jelliby knocked his walking stick against the carriage ceiling and shouted for a quickening of pace, he was thrown back into his seat by a volley of curses. Mr. Jelliby frowned and thought of all sorts of reasons why he should not be talked to so, but he didn't open his mouth for the rest of the journey.

Westminster's great new clock tower was ringing thirty-five minutes when he alighted on the curb in

Great George Street. *Drat.* He was late. Five minutes late. He dashed up the steps to St. Stephen's Porch and pushed past the doorkeeper, into the vast expanse of the main hall. Huddles of gentlemen stood scattered across the floor, their voices echoing in the rafters high above. The air stank of lime and fresh paint. Scaffolding clung to the walls in places, and some of the tile work was unfinished. It was not three months since the new Westminster Palace had been opened for meetings. The old one had been reduced to a pile of ash after a disgruntled fire spirit blew himself up in its cellars.

Mr. Jelliby hurried up a staircase, along an echoing, lamp-lined corridor. He was almost pleased when he saw he was not the only one late. John Wednesday Lickerish, Lord Chancellor and first Sidhe ever to be appointed to the British government, was also running behind the swiftly ticking hands of his timepiece. He rounded a corner from one direction, Mr. Jelliby came from the other, and they barreled into each other with some force.

"Oh! Mr. Lickerish! Do forgive me." Jelliby

laughed, helping the faery gentleman to his feet and slapping some imaginary dust from his lapels. "A bit clumsy this morning, I'm afraid. Are you all right?"

Mr. Lickerish gave Mr. Jelliby a withering look, and removed himself from Jelliby's grip with a faint air of distaste. He was dressed to perfection, as always, every button in place, every snippet of fabric beautiful and new. His waistcoat was black velvet. His cravat was cloth of silver, faultlessly knotted, and everywhere Mr. Jelliby looked he caught a glimpse of leaf stitchery, of silk stockings, and cotton starched so stiff you could crack it with a mallet. *It only makes the dirt stand out more,* he thought. He had to bite his tongue to keep from smiling. Brown half-moons looked up from under the faery's fingernails, as if he had been clawing about in the cold earth.

"Morning?" the faery said. His voice was thin. Just a rustle, like wind in leafless branches. "Young Jelliby, it is no longer morning. It is not even noon. It is almost night."

Mr. Jelliby looked uncertain. He didn't exactly know what the faery had just said, but he supposed it not very polite to be called young. For all he knew, the faery gentleman was not a day older than himself. It was hard to tell, really. Mr. Lickerish was a high faery, and like all high faeries he was the size of a small boy, had no hair at all, and his skin was as white and smooth as the marble under his shoes.

"Well," Mr. Jelliby said brightly. "We're very late, whatever the case." And much to the faery gentleman's annoyance, he kept pace with him all the way to the privy chamber, talking amiably about the weather and wine merchants and how his summer cottage in Cardiff had almost been blown into the sea.

The room in which the Privy Council was expected to meet was a small one, dark-paneled, at the heart of the building, its diamond-paned windows overlooking a hawthorn tree and the court. Rows of high-backed chairs crowded the floor, all but two of them already filled. The Speaker of the Council, one Lord Horace V. Something-or-other (Mr. Jelliby could never remember his name) sat perched at its center, at a sort of podium artfully carved with fauns and sagging clusters of grapes. The Speaker must have been dozing because he sat up with a start when they entered.

"Ah," he said, folding his hands across his ample girth and frowning. "It appears Mr. Jelliby and the Lord Chancellor have decided to grace us with their presence after all." He looked at them glumly. "Please be seated. Then, at last, we may begin."

There was much grumbling, much shuffling and pulling in of legs as Mr. Jelliby picked his way through the rows to one of the empty chairs. The faery chose the one at the opposite end of the room. When they were both seated, the Speaker cleared his throat.

"Gentlemen of the Privy Council," he began. "I bid you all a good morning."

One of the faery politician's pencil-thin eyebrows arched at this, and Mr. Jelliby smirked. (It was not morning, after all. It was *night*.)

"We have assembled today to address a matter most grave and disturbing."

Drat again. Mr. Jelliby sighed and dug his hands into his pockets. Matters most grave and disturbing were not things he liked addressing. He left that to Ophelia whenever he could.

"I daresay most of you have seen today's headlines?" the Speaker inquired, in his slow, languid voice. "The latest murder of a changeling?"

A murmur passed through the gathering. Mr. Jelliby squirmed. *Oh, not murder.* Why couldn't people simply be *nice* to each other?

"For the benefit of those who have not, allow me to summarize."

Mr. Jelliby took out a handkerchief and wiped his brow. *You needn't trouble yourself,* he thought, a little desperately. It was getting unbearably hot. The windows were all closed, and there seemed not a breath of air in the room.

"There have been five deaths in the past month alone," the Speaker said. "Nine in total. Most of the victims appear to be from Bath, but it is difficult to say as no one has stepped forward to claim the bodies. Whatever the case, the victims are being found in London. In the Thames."

A small, stern-looking gentleman in the front row

sniffed and raised his hand with an angry flourish.

The Speaker eyed him unhappily, then nodded, giving him permission to speak.

"Petty crimes, my lord. Nothing more. I'm sure Scotland Yard is doing all they can. Does the Privy Council have nothing more important to discuss?"

"Lord Harkness, we live in complicated times. These 'petty crimes,' as you call them, may have dark consequences a little ways down the road."

"Then we shall step over them when they are lying across our path. Changelings have never been popular. Not with their sort, and not with ours. There will always be violence against them. I see no reason to give these new incidences any undue significance."

"Sir, you do not know the half of it. The authorities think the murders are related. Planned and orchestrated with malicious intent."

"Do they think that? Well, I suppose they must earn their wages somehow."

"Lord Harkness, this is not the *time*." A trace of unease broke the Speaker's sleepy manner. "The victims are . . ." He faltered. "They are all children."

Lord Harkness might have said "So?" but it would not have been polite. Instead he said, "From what I hear, there are very few changelings who are *not* children. They don't generally last long."

"And the method of murder—it is also the same."

"Well, what is it?" Lord Harkness seemed to be intent on proving the entire meeting a ridiculous waste of time. Nobody wanted to hear about changelings. Nobody wanted to discuss changelings, or even think about changelings. But nobody wanted to hear how they died, either, and all Lord Harkness got for his efforts was a storm of black looks from the other gentlemen. Mr. Jelliby was tempted to cover his ears.

The Speaker's nose twitched. "The authorities are not exactly sure."

Ah. Thank goodness.

"Then how can they possibly claim the murders are related?" Lord Harkness's voice was acid. His handkerchief was in his hands, and he looked as if he wanted to wring the old Speaker's neck with it.

"Well, the corpses! They're— Why, they're . . ."

"Out with it, man, what is it?"

The Speaker looked straight ahead, and said, "Lord Harkness, they are hollow."

For several heartbeats the room fell completely still. A rat scurried under the polished floorboards and its hurrying feet rattled like a burst of hail in the silence.

"Hollow?" Lord Harkness repeated.

"They are empty. No bones or internal organs. Just skin. Like a sack."

"Good heavens," breathed Lord Harkness, and fell back into his chair.

"Indeed." The Speaker's eyes passed over the other gentlemen in the room, as if daring anyone else to disrupt the proceedings. "The newspapers said nothing of that, did they? That is because they do not know. They do not know many things, and for the time being we must keep it that way. There is something strange about these murders. Something wicked and inhuman. You will not have heard it, but the changelings were covered in writing, too. Head to toe. Little red markings in the faery tongue. It is an old and different sort of faery dialect that could not be deciphered by any of the Yard's cryptographers. I am sure you can all see what sort of unpleasantness this might lead to."

"Oh, certainly," the Earl of Fitzwatler mumbled from behind his drooping walrus moustache. "And I think it should be quite clear who is responsible. It is the anti-faery unions, of course. They had some waifs murdered and then scribbled up the bodies with faery words to put the blame on the Sidhe. It's very plain to me."

There was a great hissing at this, and just as many sage nods. Approximately half the council were members of one anti-faery group or another. The other half thought being anti anything narrow-minded, magic absolutely fascinating, and faeries the key to the future.

"Well, I say it *is* the faeries' doing!" the ancient Lord Lillicrapp cried, hammering his cane into the floor so hard a splinter of wood flew up like a spark. "Little beasts. Devils straight from Hell, if you ask me. They're the reason England's in the state it is. Look at this country. Look at Bath. It's going wild, it is. Soon we'll have rebellion on our hands, and then where'll we be? They'll turn our cannons into rosebushes, take the city for themselves. They don't understand our laws. They don't care about murder. A few dead men here and there? *Pshaw.*" The man spat contemptuously. "It's not wrong to them."

A bobbing of heads followed this outburst. Mr. Jelliby pinched the bridge of his nose and prayed it would end soon. He wanted very much to be somewhere else, somewhere cheerful and loud, preferably with brandy and people who talked about the weather and wine merchants.

The Archbishop of Canterbury was the next to speak. He was a tall, grim-looking man with a haggard face, and his tweed suit—no longer very new— stood out sorely against the cravats and colored waistcoats of the other gentlemen.

"I would not be so quick to judge," he said, leaning forward in his chair. "And I do not know why we must insist upon this word 'changeling.' As if we are still children, whispering over faery tales in the nursery. Peculiars, they are called, and they are quite real. They are not waifs put into the cradles of human children while the true infants are stolen into the Old Country. They will not wrinkle and waste away in a few years' time. They will be hanged. They are forever being hanged in our more remote villages. And no wonder, if we speak of them as if they were nothing but wind and enchantments. Humans think they are curses in child's form. Faeries are disgusted by their ugliness and are in the habit of burying them alive under elderberry bushes in case it's catching. I rather think both parties are sufficiently foolish and ill-informed to kill."

Up until then, Mr. Lickerish had been listening to the discussion quite impassively. But at the archbishop's words he stiffened. His mouth formed a thin line. Mr. Jelliby saw his hand go to his waistcoat pocket. The fingers slipped in, twitched, and were still.

The faery stood. Mr. Jelliby thought he smelled wet earth. The air didn't feel so close anymore, just old and damp and rotten-sweet.

Without bothering to wait for the old councilman's

permission, Mr. Lickerish began to speak.

"Gentlemen, these matters are indeed most troubling. But to say that the *fay* are murdering *changelings?* It is deplorable. I will not sit silent while the blame for yet another of England's woes is laid upon the shoulders of the fay. They are citizens! Patriots! Have you forgotten Waterloo? Where would England be without our brave faery troops? In the hands of Napoleon, together with all her empire. And the Americas? Were it not for the tireless efforts of trolls and giants, forging our cannon and pouring our musket balls in the infernal heat of the factories, building our warships and aether guns, it would still be a rebel nation. We owe so *much* to the faeries." Mr. Lickerish's face remained smooth, but his words were strangely beguiling, full of nuance and subtle passion. Even the council members who were distinctly anti-fay sat up in their chairs.

Only the man next to Mr. Jelliby—a Lord Locktower—clicked his tongue. "Yes, including forty-three percent of our crime," he said.

Mr. Lickerish turned on him. He flashed his

pointed teeth. "That is because they are so poor," he said. He stood a moment, considering Lord Locktower. Then he spun sharply, addressing instead the gentlemen on the other side of the room. "It is because they are being exploited!"

More nods and only a few hisses. The smell of damp was very strong now. Lord Locktower scowled. Mr. Jelliby saw him pull out a heavy old pocket watch and examine it angrily. The watch was an antiquated thing, scrolled and made from iron. Mr. Jelliby thought it somewhat unfashionable.

The faery politician began to pace. "It has been this way since the day we arrived," he said. "First we were massacred, then we were enslaved, then we were massacred again. And now? Now we are your scapegoat, to be accused of all the crimes you find too distasteful to blame on your own people. Why does England *hate* us? What have we done that your world loathes us so? We do not *want* to be here. We did not come to stay. But the road home has vanished, the door is closed."

The faery stopped pacing. He was watching the

assembled gentlemen, watching them very closely. In a voice that was barely a wisp, he said, "We will never see our home again."

Mr. Jelliby thought this unbearably sad. He found himself nodding gravely along with most of the others.

But Mr. Lickerish was not finished yet. He walked to the center of the room, right up next to the Speaker's podium, and said, "We have suffered so much at the hands of fate. We live here in chains, locked into slums, among iron and bells that harangue against the very essence of our beings, but is that enough for you? Oh, no. We must be murderers as well. Murderers of innocent children, children who share our very blood." He shook his head once, and as the light shifted across it, his features seemed to change and the angles soften. He didn't look so cold anymore. He looked suddenly tragic, like the weeping angels under the trees of Hyde Park. "I can only hope justice will prevail in the end."

Mr. Jelliby gave the faery politician what he hoped was a look of deep and heartfelt sympathy. The other gentlemen tutted and harrumphed. But then Lord Locktower stood up and stamped his foot.

"Now stop all this!" he cried, glaring at everyone at once. "Whining and sniveling, that's what this is. I, for one, shall have none of it." The gentleman two chairs over tried to shush him. He only spoke louder. Other men broke in. Lord Locktower began to shout, his face flaring red. When Baron Somerville tried to pull him back into his seat, he brought up a glove and slapped him hard across the face.

The whole room seemed to draw in a breath. Then it exploded into pandemonium. Chairs were overturned, walking sticks were hurled to the floor, and everyone was on his feet, bellowing.

Mr. Jelliby made for the door. Barons and dukes were everywhere, jostling and elbowing, and someone was crying "Down with England!" at the top of his lungs. Mr. Jelliby was forced to turn aside, and when he did he caught sight of Mr. Lickerish again. The faery was standing in the midst of the commotion, a pale slip in the sea of red faces and flailing black hats. He was smiling.

CHAPTER III
Black Wings and Wind

BARTHOLOMEW lay in the attic, curled up, still as stone. Daylight slipped away. The sun began to sink behind the looming bulk of New Bath, the light from the little round window stretched its fingers ever farther and ever redder across his face, and still he did not move.

A hard, cold fear had moved into his stomach, and he couldn't make it go.

He saw the lady in plum again, over and over in his mind, walking in the alley. Her hair was pulled away, the little face staring, dark and knotted, and the bramble-haired boy followed her in shadows shaped like wings. *Jewels, and hats, and purple skirts. A blue hand grinding glass. Wet black eyes, and a smile under them, a horrid, horrid smile.*

It was too much for him. Too much, too quickly, a rush of sound and fury, like time sped up. Bartholomew had seen thieves from that attic window, an automaton with no legs, a pale corpse or two, but this was worse. This was dangerous, and he had been seen. *Why had the lady come? And why had she taken his friend away?* Bartholomew's head ached.

He stared at the floorboards so long he could make out every rift and wormhole. He knew it wasn't the magic that had shaken him. Magic was a part of life in Bath, always had been. Somewhere in London, important men had decided it would be best to try to hide it, to keep the factories heaving and the church bells clanging, but it hadn't done much good. Magic was still there. It was simply underneath, hidden in the secret pockets of the city. Bartholomew saw a twinkly-eyed gnome in Old Crow Alley now and again, dragging behind him a root in the shape of a child. Folk would open their windows to watch, and when someone dropped the gnome a penny or a bit of bread, he would make the root dance, and make it wheel around and sing. Once in a blue moon the oak on Scattercopper Lane was known to mumble prophecies. And it was common knowledge that the Buddelbinsters' faery mother could call the mice out of the walls and make them stir her soups and twist the wool for her spinning wheel.

So a whirling pillar of darkness was not really dreadful to Bartholomew. What was dreadful was that it had happened here, in the muddy confines of his own small street, to someone just like him. And Bartholomew Kettle had been seen.

The sun was completely gone now. The shadows were beginning to slink from behind the rafters, and that made Bartholomew get up. He crawled out of the attic and made his way downstairs, trying not to let the groaning, sagging house give him away. *Don't get yourself noticed, and you won't get yourself hanged.*

At the door to their rooms, Bartholomew paused. Oily yellow light seeped from under it. The rhythmic clank of the mechanical wash wringer sounded dully into the passage.

"Come now, Hettie," Mother was saying. Her voice was loud and cheerful, the way it was when nothing was well and she was determined not to show it. She was trying to keep Hettie from worrying. "Drink your broth down quick-like, and then off to bed. This lamp's not got more 'n fifteen minutes in it, and I'll be needing it another night or two."

There was a slurp. Hettie mumbled, "It doesn't taste like anything."

That's because it's only water, thought Bartholomew, leaning his head against the door frame. *With wax drippings so we think there's meat in it.* It was why the saucers at the base of the brass candlesticks were always empty in the mornings. Mother thought she was careful about it, but he knew. They were scraped clean by the kitchen spoon.

"Mummy, Barthy isn't back yet."

"Yes . . ." Mother's voice was not so loud anymore.

"It's dark outside. It's past bedtime. Isn't it?"

"Yes, dearie, it is."

"I suspect something, Mummy."

"Oh . . ."

"Do you want to know what I suspect?"

"There isn't any salt left."

"No. I suspect a kelpy got him and dragged him down into his bottomless puddle."

Bartholomew turned away before he could hear his mother's reply. She wasn't really thinking about the salt. She was thinking about where he might be hiding, where she hadn't searched yet, and why he hadn't returned. He felt cruel suddenly, slinking around outside their door while she worried inside. Soon she would start to panic, knock on the neighbors' walls, and go into the night with the last fifteen minutes of the lamp oil. He had to be back before then.

Tiptoeing the rest of the way downstairs, he scraped himself along the wall toward the alley door. A goblin sat by it, fast asleep on a stool. Bartholomew went past him and brushed his hand over the door, feeling for the bolt. The door had a face in it—fat cheeks and lips and sleepy old eyes growing out of the gray and weather-beaten wood. His mother said the face used to demand beetles from folks who wanted to come in and spat their shells at folks who wanted to go out, but Bartholomew had never seen it so much as blink.

His fingers found the bolt. He pulled it back. Then he slipped under the chain and onto the cobbles.

It was strange being in the open again. The air there was close and damp. There were no walls or ceilings, just the alley splitting into other alleys, on and on into the great world. It felt huge, frightening, and endlessly dangerous. But Bartholomew didn't suppose he had a choice.

He scurried across the alley to the low arch in the Buddelbinsters' wall. The yard was dark, the crooked house as well. Its many windows had been thrown open. They looked as if they were watching him.

He leaped over the broken gate and pressed himself to the wall. The night was not cold, but he shivered anyway. Only a few hours ago, the lady in plum had stood here, so near where he was standing now, luring his friend to her with blue-gloved fingers.

Bartholomew shook himself and moved on. The circle the lady had poured onto the ground was still there, a few steps to the right of the path. From his attic window Bartholomew had been able to see it clearly, but up close it was very faint, practically invisible if you didn't already know it was there. He knelt down, pushing aside a tuft of weeds to examine it. He frowned. The ring was made of mushrooms. Tiny black mushrooms that looked like no sort of mushroom he would want to eat. He plucked one up. For a moment he could feel its shape, soft and smooth against his fingertips. Then it seemed to melt, until it was only a droplet of black liquid staining the whiteness of his skin.

He stared at his hand curiously. He waved it over the circle. Nothing happened. One more hand and his forehead. Still nothing. He almost laughed then. It didn't work anymore. They were just mushrooms now.

Standing up, he dug his bare toe into the cold soil inside the ring. Then he stomped a few of the mushrooms. He wasn't sure, but he thought he heard a soft titter at that, like a crowd of whispers, far away. Without another thought, he leaped up and landed in the middle of the mushroom ring.

A hideous screeching erupted all around him. There was a burst of darkness, and wings were everywhere, flapping in his face, battering him. He was falling, flying, a fierce and icy wind tearing at his hair and his threadbare clothes.

"Idiot!" he screamed. "You stupid, stupid, what were you thinking, you—" But it was too late. Already the darkness was subsiding. And what he saw then was not Old Crow Alley or the Buddelbinsters' yard. It was not anything in the faery slums. Flashing through the wings like scraps of sunlight was warmth, luxury, the gleam of brass and polished wood, and heavy green drapes stitched with leaves. A fire was somewhere nearby. He couldn't see it, but he knew it was there, crackling.

With a desperate lunge, he tried to throw himself free of the wings. *Please, please put me back.* The magic couldn't have taken him far in those few seconds, could it? Maybe a few miles, but if he hurried he could find his way back before the faeries and the English filled the streets.

The wings slashed past his face. Gravity seemed to become unsure of its own laws, and for a moment he thought his plan might have worked; he was soaring, weightless. And then the wings were gone. The screeching stopped. His head thudded against smooth wood, and the air was knocked from his lungs.

Bartholomew propped himself up on his elbows dizzily. He was on the floor of the loveliest room he had ever seen. There were the green drapes, drawn against the night. There, the fireplace and the flames. Woodsmoke drifted from the grate, making the air warm and hazy. Books lined the walls. Lamps with painted silk shades threw a soft glow about them. A few feet away from where Bartholomew had fallen, a circle had been carefully drawn with chalk on the bare floorboards. Rings of writing surrounded the circle, thin twining letters that seemed to spin and dance as he looked at them.

That was where I was supposed to land, he thought, feeling the bump that was growing on his head.

Shakily, he got to his feet. The room was a study of some sort. A heavy wooden desk took up most of one end. It was carved with bulbous frogs and toads, and they all looked to be in the process of eating one another. On top of the desk, in a neat row, were three mechanical birds. They were each a slightly different size, and were built to look like sparrows, with metal wings and tiny brass cogs that peeped out from between the plates. They sat utterly still, obsidian eyes staring keenly at Bartholomew.

He took a few steps toward them. A little voice at the back of his mind was telling him to run, to get away from that room as fast as he could, but he was feeling dull and silly, and his head still hurt. A few minutes wouldn't make any difference, would they? And it was so pleasant here, so shiny and warm.

He walked a little closer to the birds. He had the strongest urge to reach out and touch one. He wanted to *feel* those perfect metal feathers, the delicate machinery, and the sharp black eyes. . . . He uncurled his fingers.

He froze. Something had shifted in the depths of the house. A floorboard or a panel. And then all Bartholomew heard was the *clip-clip* of feet approaching briskly from the other side of the door at the far end of the room.

His heart clenched, painfully. *Someone heard.* Someone heard the noise, and now he was coming to investigate. He would find a changeling in his private chambers, a pauper from the faery slums clearly breaking into his house. A constable would come, beat Bartholomew senseless. Morning would find him swinging by the neck in the hot breath of the city.

Bartholomew flew across the room and wrenched at the doorknob with desperate fingers. It was locked, but the person on the other side would have a key. He had to get out.

Racing back to the chalk circle, he leaped and landed squarely in the middle. His heels struck the floor, the force jarring his legs.

Nothing happened.

He threw a frantic look back at the door. The footsteps had stopped. Someone was right there, right on the other side, breathing. Bartholomew heard a hand being placed on the knob. The knob began to turn, turn. *Click.* Locked.

Panic slithered in his throat. *Trapped. Get out, get out, get out!*

For a moment the person outside was silent. Then the knob began to rattle. Slowly at first but becoming more insistent, getting stronger and stronger until the whole door was shivering in its frame.

Bartholomew stamped his foot. *GO!* he thought desperately. *Work! Take me away from here!* His chest began to ache. Something was pricking the back of his eyes, and for a moment he wanted nothing more than to sit down and cry like he had when he was little and had lost hold of his mother's hand at the market.

The person outside began to beat viciously against the door.

It wouldn't do any good to cry. Bartholomew ran his hand over his nose. A crying thief would still be hanged. He looked down at the markings all around him and tried to think.

There. A section of the chalk circle was smeared across the floor. The ring didn't go all the way around anymore. He must have ruined it when he fell.

Dropping to his knees, he began scrabbling the chalk dust together, piling it in a rough line to close the circle.

A dull snapping sounded from the door. The wood. *Whoever is outside is breaking down the door!*

Bartholomew couldn't hope to copy all the little marks and symbols, but he could at least complete the ring. *Faster, faster* . . . His hands squeaked against the floor.

The door burst inward with a thunderous crash.

But the wings were already enveloping Bartholomew, the darkness howling around him, and the wind pulling at his clothes. Only something was different this time. Wrong. He felt *things* in the blackness; cold, thin bodies that darted against him and poked at his skin. Mouths pressed up to his ears, whispering in small, dark voices. A tongue, icy wet, slid over his cheek. And then there was only pain, horrid searing pain, tearing up his arms and eating into his bones. He kept down his scream just long enough for the room to begin to flit away into the spinning shadows. Then he shrieked along with the wind and the raging wings.

CHAPTER IV
Nonsuch House

NONSUCH House looked like a ship—a great, stone nightmarish ship, run aground in the mire of London at the north end of Blackfriars Bridge. Its jagged roofs were the sails, its lichened chimneys the masts, and the smoke that curled up from their mouths looked like so many tattered flags, sliding in the wind. Hundreds of small gray windows speckled its walls. A pitted door faced the street. Below, the river swirled, feeding the clumps of moss that climbed its foundations and turning the stone black with slime.

A carriage was winding its way toward the house through the evening bustle of Fleet Street. Rain was falling steadily. The streetlamps were just beginning to glow, and they reflected on the polished sides of the carriage, throwing tongues of light onto the windows.

The carriage shuddered to a halt in front of Nonsuch House, and Mr. Jelliby ducked out, leaping a puddle to get into the shelter of the doorway. He brought up his walking stick and knocked it twice against the pockmarked black wood. Then he wrapped his arms around himself and scowled.

He didn't want to be here. He wanted to be anywhere *but* here. Scattered on his desk at home were gilt-edged cards and monogrammed invitations that would gain him entrance to a whole parade of lively and fashionable drawing rooms. And what was he doing but standing in the wind and rain outside the house of Mr. Lickerish, the faery politician. There ought to be laws against such things.

Drat these ale meetings. . . . They were a very old tradition, but that didn't mean Mr. Jelliby had to like them. Members of the Privy Council, two or three at a time, met at each other's townhouses for drink and pleasant discussion, in the hope that it would breed fellowship and respect for differing opinions. Mr. Jelliby's scowl deepened. *Fellowship, indeed.* Perhaps it had done so four centuries ago when the members still drank ale. But it was all tea these days, and the meetings were frosty affairs, much dreaded by host and guests alike.

Mr. Jelliby stood up straighter. A rattling of locks had begun on the other side of the door. He must at least *look* as if he didn't want to be anywhere else. He raised his chin, folded his gloved hands across the head of his walking stick, and assumed an expression of pleasant inquiry.

With a final, thudding *clank*, the door opened. Something very tall and thin thrust its head out and blinked at Mr. Jelliby.

Mr. Jelliby blinked back. The creature leaning out of the shadows of the doorway must have been seven feet tall, and yet it was so bony and starved-looking it seemed barely able to support its own weight. The pale skin on its hands was thin as birch bark, and all the little knuckles pushed up underneath. He (for it was a he, Mr. Jelliby saw now) wore a shabby suit that ended several inches above his ankles, and the air around him smelled faintly of graveyards. But that was not the oddest part about him. One side of his face was ensconced in a web of brass, a network of tiny cogs and pistons that whirred and ticked in constant motion. A green glass goggle was fixed over the eye. Every few seconds it would twitch, and a lens would flick across it like a blink. Then a thread of steam would hiss out from under a screw in its casing.

"Arthur Jelliby?" the creature inquired. He had a high, soft voice, and his other eye—the slanted, faery eye—squeezed almost shut when he spoke. Mr. Jelliby did not like that at all.

"Ah . . ." he said.

"Enter, if you please." The faery ushered him in with a graceful sweep of his hand. Mr. Jelliby stepped in, trying not to stare. The door boomed shut behind him, and instantly he was plunged into silence. The clatter of Fleet Street was cut off. The noise of the rain was very far away, only a faint drum at the edge of his hearing.

Mr. Jelliby's coat dripped onto black-and-white

tiles. He was standing in a high, echoing hall, and the shadows pressed around him, heavy and damp from the corners and doorways. There was not a lit wick to be seen, not a gaslight or a candle. Mildew streaked the paneling in long, green trails. Faded tapestries clung to the walls, barely visible in the gloom. A grandfather clock with little faces where the numbers should have been stood silently against the wall.

"This way, if you please," the faery said, setting off across the hall.

Mr. Jelliby followed, tugging uncertainly at his gloves. The butler should have taken them. In a proper house he would have, along with Mr. Jelliby's hat and overcoat. Mr. Jelliby was suddenly aware of how loud his shoes sounded, slapping wetly against the floor. He didn't dare look, but he imagined himself leaving a slippery trail over the tiles like a massive slug.

The faery butler led him to the end of the hall and they began to climb the stairs. The staircase was a mass of rotting wood, carved with such cruel-looking mermaids that Mr. Jelliby was afraid to put his hand on the banister.

"Mr. Lickerish will be seeing you in the green library," the butler said over his shoulder.

"Oh, that's nice," Mr. Jelliby mumbled, because he didn't know what else to say. Somewhere in the house the wind moaned. A casement must have been left open, forgotten.

The oddness of Nonsuch House was unsettling him more with every step. This was obviously not a place for humans. The pictures on the walls were not of landscapes or ill-tempered ancestors as in Mr. Jelliby's house, but of plain things, like a tarnished spoon, a jug with a fly sitting on it, and a bright red door in a stone wall. And yet they were all painted with so much shadow that they looked decidedly sinister. The spoon might have been used to murder someone, the jug was full of poison, and the red door doubtless led into a tangled garden of flesh-eating plants. There were no photographs or bric-a-brac. Instead there were many mirrors, and drapes, and little trees growing from cracks in the paneling.

He was almost at the top of the stairs when he saw a small, hunched-up goblin rushing along the balcony that overlooked the hall. Something was jangling in the goblin's hands, and he paused at each door, clicking and scraping, and Mr. Jelliby saw that he was locking them, one by one.

On the second floor, the house became a maze, and Mr. Jelliby lost every sense of direction. The butler led him first down one corridor, then another, through sitting rooms and archways and long, gloomy galleries, up short flights of stairs, ever farther into the house. Now and then Mr. Jelliby caught a glimpse of movement in the darkness. He would hear the scamper of feet and the titter of voices. But whenever he turned to look there was nothing there. *The servants, most likely*, he thought, but he wasn't sure.

After a few minutes they passed the mouth of a corridor, long and very narrow, like the sort inside a railway carriage. Mr. Jelliby froze, staring down it. It was so brightly lit. Gas lamps fizzled along its walls, making it look like a tunnel of blazing gold cutting into the darkness of the house. And a woman was in the corridor. She was hurrying, her back toward him, and in her haste she seemed to be flitting like a bird, her purple skirts billowing out behind her like wings. Then the butler was at Mr. Jelliby's side, herding him up a winding stair, and he was surrounded again in shadow.

"Excuse me?" Mr. Jelliby said, pulling himself from the faery's grasp. "Excuse me, butler? Does Mr. Lickerish have a wife?"

"A wife?" said the butler, in his sickly, sticky voice. "Whatever would he want a wife for?"

Mr. Jelliby frowned. "Well . . . Well, I don't know, but I saw a—"

"Here we are. The green library. Tea will be served directly."

They had stopped in front of a tall pointed door made from panes of green glass that were shaped like eels and seaweed and water serpents, all twisting and writhing around one another.

The butler tapped against it with one of his long yellow fingernails. "*Mi Sathir?*" he whined. "*Kath eccis melar.* Arthur Jelliby is arrived." Then he turned and melted away into the dark.

The door opened silently. Mr. Jelliby felt sure the

faery politician would poke his head out and greet him, but no one appeared. He poked his own head in. A very long room stretched away in front of him. It was a library, but it did not *look* very green. A few lamps had been lit, making the room almost welcoming compared to the rest of the house. Chairs and carpets and little tables filled the floor, and every inch of the walls was covered with . . . Oh. The books were green. All of them. They were many different shades and sizes, and in the half-light they had looked like any other books, but now that Mr. Jelliby's eyes had adjusted he could see that this was indeed a library of green books. He took a few steps, shaking his head slowly. He wondered whether in this strange house there was also a blue library for blue books, or a burgundy library for those of the burgundy persuasion.

At the far end of the room, silhouetted against the glow of a fire, three figures sat.

"Good evening, young Jelliby," the faery politician called to him as he approached. It was a very quiet call, if such a thing were possible, spoken very coldly. Mr. Lickerish was obviously not about to make a lie of the fact that none of them were welcome here.

"Good evening, Lord Chancellor," said Mr. Jelliby, and managed a halfhearted smile. "Mr. Lumbidule, Mr. Throgmorton. What a pleasure." He bowed to the two men, and they nodded back. Apparently they were not going to make a lie of anything, either. After all, they were in opposing parties to Mr. Jelliby's. He sat down hastily in one of the empty chairs.

A low table had been laid with edibles. The faery butler drifted in with a silver kettle, and then everything looked very respectable and English-like. It didn't taste English, though. It didn't even taste French. What had seemed to be proper liver-paste sandwiches tasted remarkably like cold autumn wind. The tea smelled of ladybeetles, and the lemon tart was bitter in a not-at-all lemony way. To make matters worse there were two sumptuous onyx perfume burners on either side of the little gathering, spewing a greenish smoke into the atmosphere. It was so sweet and cloying, and it made Mr. Jelliby think of splitting overripe fruit, of mold, and buzzing flies. Almost like the smell in the chamber of the Privy Council, after Mr. Lickerish's fingers had twitched in his waistcoat pocket.

Mr. Jelliby laid his lemon tart aside. He stole a look at the other two gentlemen. They didn't seem to be in any discomfort at all. They nipped at their ladybeetle tea, smiling and nodding as if to show their appreciation for everything in general. When one of them spoke, it was to say something so pointless that Mr. Jelliby could not remember it two seconds afterward. As for the faery, he sat perfectly still, arms folded, not eating, not drinking.

Mr. Jelliby took a small, gasping breath. The green fumes wriggled in his throat, making his lungs feel as if they were being stuffed with silk. A fog began to creep about the corners of his vision. The room felt suddenly unsteady. The floor swayed, bucked, like wooden waves in a wooden sea. Vaguely he heard Mr. Throgmorton asking after the weight of Mr. Lumbidule's mechanical hunting boar. "It must be shot with a special sort of gun," Mr. Lumbidule was saying. ". . . has real blood inside, real meat, and if you are tired of hunting it, it will lie down on its iron back and . . ."

Mr. Jelliby could take it no longer. Wiping his brow he said, "Forgive me, Mr. Lickerish, but I am feeling unwell. Is there a water closet nearby?" The two other men stopped their blathering long enough to smirk at him. Mr. Jelliby barely noticed. He was too busy trying not to vomit.

The faery's mouth twitched. He regarded Mr. Jelliby sharply for a moment. Then he said, "Of course there is a water closet. Left of the door you'll find a bellpull. Someone will come to escort you."

"Oh . . ." Mr. Jelliby lurched out of his seat and stumbled away from the chairs. His head was spinning. On his way across the room he thought he might have knocked something over—he heard a clatter and felt something delicate grind to glassy shards under his feet—but he was too dizzy to stop.

He staggered out of the library, fumbling along the wall for the bellpull. His fingers brushed a tassel. His hand closed around a thick velvet cord and he tugged it with all his might. Somewhere deep in the house a bell tinkled.

He waited, listening for the sound of footsteps, a door opening, a voice. Nothing. The bell faded away. He heard the rain again, drumming on the roof.

He pulled a second time. Another tinkle. Still nothing.

Fine. He would find the privy himself. Now that he was out of the green library, he was feeling better anyway. His head was beginning to clear, and his stomach had settled. A splash of cold water, perhaps, and he'd be well enough. He began wandering back the way he had come, down the winding staircase and into the passageway below, trying the doors as he passed them to see if there might be a privy behind one. His mind went back to the brightly lit corridor, the woman hurrying down it. He wondered who she was. She hadn't been a servant. Not with those rich clothes. Nor had she looked like a faery.

Mr. Jelliby came to the end of the hallway and turned down another one. It was the same one he had been in not twenty minutes before, but now that he was alone it looked somehow darker and more forbidding. It led to a large dingy room, with furniture all covered in dust sheets. That room led to another hallway, which led into a room full of empty birdcages, and then a smoking room, none of which looked anything like the rooms he remembered passing through earlier. He realized he wasn't looking for a privy anymore. He was looking for the gaslit corridor, wondering if the woman might still be there, wondering if he could find out who she was. He was just about to turn back and search in a different direction when one room opened into another and he found himself standing at the mouth of the brightly lit corridor.

He could have sworn it had been in a different place before. Hadn't there been a pot of withered roses to the left of it? And a sideboard with a bone-white bowl? But here it was—the long, narrow corridor that looked so very like those in railway carriages. It was not as if it had moved.

The corridor was empty now. The doors on both sides were closed, no doubt locked by the goblin Mr. Jelliby had seen earlier. He stepped forward, listening. The distant patter of the rain was gone. There was no sound at all. Only a slight vibration, a hum more felt than heard. It was in the paneling, and the floor, and it tickled the inside of his forehead.

He walked all the way down the corridor, passing his hand over each door as he went. The wood of the last door was warm. A fire must be lit in the room beyond. He laid his ear against the door, listening. A heavy thud came from the other side, as if some large object had fallen to the floor. *Was the lady there, then? Was she* the object that had fallen? Oh dear. Suppose she had tumbled from a chair while reaching for something and was now lying broken on the floor. He turned the doorknob. It was locked. Gripping the knob with both hands, he began to shake it. Another sound came from behind the door, quick breaths and something like scratching. He began pounding. *She certainly isn't unconscious. But is she deaf? Or mute?* Perhaps he should run and fetch a servant. But before he could rightly entertain this idea, there was a tremendous noise of splintering and breaking, and then the door lay in pieces at his feet. He was looking into a room that had a beautiful blazing fire and a desk carved with toads. It was empty. Far, far away he thought he heard a cry. So very far away he didn't know if he had imagined it.

And then the faery butler was at the mouth of the corridor, his one green eye blazing, the machinery across the side of his face skippering madly. "What is *this*?" he cried. "What have you done?" He began to run, long arms stretched out in front of him like the talons of a horrible insect.

"Oh. Oh, good heavens," Mr. Jelliby stammered. "Do forgive me, I didn't mean to—"

"Mr. *Lickerish*!" the butler screeched. *"Sathir, el eguliem pak!"* His voice rose to such a desperate height on the final word that it made Mr. Jelliby wince. A door opened somewhere in the house, then another. Footsteps sounded in the passageways, on the stairs, not loud but steady, approaching quickly.

Oh dear, thought Mr. Jelliby.

The faery butler reached him and took hold of his arm, his face so close Mr. Jelliby could smell his putrid breath.

"Come away from here this instant!" the butler hissed. "Come back into the house." And he practically dragged Mr. Jelliby down the corridor, out of the blazing gaslight, into the solid gloom beyond. Someone was waiting for them there. A whole group of someones. Mr. Throgmorton and Mr. Lumbidule, a wide-eyed Mr. Lickerish, and in the shadows, a huddle of lower faeries, whispering *"Pak, pak"* over and over amongst themselves.

"It—it was not the water closet," Mr. Jelliby said weakly.

Mr. Throgmorton gave a bark of laughter. "Oh, the surprise! And yet you broke down the door. Mr. Jelliby, privy doors are locked for a reason, I think. They are locked when they are being used, when they are not meant to be used, or when they are not, in fact, a privy."

Mr. Throgmorton started laughing again, fat lips quivering. Mr. Lumbidule joined in. The faery folk only watched, faces blank.

Suddenly Mr. Lickerish clapped his hands, producing a clear, sharp sound. The chortles of the two politicians lodged in their throats.

The faery turned to Mr. Jelliby. "You are leaving now," he said, and his voice made Mr. Jelliby want to shrivel up and fall through the cracks in the floorboards.

Mr. Jelliby couldn't remember afterward how he came to be back in the hall with the mermaid staircase. All he remembered was walking, walking through endless corridors, head lowered to hide the burning of his face. And then he was at the front door again, and the butler was letting him out. But before stumbling into the streaming misery of the city, he recalled looking back into the shadows of Nonsuch House. And there, on the staircase landing, stood the faery politician, a flicker of white in the darkness. He was watching Mr. Jelliby. His pale hands were folded across the silver buttons of his waistcoat. His face was a mask, flat and inscrutable. But his eyes were still wide. And it struck Mr. Jelliby that a wide-eyed faery was not a surprised faery. It was an angry, angry faery.

CHAPTER V
To Invite a Faery

BARTHOLOMEW'S eyes snapped open. The air was foul. He was in his own bed and sunlight was pouring through the window. Mother was standing over him. Hettie clung to her skirts, staring at him as if he were a wild beast.

"Barthy?" Mother's voice shook. "Well, Barthy?"

He tried to sit up, but pain roared inside his arms and he collapsed, gasping. "Well what, Mother?" he asked quietly.

"Don't play daft with me, Bartholomew Kettle, who did this to you? Did you *see* who did this to you?"

"Did *what*?" His skin hurt. Oh, why did it hurt

so? The pain went all the way to the bone, aching and throbbing as if there were maggots underneath, chewing.

His mother turned her face away and moaned into her hand. "Larks and stage lights, he's amnesiagactical." Then she whirled back on Bartholomew and practically screamed, "Scratched you to ribbons, that's what! Scratched my poor little darling baby to *ribbons!*" She lifted the corner of his old woolen blanket.

Hettie hid her face.

Bartholomew swallowed. All down the front of his body, down his arms and on his chest, were bloodred lines, thin scratches that looped and whirled across his white skin. They were very orderly. They made a pattern, like the writing in the room with the clockwork birds. In a violent, frightening sort of way they looked almost beautiful.

"Oh . . . ," he breathed. "Oh, no. No, no, I—"

"Were it faeries or people?" There was fear in his mother's voice. Raw, desperate fear. "Did one of the neighbors find out what you are? John Longstockings, or that Weevil woman?"

Bartholomew didn't answer. Mother must have found him in the street. He remembered crawling, half-numb with pain, out of the Buddelbinsters' yard. *The filthy cobbles against my cheek. Wondering if a cart would come and roll me over.* He couldn't tell Mother about the lady in plum. He couldn't tell her about the change-ling boy, or the mushrooms, or the room with the birds. It would only make things worse.

"I don't remember," he lied. He tried rubbing at the lines, as if the red might come off on his fingers. The pain became worse, so bad that spots blossomed in front of his eyes. The lines remained the same, bright and unbroken.

He looked up. Hettie was peeking at him again. Mother's face was drawn, her mouth pinched to keep from shaking, the fear in her eyes about to spill over in another fit of hysterics.

"I need to go," he said. "Mother, I can ask some-one. I'll make everything better." He got up, swaying a little as the ache struck him full force. He snatched his dirty clothes off the top of the bedpost. Then he made for the door, hobbling as quickly as he could.

His mother tried to stop him, but he pushed past her, out of the flat and into the passage.

"Bartholomew, please!" Mother whimpered from the doorway. "Come back inside. What if someone *sees?*"

Bartholomew began to run. He was going to summon a faery. He *had* to. It was clear as rain to him now. A house faery could tell him what the ring of mushrooms was, where it led, and why the little creatures in the wings had written on him. It could keep them all safe, and bring them luck. And it could be his friend. A real friend that didn't just wave at him through windows.

I'll make everything better.

He limped up the stairs toward the roof. The house always felt safe in the morning hours, when the passages were empty and the dust motes whirled slowly through the yellow light from the windows. But it wasn't safe. No one in the faery slums slept past five, if they slept at all, and Bartholomew didn't want to know all the things that were happening just beyond the rotting walls. A sharp, metallic tang filled the corridor outside the Longstockings' door, and behind it, what sounded like knives sliding against each other. Piskies were wailing and scampering inside the Prickfinger flat. On the third floor, where the heat rose and the air was thick as blankets, the smell of boiled turnips and musty bedding was strong enough to smother him.

A door opened in front of him, and he only barely managed to skid around it. An old faery matron stepped out. She kicked the door closed.

Bartholomew's throat constricted like a wire trap. *Not this, too.*

She was so close. Bartholomew could see every wrinkle in her apron, the blue cornflowers stitched into her faded ruffled cap. For a terrible moment she paused, head raised, as if listening. If she flicked her eyes around, even just a hair's breadth, she would see him standing there, stock still in the middle of the passageway. She would see his pointy face, the tracery of lines, bloody along his arms.

One. Two. Three . . .

Finally the old faery sniffed and began lumbering

away down the passage. Behind her, a scuffle, then a bang. She stopped midstep and whirled.

But Bartholomew's heels had already disappeared up through the trapdoor into the attic.

Once inside the secret gable, he pulled an old coffee tin from its hiding place in the rafters and opened it, laying out its contents quickly on the floor.

His mother had forbidden him to invite a house faery, but she didn't know everything. She was just afraid of faeries, had been ever since their Sidhe father had danced off into the night and never come back. That was different though; Bartholomew wished she could see that. His father had been a high faery, sly and selfish, and had whisked Mother away from her theater troupe when she was young and pretty and full of life. Mother had given everything up to be with him. And then, when her pretty face was gone, and her hands were cracked from the lye, from drudging to feed their children, he had simply left. Mother hadn't spoken to a faery since.

Bartholomew's fingers found a slip of ribbon in the box, and he lingered a moment. Memories of his father were dim, but he knew he had been afraid of him, of those black eyes always turned toward him with disgust, and perhaps the hint of a question. One time his father had spoken to him in a strange language, on and on for what seemed like hours, and when he had finished and Bartholomew had simply stood there, dumb and wide-eyed, his father had flown into a rage and thrown all Mother's dishes against the wall. House faeries weren't like that, Bartholomew told himself. Nothing so cold and flighty. They were more like animals, he decided, like very intelligent birds.

He looked darkly at the items before him, trying to ignore the pain in his arms. The faery wouldn't throttle them in their sleep. It *wouldn't*. Scratched out in black ink in one of Bartholomew's books was a tiny shimmery creature, barely as tall as the candlestick it stood by. The faery wore a cap with a feather in it and had snowdrop petals growing out of its back. It looked *nice*.

Bartholomew picked up one of his twigs and then threw it down again. *Why did Mother have to go and forbid things?* It just made everything worse. She was wrong. She would see that soon enough when the domesticated faery became the end of all their troubles. Once Bartholomew had the faery whisper away the red lines and tell him things and play hide-and-seek in the attic, he would make it work. It could help with mending, and run errands, and stoke the potbellied stove for the wash kettle. Mother wouldn't have to work so hard, and maybe someday they could get out of the faery slums and live in a beautiful room like the one with the green drapes and the fireplace.

Then she would see.

Banging open a dusty volume, Bartholomew began to invite a faery.

The domesticated fayrye, or "house fayrye," is a magikal being originating from the Old Country, that lies beyond the fayrye door. It is immaterial and can appear in all shapes and syzes. The appearance of your fayrye will depend entirely on its personal charactre and mood.

To invite this fayrye, you must find a quiet place, secluded and very stille. The dark and mossy hollows that form near woodland streams are particularly suited. (*Have no fear, the fayrye will follow you home.*) Gather an assortement of leaves, straw, twigs, and other plant-ish fibre. Weave them together into a hollow mound, leaving a little openning at its base. (*This is the door so that the fayrye may entre.*) Tangel scraps of naturel food (such as elderberries and annis) into the walls of the dwelling. Place inside:

One spoon (*NOT iron*)

One ribbon, prettily coloured

A thimble

A shard of glass

Bits of domestic food (*such as bread, or cheese*)

Lastly, sprinkle a pinch of salt over it all. Fayryes despise salt above all elss, but in putting it over your offering you will give them cause to respect you. Do not strew **too** much salt, however, or the fayrye will fear you as the Devil Himself and be of no use.

Note: the higher the quality of each item, the better chance one has of attracting this fayrye. Also, the quality of the items is directly related to the quality of the fayrye swayed by them. A silver spoon and silken ribbon will likely get you a house fayrye kind and good.

And then, in very small and faded type:

To Invite a Faery

Excerpt from the original "Encyclopaedie Fayrye" by John Spense, 1779. Thistleby & Sons Ltd. can make no guarantee as to the efficacy of the above-stated actions, nor can it take responsibility for any undesired results they might procure.

Bartholomew had read all this so many times he could almost have said it from memory, but he read it again one last time. Then he picked up the ingredients and set to work. Each of the things on the list he had gathered over the course of many months, searching them out and hiding them away in his treasure box. The leaves were from the rope of ivy that clung to the back of the house. The straw he had taken from his own pillow. Spoon, breadcrumbs, three dried cherries, and the last of the salt, were all snitched from Mother's kitchen.

Twenty minutes later, Bartholomew clapped the dust from his hands and sat back to inspect his work. The faery dwelling didn't look like much. In fact, it looked dejected, as if someone had simply emptied a pail of rubbish on the floor. He began to wonder if perhaps this was just silly and hopeless. His skin hurt so terribly. He didn't know how long it took a faery to find such a dwelling, and he didn't know if he should wait for it, or if he should go away and come back later. And what if the faery *didn't* help him? What if it didn't want to be his friend, and soured the milk like his mother had said it would? The more Bartholomew thought about it the more miserable he became, until finally he shook his head and crouched down in front of the round window. Hugging his knees to his chest, he looked out.

A mangy black dog was wandering along the gutter, searching for a cabbage leaf or a bone. At the far end of the alley, two men were conversing quietly in the blue-gray shadows of some eaves. Light the color of lamp oil drifted down from the slit of sky. Across the way, the Buddelbinsters' house stood hunched around itself. The sour-looking woman was in the yard, a basket of washing against her hip. She was laying sheets out on the grass to dry. She shuffled across the place where the circle of mushrooms had been, once, twice, a dozen times, but nothing happened. No wings, or wind. It didn't work anymore. The magic was gone.

Bartholomew's gaze traveled on to the house. Something stirred in an upper window. He tensed, half expecting to see the figure again, the dark one that had stood there the day his friend had been taken. The window swung open. Some flimsy curtains were brushed aside. It was the faery mother, seated on a straight-backed wooden chair, head up, hands in her lap, looking out.

Bartholomew pulled back from the glass. He had hardly ever seen her before. But then he hardly ever saw anyone. She was a wood spryte, small and delicate, with a crown of antlers growing out of her head. She was almost pretty. All but her eyes. They were flat, empty, staring out onto the yard as sightless as marbles. She had been weeping.

Bartholomew squinted at her, puzzled. *Does she miss her son? Was he kidnapped, after all?* He had almost managed to persuade himself that the lady in plum was a magician of some sort, and a relative, and had taken his friend away with her to give him a better life. But all in an instant he wasn't so sure. That was not the face of a lonely mother. That was the blank, disbelieving face of someone with so much grief locked up inside her that she didn't know what to do with it, someone with a barb in her heart that no amount of crying or screaming could ever dull.

In the yard, the sour-looking woman continued to lay out the washing. She faced the house, even walked under the window several times, but she never even glanced at the faery in it. *What a rude, mean person,* Bartholomew thought. He looked back at the faery mother.

Her mouth had begun to move. Her lips were forming words, but he was too far away to make sense of them. In her lap, her hands folded, unfolded. Slowly she began to rock back and forth in the chair. The sour-looking woman was laying out bedding now, turning the yard into a checkerboard of pillowcases and withered grass.

Bartholomew inched closer to the windowpane. A breeze was picking up. Wisps of the white curtain were blowing across the faery mother's face, into her antlers and eyes. She didn't move from her chair.

The breeze gathered in strength. Sheets and

bedclothes began to shift, skittering gently across the weeds in the yard. A shadow passed overhead. Bartholomew glanced up and saw that the summer sky had become low and angry, darkening with sudden weather. The sheets began to curl over themselves, piling up into heaps.

The sour-looking woman worked on, flicking out more sheets, even as the other ones twisted across the yard. At the end of Old Crow Alley, the two men were still deep in conversation. The dog had found a scattering of slop and was scratching through it lazily. All seemed oblivious to the flooding darkness.

The breeze was a wind now, churning the bedclothes, picking them up and hurling them into the air. Curtains slashed and flew across the window where the faery mother sat, now obscuring her, now revealing her stark against their whiteness.

Suddenly there was a vicious shriek, like metal grinding against metal. The faery mother's face exploded inches from his own, flat against the other side of his window. Her eyes were huge, dead-black, and sunken. Tears flowed from them, too many tears, streaming over her cheeks. Her mouth gaped open.

Bartholomew screamed. He tried to jerk back from the glass, but he couldn't move. His body had gone cold, stiff as the water pump in winter. The faery mother's mouth opened even wider, and a horrid keening wail snaked from within.

"You won't hear it come!" she screamed, and her eyes began to roll back in her head.

Bartholomew was crying, trembling, terror strangling the air from his lungs.

"You won't hear a thing. The cloven hooves on the floorboards. The voice in the dark. It'll come for you, and you won't hear a thing."

Bartholomew clamped his hands across the window, trying desperately to block out the face.

But she only laughed a hopeless, anguished laugh, and sang:

"You won't hear it calling. You won't know until it's too late, too late, TOO LATE!"

With a start, Bartholomew fell back and struck his head hard upon the floor.

~ ~ ~

The next morning, while Bartholomew was still in bed, his mother came in with a smelly, boiled poultice, and a wet rag for his head. She didn't ask where he had been. When he thought of it—the little faery house in the attic, the round window, and the face—it made him feel a million times worse.

"Mother?" he said quietly. "Mother, did you hear anything about the Buddelbinsters?"

"The Buddelbinsters?" Her voice was almost as hoarse as his own. "Don't bother about them. There's enough of bad luck in this house. We don't need anyone else's."

"Bad luck?" Bartholomew sat up a little. "About their son?"

"Shush now, Barthy. Lie still. Not the son. The mother. Driven mad with grief, Mary Cloud says, but that's just talk. Likely she died of the cholera. It's all a-raging in London now."

His mother finished patting down the poultice and left. The flat door banged shut, then the door to the alley. He heard Hettie pattering in the kitchen, and the clink of a bowl. A few minutes later she came into the tiny room. Her arms were bare. She had pressed the juice from the red bird-berries Mother used to brighten the colors in the washing and had painted her arms in sloppy, twining lines.

"Hallo, Barthy," she said. She smiled at him.

Bartholomew stared back. He almost shouted at her. *What a silly thing to do. What a silly, know-nothing little person you are!*

Hettie kept smiling.

"Where'd Mother go?" he asked after a while.

She stopped smiling and climbed up beside him on the bed. "To find some turnips for breakfast. It'll be all right, Barthy."

Bartholomew looked down at their arms, Hettie's dripping red, right next to his own delicate swirls. He knew why she had done it then.

"Well, aren't we the finest-looking people in Bath," he said, and then they went to the wash tub and he helped her scrub away the red, and they were both smiling by the time Mother came back with the turnips.

CHAPTER VI
Melusine

PAK, *n. Faery vernacular meaning "one who has a long nose," or spy. (Not to be confused with the breed of faery called "puck" or "pooka," those wicked shapeshifters whose cunning, and shocking lack of moral restraint, do yet again illustrate for us the debased nature of the fay.)*

Mr. Jelliby slammed the dictionary closed and buried his head in his hands, letting the leather-bound volume slip from his lap. It fell to the carpet and lay there, spine up, its pages crumpled.

A low moan escaped his lips. They thought he had been spying. Mr. Lickerish, Lord Chancellor to the Queen, thought he was a spy. He, of all people. No doubt the Throgmortons and Lumbidules of this world would think nothing of breaking down a door or two in order to inform themselves on other people's business. But Mr. Jelliby, who thought simply getting out of bed quite tiring enough and had no wish to pry into other people's business, was now the one under suspicion. He was not used to being distrusted, and it upset him very much.

For days after his disgraceful departure from Nonsuch House he was in a glum mood. Ophelia noticed almost at once, but when she asked what was troubling him he wouldn't say. He stopped going to his club. He stopped seeing the visitors who came to the house on Belgrave Square. For the Covent Garden performance of *Semiramide,* he was absent from the family box, and he even stayed home from service on Sunday morning. When Ophelia at last confronted him and told him she had heard what had happened from some dear and trusted friends and that he needn't worry himself over it, he locked himself in his study and refused to come out.

He knew most of Ophelia's "dear and trusted friends." He knew them quite well. Gossips, the lot of

them. They made it their business to find out everything about everyone, and then to toss this informa-
tion around them like flowers at a wedding. If they had
obtained some scandalous bit of news, every drawing
room in London would have heard of it by now. What
humiliation. What dishonor to his name. People had
always thought him a pleasant, vacant sort of person.
The sort of person you could invite to parties without having to worry about his bringing up sore top-
ics like faery integration or Charles Dickens's novels.
No one had ever taken much notice of Mr. Jelliby,
but at least they hadn't thought ill of him. And now?
Now they would be inventing all sorts of stories. He
had an image in his mind of a gaggle of long-necked
geese, all done up in petticoats and crinolines, sitting around a stuffy parlor and talking about him.

"Did you hear, Jemima, he broke down a door? Oh, yes! In the
Lord Chancellor's house! You know, behind all those handsome looks
and broad smiles he must be secretly quite the violent fellow."

"Almost certainly, Muriel. One has to be in his profession. And
how poor Ophelia is faring, with that hanging over her head like a
veritable Sword of Damocles, heaven only knows. She's a perfect

angel, not carrying on and saying only good of him. The silly dear. When he's so obviously a wicked spy . . ."

And they were not even the worst. He absolutely dreaded the next meeting of the Privy Council. Mr. Lickerish would be there. The other members would be there, all quite well-informed, all wondering whether he worked for the Americans or the French or some radical anti-faery formation. All wondering how well it paid.

But the day came whether he wanted it to or not, and when Ophelia pressed her ear against his door and told him he must make himself ready, he growled at her to send the valet with a note.

"Arthur, that will only make things worse," she said, leaning her head against the door. "You must go out and confront them! You have nothing to fear." She waited for a reply, and when none came she added gently, "*I* don't believe you were spying on Mr. Lickerish. And you *know* you weren't. You did no wrong other than that little accident with the door, and I've already sent Mr. Lickerish a sincere apology with six guineas for the repairs."

Mr. Jelliby grunted and stabbed at the cold ashes

in the grate with the poker. "Six guineas. Six guineas won't mend my reputation. I won't ever be able to show my face again. Thanks to your daft friends it may as well have been printed front page in the *Times*."

Ophelia sighed. "Oh, Arthur, you're making it out to be far worse than it really is. People will always talk! They will always invent and embellish things to make them more interesting. Why, you remember the time I wore the blue silk instead of the mourning colors for Father's passing, and it was quite by mistake, but a tale started up that Papsy had not been my father and that I was in fact adopted from India. From India, darling! The only thing one can do against these things is ignore them. Present yourself cheerfully and confidently and . . ."

She was forced to go on like this for a good fifteen minutes, reassuring him patiently while he sulked and grumbled. But there are few things quite so persuasive as time, and in the end he said, "Oh, confound it all," and dressed himself, and combed his hair, and left his room rather cautiously, as if he expected the whole house to pounce on him the instant he stepped into the hall. He was almost surprised when the maid only curtseyed, Brahms was cheerful, and the ancient gnome, whom he again had the misfortune of having as his driver, was no more ill-disposed toward him than usual.

Wagons and steam carriages clogged the thoroughfares more thickly than the smoke that day, but the gnome took a roundabout down Tothill Street and Mr. Jelliby arrived at Westminster in good time. He stepped down from the carriage in front of the South Gate and stood for a few moments, very still, in the usual gaggle of protesters and newsboys that collected there. He let the chimney ash drift onto his coat. Then he took a deep breath and plunged into the cool of the hall.

All Ophelia's gentle coaxing and encouragements melted away as he stepped onto the massive stone slabs of the floor. Suddenly he was a boy again, the new one entering the boarding school refectory for the first time, and every titter and sideways glance set off little pangs of embarrassment around his temples. He kept his eyes fixed on the tips of his shoes as he walked, wishing he could simply fly past all those staring faces. It was only when he was seated in the farthest, darkest corner of the Privy Council's chamber that he dared raise his eyes again. A servant looked back at him from where he was waxing the chair legs. For a moment they stared at each other. Then the servant shrugged and returned his attention to his wax cloth. Mr. Jelliby slumped back. *Drat.* Except for him and the servant the room was empty. He was ridiculously early.

He couldn't just sit there for twenty minutes. Not while the lords and barons trickled in with their noses in the air and bemusement in their eyes. He got up and left the room, walking down the hall at a brisk pace so that everyone who saw him would think he was actually going somewhere. There were miles of corridors in the new palace, all very wide and slightly dim despite the gasoliers burning along the walls. At first there were people crowding everywhere and the air was full of voices, but the farther he walked the more deserted the halls became until he could hear nothing but the distant ticking of a clock, echoing in time with his shoes. After several minutes he began to feel foolish hurrying down corridor after empty corridor. He sidestepped quickly into a doorway, listened, and hearing nothing, let himself in.

The room was small, just a closet compared to some of the other chambers in the palace. The wall facing the river was all windows, and the rest was all empty bookcases except for a large walnut cabinet that stood next to the door. There were no drapes, no papers or photographs. Mr. Jelliby decided it must be a clerk's office not yet moved into. All the better. He sat down on the bare floorboards and resolved to wait. In ten minutes he would hurry back to the council chamber and enter unnoticed during the main crush of gentlemen.

It was very quiet in the room. The absence of books on the shelves made it feel hollow somehow, not lived in. He pulled out his timepiece and waited for the minute hand to move. It took an eternity. *Tick.* He set to drumming his fingers against the floor. *Tick.* Two people passed by the door, deep in conversation. "Most unbecoming . . ." he heard, before the voices receded again. *Tick.* More footsteps. Another person was coming down the hallway, pattering lightly. Mr. Jelliby stood, stretching. The footsteps came closer. *Are they slowing? Oh heavens, they won't stop. They will go past. They must go past.*

The feet stopped, directly in front of the door to the empty clerk's office.

Mr. Jelliby clutched his watch so hard he almost cracked its glass face. His eyes flickered around the room. *What am I to do?* He could go to the door and face whoever was about to enter. Or he could hide. Hide in the cabinet and hope upon hope that whoever it was, he was a quick fellow utterly uninterested in walnut closets. Mr. Jelliby chose the cabinet.

It was one of those odd desk cabinets that is actually a tiny closed chamber, with drawers and compartments for ink and envelopes all up its walls. It had a little padded bench and a paraffin lamp to see by. A pane of warped glass looked out its door. Mr. Jelliby scooted in clumsily, and when he was pressed back as far as he could get, he shut himself in.

Not a moment too soon. The door to the hallway

opened quietly. Mr. Jelliby held his breath. And John Wednesday Lickerish slipped into the room.

It took Mr. Jelliby a second to fully grasp his own bad luck. This was a dream, surely. Perhaps there was a gas leak in the palace and he had breathed the fumes, or contracted lead poisoning, and the effects were coming on now in hallucinations and headaches. But no. This was his life. And it made him angry.

Confound it! Confound everything! Of course it would be the faery politician. And of course the bulb-headed blighter would choose this room to enter, out of all the hundreds of rooms in Westminster. Now if Mr. Jelliby were to be discovered it would mean more than just humiliation. It would mean an investigation, banishment from his club and all his favorite drawing rooms, perhaps even arrest. Hiding inside the furnishings of a private Parliament chamber only days after widespread rumors of spying was not something that could be interpreted favorably. With a few well-placed words, his opponents could easily have him thrown out of Parliament altogether. Mr. Jelliby had half a mind to burst from the cabinet then and there, and shout at the faery that he was bringing him ill fortune by the buckets and Mr. Jelliby wanted nothing to do with him. But of course he could never have brought himself to do it. He simply sat, rooted to the bench, and watched through the glass pane.

The faery politician walked to the center of the room. He glanced around him. Then he moved toward the large mullioned windows that looked out over the Thames and undid a latch, throwing wide the casement. His hand went out. Something moved in his palm—metal feathers and mechanics. A clock-work sparrow. It rose out of Mr. Lickerish's palm, fluttering for an instant in the air. Mr. Jelliby saw a brass capsule catch the sunlight and glint from one brass leg. Then the bird shot away across the river and was lost in the ribbons of smoke rising from the city's roofs.

Mr. Jelliby took a very small, very careful breath. *A capsule.* It was carrying a message. The bird was a mes-senger bird, like the sort his grandparents had used when there were no such things as speaking-machines and telegraphs. Only the ones his grandparents had used had pumping hearts and soft feathers. A contraption of the sort the faery had just launched did not come cheaply. Mr. Jelliby's own household didn't have any. Ophelia wasn't taken with such things, being sophisticated, and far more interested in magic than in machinery. But he had seen them often while promenading: automatons shaped like dogs, like crows and spiders and even people, staring with beady eyes from the windows of the fine mechanical-chemist's shops on Jermyn Street. Clockwork horses were the newest craze. They were hideous and loud, shot steam from every joint, and looked rather more like rhinoceroses than horses, but the king of France owned a stableful, and the Queen of England, not to be outdone, had purchased a fieldful, and soon every duke and minor noble owned at least one mechanically drawn coach.

The faery refastened the window and turned to go, again casting a wary look around the room. He was only steps from the door to the hallway when it was thrown open again. It only barely missed knocking out a few sharp faery teeth.

Mr. Jelliby couldn't see the visitor from his hiding place in the cabinet, but he did see the Lord Chancellor's face go sharp, saw his eyes harden and his hands grasp at the fabric of his coat. It was someone the faery knew, then. Someone he didn't want to see.

"You stinking candle," Mr. Lickerish hissed. "What are you doing here? Melusine, we must *not* be seen together! Not in public!"

It was the lady. The lady Mr. Jelliby had seen rushing down the brilliant passage in Nonsuch House. Mr. Lickerish pulled her into the room and shut the door behind her, drawing the bolt with a sharp *clank*.

She stepped into the middle of the room. "We are not *in* public," she said, turning to face the faery.

Mr. Jelliby stared. Her lips, bright red in the powder of her face, had not moved. The voice had come from somewhere in her vicinity, but it was not the voice of a lady. It was not even the voice of a man. It was a thin, cold, lazy-sounding voice that made Mr. Jelliby think of frosty leaves against stone. And it was unmistakably the voice of a faery.

Mr. Lickerish stamped his foot. "Melusine, we—"

"*Don't* call me that," the voice snapped. Again the red lips were motionless.

Mr. Lickerish's eyes went wide, expanding into two black moons. With savage suddenness, he lifted his walking stick and struck it hard across the back of the lady's head. There was a yelp. The lady bent forward under the force of the blow, but her face remained stiff.

"Never are you to give me orders," Mr. Lickerish said, lowering the walking stick. "*Melusine.*" He spat the name.

"Forgive me, *Sathir.*" The voice was subdued again. "That is her name. It is not mine. It brings back memories to her. Ones I do not wish her to recall."

Mr. Lickerish began to pace to and fro behind the lady's back. She remained still as waxwork, a shadowy statue in the center of the room. With a start, Mr. Jelliby realized her face was directed straight at his hiding place. She wore a little top hat that hid her eyes, *but was she watching him? Right that very moment?* He stared at her, wondering who she was. Her clothes had been sumptuous once, all those yards of velvet, the seed buttons and swirling stitchery. They weren't anymore. The plum-colored skirts had become filthy, every swish bringing to light layers upon layers of lace and petticoats, discolored with dirt. One of her gloves was torn and flecked with what looked like dried blood. He tried to make out her features, but all he could see was a dainty chin and that red, red mouth.

"Why are you here, Jack Box?" Mr. Lickerish stopped pacing long enough to glare at her back. "Speak quickly and beg the wind-strewn stars it was important enough to disturb me. The Privy Council is convening in less than five minutes." He took a pocket watch from his waistcoat and examined it fiercely.

"Minutes," the voice said, disdain and disbelief coming together in a point. "Minutes are for *humans*."

Mr. Lickerish's eyes grew round again. The lady took a few halting steps away from him. "No matter!" the voice added quickly. "You must do as you please, of course. I have found a new one."

There was a pause.

"I saw it the day I took Child Number Nine, watching from a window. It lives right across from Nine, in the same alley"

Another pause. Still Mr. Lickerish said nothing.

"The faery districts are a boon to us, *Sathir*. Tens and hundreds of changelings just waiting to be plucked up. And no one gives a tinker's thumb if they live or die." A brittle, unpleasant laugh sounded in the room. "The last one I didn't even have to steal. I bought it right from under its mother's nose. For a purse of rose hips."

Mr. Jelliby, who had developed a cramp and was trying every possible way to relieve it without making a sound, pricked his ears. *Changelings. Where have I last heard about—* Oh. Oh dear. It was John Lickerish, then. He was a part of it. The Lord Chancellor of England, and all tangled up with the deaths of nine half-bloods.

All Mr. Jelliby could think of was his awful luck at having to know this. *If only I had stayed out of this accursed room.* He might have chosen a different door, or pretended to be lost, or simply stayed in the council chamber and faced the stares. He might have gone home a few hours from now and spent a pleasantly uneventful evening complaining to Ophelia about his many woes. Because Mr. Jelliby didn't *want* to know who was murdering the children. They were changelings, after all. They were far away, and he had never known them, and he had his own troubles. But the conversation went on, and Mr. Jelliby was forced to hear every word.

"I don't want hundreds," Mr. Lickerish was saying, and his voice was angry and very soft. "I want one. Just *one* that actually works. I tire of this. I tire of the endless failure. It has gone on far too long, do you hear me? Too much attention, too many people coming to know about it. Last week the Privy Council was convened to discuss this very operation." He turned back to the window, his face taut. "If you pay any attention at all to what is happening around you, you will have heard that the failed changelings were found. I knew they would be. The river does not keep his dead for long. But that it would cause such a stir! There have only been nine. Nine sniveling, worthless little

Peculiars, and the whole country goes into hysterics. It must end. You must find me a changeling that works, one that meets every qualification. I want no more *almosts*. No more *very nears*." Mr. Lickerish stood on the tips of his polished shoes and whispered up into the hair at the back of the lady's head, so quietly that Mr. Jelliby could hardly hear the words. "I want one that is everything, Jack Box. Do not bring me another until you are sure."

The lady shied away again, away from Mr. Lickerish. "I thought I was sure last time," the voice said. "I *was* sure. And yet— No. There will be no more mistakes, *Sathir*. I will make doubly certain this time. Beyond a shadow of a doubt."

Mr. Jelliby's leg twitched. It was only a very tiny twitch, of a muscle or a sinew, but it disturbed the cabinet. The padded bench creaked such a little bit. Mr. Lickerish spun.

"Did you hear that?" he whispered, eyes darting around the room.

Mr. Jelliby blanched.

"Yes," the voice said. "Yes, I heard it."

Mr. Lickerish took a step toward the cabinet, his lips pressed so tight they were bloodless. He lifted his hand, long fingers reaching for the handle. He was too small to see through the little glass pane, but it made no difference. Another step and he would open the door. He would see Mr. Jelliby cowering in the darkness and then—

A spasm passed over the lady's face, a flicker under the surface of her skin, and suddenly her expression was no longer blank. Her eyes fixed on Mr. Jelliby's through the glass. He could see them now, shining bright and full of pain. Then her red lips parted and she was speaking in a creamy soft voice that held the faintest hint of an accent. "It is only the woodwork, my lords. It expands in the heat of the day."

Her voice stopped, but she continued to stare at Mr. Jelliby, and her mouth continued to move. It formed two words. Two soundless words, just once, but they rang clear as crystal in his head.

Help me.

CHAPTER VII
A Bad One

"MUMMY, do you have pennies behind your eyes?" Hettie didn't even look up as she asked it. Her bony hands were wrapped around a chipped mug of broth, and she was staring at something at its bottom.

Mother said nothing. She was stabbing a woolen stocking with a long needle. Her mind was far, far away.

"Do you have pennies behind your eyes?" Hettie asked again, louder this time.

Bartholomew looked up from his own broth. Normally he would have laughed at her. He would have pinched her under the table and repeated her question in a high, foolish voice until she giggled.

But he didn't think he could do that anymore. He felt old now, and frightened, and laughing and pinching seemed such long-ago things.

The red symbols were not healing. Mother had bathed them in hot water, rubbed them with smelly leaves, packed them with poultices, and wrapped them in the cleanest linens that could be found, but even now, days later, they looked much the same. The flesh around them was not as swollen as before, and oddly enough he only felt them when there was a piercing noise like the creak of a floorboard or the cry of a bird. But they weren't fading; they weren't scarring or growing scabs. They were just there, a pattern of bloodred lines whirling across his skin.

"Mother!" It was Hettie.

The needle pricked Mother's finger just below the nail and she brought her head up with a little gasp. "Hettie, what *are* these strange ideas you have?" She sucked her finger. "Why would I have pennies behind my eyes?"

Hettie sank her face into her mug. "Someone told me you did," she said, and her voice echoed. "He said

I should pick them out and buy brown-sugar toffee with them."

Bartholomew sat up. Mother was going to scream at Hettie now, cry and weep, and beg that it wasn't true, that Hettie hadn't been talking to strangers. But Mother hadn't heard the last bit. Instead her eyes lit up with a rare twinkle and she asked, "Oh, and what sort of someone would that be? A little prince, perhaps, upon a wild boar?"

Hettie looked at her reproachfully. "No. A raggedy man."

"A raggedy man?" Mother knocked her wounded finger once against the table, as if to make sure it was still functioning, and then hunched back over her stitching. "That's not very enchanting."

"Of course he's not enchanting, Mummy, he's a raggedy man." Hettie was being very sullen this morning. *What did she have to be peeved about*, Bartholomew wondered. She hadn't come within a hairsbreadth of being hanged. She hadn't had her friend stolen, or been magically written on, or had a dead faery screech at her some nonsense about hooves and voices.

Mother looked at Hettie sadly. "Oh, deary." She dropped her needlework and gathered Hettie into her lap. "Deary, deary, deary. I do wish you could have real friends. I wish you could go into the street and chase after the wood sprytes and run errands to the market like other children do, but— Well, you just can't. Folks out there, they don't— They would . . ." Mother trailed off.

They would kill you, Bartholomew thought, but Mother wasn't going to tell Hettie that. She wasn't going to tell Hettie that she would never be able to play in the street, or go to market, or chase after the wood sprytes. Not in Bath. Hettie would be snatched up and hanged faster than you could say "gentleman jack."

"I'm afraid you'll just have to make do with made-up friends for a while longer" was all Mother said.

"Mummy, the raggedy man is *not* my friend," Hettie corrected her sternly.

Mother lifted Hettie off her lap and set her squarely on the floor.

"Well, why did you invent him then?" she said shortly, and by the sharp way she jabbed her needle into the stocking it was clear she didn't want to hear the answer.

Hettie couldn't see that, though. "I didn't!" she said, going to the wash pot next to the stove and drowning her mug in the cold soapy water. "He came by himself. He comes every night, through the keyhole in the door." Her voice became quiet. "He sings songs to me. Long, sad songs." The mug hit the bottom of the pot with a *thunk*. "They're not pretty songs."

Mother set down her needlework slowly. She was watching Hettie, staring at her back. "Child, what are you talking about? Who is this person?"

Bartholomew saw the fear in the lines of her face, heard it in the lowness of her voice. And then everything Hettie had said snapped together in his mind. *A stranger . . . comes through the keyhole . . . comes in the night.*

He jumped up, scraping his stool noisily. "That was a fine breakfast, Mother. Don't mind Hettie, she's just playing pretend. Should we go find you some sand from behind the house? Should we, Hettie? Come on. Now."

Mother picked up the stocking again, but she was still

eyeing Hettie. "Sand. Yes. Go and get me some. But Bartholomew . . ." His mother's hands were tight round the wool, so tight her knuckles poked up. "If anyone even looks at Hettie you run her back here, d'you hear me? Straight back through that door, sand or no sand."

"Yes, Mother. We'll be all right. We'll be back before you know it."

Mrs. Kettle did laundry for the few people who could afford not to do it themselves, the few people she could trick into believing she had a proper laundry service and didn't trundle their nighties and undergarments into the depths of the faery slums in a green-painted wheelbarrow. She bought the lye from peddlers, but it had always been the children's job to dig for scrubbing sand in the little courtyard behind the house.

Hettie tied her hood under her chin and went to Bartholomew, ignoring his outstretched hand.

"Let's *go*!" he said under his breath, taking hold of her shoulder and bundling her toward the door. He unbolted it, peeked out to make sure no one was there. Then he crept into the passage and motioned for Hettie to follow. As soon as they were out of earshot, Bartholomew pulled her into a hollow under a flight of steps and knelt down next to her, whispering, "Where does he live, Het? Can he fly? Was he very nice?"

Hettie looked at him dumbly. "Nice?" she repeated. "We're supposed to get sand. Why are we under the stairs?"

"Yes, and when was the first time you saw him? And what were you thinking, startling Mother like that?" He gave her shoulder a shake. "Come *on*, Hettie, tell me!"

"The day before yesterday," she said, shoving his hand away. "And Barthy, you don't need to joggle me. You'll shake my head loose."

The day I built the faery dwelling. Bartholomew scrabbled out from under the stairs.

"Run back quick as you can, Hettie, we'll get sand later."

Mother would clout him for leaving Hettie by herself, but he couldn't be bothered with that right now. His invitation had worked. It had *worked*. He ran down the passage, up another staircase, taking the steps two at a time. And for one bright moment as he flew up the steps, he was happy. Completely and utterly happy.

Then he pulled himself into the attic and the dusty darkness, and he thought of how the faery had only shown itself to Hettie and not him, and a little thistle of envy buried itself between his ribs. *She* shouldn't have seen it first. It was his faery. It should have come to him.

He stole across the floor and squirmed into his secret gable. The faery dwelling was exactly as he had left it. The shriveled cherries were still tangled in its walls. The salt he had sprinkled over its roof sparkled in the sunlight like snow, undisturbed. The last few days, Bartholomew had come up there every chance he'd gotten, searching the little room for the slightest change, the slightest hint that his faery had come. Each time there had been nothing. And there was still nothing.

He went down on his knees, huffing, blowing a cobweb back and forth, back and forth. *What could* that *mean*? If the invitation had been successful, why hadn't the faery eaten Bartholomew's offerings? He had spent enough time collecting them for the stupid thing. And shouldn't it have announced itself? His breathing slowed. The happiness of a few moments went out like a candle. *How long will I have to wait?*

He thought back to the words in the tattered book, about the faery and how it was supposed to have followed its summoner home. He hadn't seen any faery. Hettie had. And if it could follow him home from a stream in some wild wood, it ought to be able to find its way down a few flights of stairs.

But what if the faery didn't want to make itself known? What if that was not how house faeries worked, and Bartholomew had to be nice to it first and gain its trust? The book had been very vague on all that. He supposed he could try it. He could write the faery a letter, ask it a question or two, place the paper inside the faery dwelling, and hope upon hope it would answer him. He didn't know if domesticated faeries could even read. But he could think of nothing else to do.

His first question would be what the patterns on his skin meant. They were words, he was sure of that, but in what language? They looked a lot like the writing he had seen on the floor of the room with metal birds. Not nearly as complicated, though. In fact, they appeared to be just two or three of the same symbols, repeated over and over again.

One of his old books had a blank page between the cover and the title page, and this he separated from the spine, very carefully so as not to crack the glue. He was not especially good at writing. When he was very small—what seemed like ages ago—a young man who wore garish waistcoats and looked perpetually ill had lived in the flat next door. He was a poverty-stricken painter who, for some unfathomable reason, found the filthy streets and leaning houses of the faery districts picturesque. He hadn't been like other people. When he had spotted Bartholomew running up to the attic, he hadn't been afraid of him or buried him under an elderberry bush. He had told Bartholomew stories, taught him how to read. He had given him the books Bartholomew now kept behind the stove. He had been rather like a friend. But then he had left in a pine box and Bartholomew had forgotten much of what he had taught him. No, Bartholomew was not very good at writing. But he did it anyway.

Dear Mr. Fayrye, he wrote. He was using a quill rubbed in the tar from the window frame. The tar was used to seal the chinks and keep the rain from dripping in, but during the summer months it turned almost liquid under the hot sun. It didn't make very good ink. It was sticky and difficult to direct across the paper, but proper ink was not to be had.

I have an important question. I would be very happy and grateful if you would answer it. What do these signs mean?

Here he copied the markings on his skin as exactly as he could onto the paper. It was much easier than writing in English. It was like a drawing, and he didn't have to worry about how the letters fit together or what sounds they made. Then he wrote:

Thank you very much, and good day,

And signed the whole thing,

Bartholomew Kettle

He made a flourish under his name that made him very proud, and pushed the paper carefully into the faery dwelling. Then he went down to the flat and was clouted for leaving Hettie by herself.

> > >

That night, as Bartholomew lay on his cot half thinking, half dreaming about faeries and quills and question marks, he heard a sound. A gentle clicking in the kitchen, like old, rusty metal grinding against itself. The door to the flat. Someone was fiddling with the lock.

He sat bolt upright. More clicks. Swinging his legs over the edge of the bed, he got up and padded silently to the door of his room. The sound stopped. He knelt down and pressed his eye to the keyhole. The kitchen beyond was eerie, dead. The fire had gone out completely. Mother was fast asleep in her narrow bed, and all the keys were hanging in their place on the far wall: the big toothy key to the flat door; the key to his room; the keys to the soap cupboard and the back gate, all there on a spike in the plaster.

Something was wrong. His eye made another sweep of room. *The door to Hettie's cupboard bed.* It was open, just a crack. And inside, someone was singing.

His heart dropped into his belly. It was not

Hettie's voice. It was not like any voice he had ever heard before. It was hollow and earthy, and it sang in a thin, pointy language that for some reason made Bartholomew feel wicked for listening to it, as if it was not meant for him to hear, as if he were eaves-dropping. But the melody was paralyzing. It went up, then fell, now tempting, now wild, snaking out of the cupboard and filling the whole flat. He was sur-rounded by it, swimming up through swirling black ribbons of sound. It filled his head, becoming louder and faster until it was all there was, all he heard, all he knew.

His eyelids had gone heavy as lead. Inky spots bloomed across his vision. The last thing he remem-bered before his eye fell away from the keyhole and he slid to the floor was seeing the door to Hettie's cup-board bed open a bit more. A dark and gnarled hand curled around from inside. Then Bartholomew's head hit the floor like a stone and he was asleep.

It was the door that woke Bartholomew the next morning. Mother came into the room with a heap of yarn ends, and the worm-eaten wood knocked soundly against his head. He leaped up with a cry.

"Bartholomew Kettle, what are you doing on the *floor*? Larks and stage lights, what's your bed for? Why, I've got half a mind to—"

He didn't stay to hear what exactly she had half a mind for. He was already running, out the door and up the stairs toward the attic, his legs pumping. *Please be answered, please be answered.* He had a creeping dread that the faery would just ignore him and he would find everything exactly the way he had left it.

But this time nothing was the way he had left it. His breath caught in his throat as he crawled under the gable. It looked as if a storm had blown through. His treasure box lay open, its contents strewn across the floor. The string of glass had been tied into a great knot so tight and complicated-looking that he knew he would never be able to undo it. The straw inside the mat had been torn out and stuffed between the tiles overhead. It sifted down now, gentle and golden in the light from the window. As for the faery dwelling, it was in ruins. The twigs he had spent so many months gathering had been trampled into the cracks in the floorboards. The cherries were gone. So was the spoon.

He took a few steps forward, his mind numb. Something crinkled underfoot. It was his letter, half hidden under a tangle of ivy. He knelt down and unfolded it shakily.

There was his writing, so crooked and bad he was ashamed of it now, and around it, little dirty fingerprints like those of a small child. On the other side, bleeding into the creamy paper like a stain, was a number. A single number . . .

10

And that was all.

He stared at it, the straw drifting around him, and his mother's words came unbidden into his mind. The words she had said that day, weeks ago, when the lady in plum had first swept into the shadows of Old Crow Alley and he had begged Mother to let him invite a faery.

And what if you get a bad one.

CHAPTER VIII
To Catch a Bird

TWENTY minutes after the faery gentleman prod-
ded Melusine from the room like a mangy goat,
Mr. Jelliby was still huddled inside the cabinet, eyes
closed, blood thumping a tattoo inside his head.
He felt he was going mad. His brain ached. He was
almost certain it would come sliding out of his nose
at any moment, and wriggle away across the floor on
tentacle feet.

The lady in plum had seen him. She had looked
straight into his eyes and she had not cried out, or
alerted Mr. Lickerish to his presence as one would
have expected from the henchwoman of a dreadful

murderer. No, she had implored Mr. Jelliby for help.
He could still see her lips forming the two words, the
desperation in those bright and shining eyes.

Help me. She may as well have screamed it. But help
her how? Who *was* she?

Slowly, cautiously, Mr. Jelliby opened the cabinet
door and peeked out. The room looked ridiculously
pleasant. Sunlight shone warmly through the windowpanes, making a pattern on the floor. All the
gloom and darkness seemed to have gone out with the
faery and the lady in plum.

Mr. Jelliby stepped down from the cabinet. His
legs very nearly collapsed under him, and he had to
cling to the woodwork for support, his knees all at
angles.

He didn't understand any of it. He didn't understand where that leafy voice had come from, or all
its talk of rose hips and numbers. But he couldn't
very well do nothing. After all, hadn't the lady kept
Mr. Lickerish from discovering him? He owed it to
her to do *something*. He supposed he could rescue her.
Very subtly, of course. There was no need to be all

valiant about it. Ophelia would not approve of him gallivanting after foreign ladies in dirty dresses.

He took a few unsteady steps to get rid of the needles in his legs and then made for the door.

Melusine. What a strange, shadowy sort of name. Was it French? No, that was Mélisande. He would have to look it up when he got home. Or ask Aunt Dorcas. She would know. She knew everything. Aunt Dorcas was his father's sister, was married to a clerk, and lived in three rented rooms in Fitzrovia; because she was not nearly as well-to-do as she would have liked, she consoled herself by knowing all about everyone who was. For all practical purposes, Aunt Dorcas was an encyclopaedia of society in a frock. If there was a lady of any importance at all by the name of Melusine, Aunt Dorcas was sure to know.

Putting his head out the door, Mr. Jelliby looked first up the hall, then down the hall, then slipped out and hurried stiffly away. *Drat,* he thought miserably. *Drat, bang, and smash it all.* The Privy Council. It would have started ages ago. There was no chance of his entering unnoticed now.

He retraced his steps down the echoing corridors until he was back in the wing of the building where the council chamber was. The hall was bare of people now. He laid his hand on the brass handle, putting his head against the cool wood of the door. The droning voice of the Speaker sounded from the other side. One sentence. A pause. Three sentences and another pause. A chair creaked resoundingly. No fighting or arguing. Everyone was probably bored out of their minds. *And wouldn't it be an exciting diversion if that Arthur Jelliby fellow came in right now, late of course, probably having been detained by some dastardly bit of spying.*

He couldn't open that door. He couldn't possibly. He would go to a coffeehouse and wait an hour behind a newspaper, and then he would go home and . . . Ophelia would be unhappy with him. She would ask him how it had gone, and he would have to lie endlessly. But lying seemed vastly easier than this. He simply did not have the courage to open that door and walk past all those curious eyes. Besides, Mr. Lickerish would be there. How Mr. Jelliby could ever again sit coolly in the company of that villainous creature, he did not know.

An elegant gentleman wearing a hat made out of a giant toadstool turned into the hall, instantly cutting Mr. Jelliby's conflict short. Without another thought, he walked away in the opposite direction.

Once free of Westminster's walls, out in the whirling smoke and the sunshine, with the noise of the city all around, Mr. Jelliby felt almost weightless. He took a few deep breaths of the foul air. Then he headed up Whitehall, his fingers toying with the watch chain at his side.

He would need a plan if he were to find Melusine. She might have been abducted. Or become a victim of blackmail. Aunt Dorcas would definitely know of her then. Likely she would know either way, as the lady in plum had obviously been wealthy once. Not so long ago that velvet dress had been a marvelous sight, tailored to turn heads and slacken jaws. It must have cost a fortune.

He wandered into the labyrinth of shop stalls in Charing Cross, letting the vendors swarm around him. He barely noticed their trays of wind-up toys, their pretzels and sticky apples and hand mirrors that made you look prettier than you really were. People jostled him from all sides. Dirty faces blared up close and then fell away again, lost among the coattails. A very tiny faery woman with flowing green hair like river grass materialized in front of him. Strapped to her back was what looked like a bundle of canes.

"An umbrella for the guv'nor?" she said, and flashed her pointed fangs. "An umbrella for the rain?"

Mr. Jelliby laughed. It wasn't the merry, carefree laugh he was used to performing, but it was the best he could do right then. "Rain? Madam, it's bright as bells out here."

"Aye, guv'nor, but it won't be forever. The clouds are comin' in. Down from the North. Be here by evening. A blackbird told me not one hour ago."

Mr. Jelliby paused, regarding the faery woman curiously. Then he tossed her a farthing and plunged into the crowds, a spring in his step.

A blackbird had told her. *A bird.* Birds knew all sorts of things, it seemed. And what would Mr. Lickerish's bird know—the little clockwork one that had flown from the window of the empty clerk's office? What sort of message had been in the glinting capsule on its leg? And to whom was it so swiftly headed? It might not lead him directly to Melusine, but to someone she knew? An associate perhaps? It was a trail at least, something to follow.

He had to catch the bird. Once he had the bird, he hoped it would lead him to Melusine. And once he had bravely rescued her and all that, he supposed he ought to find a way to stop Mr. Lickerish. That part sounded less appealing. In fact, it sounded a little bit dangerous. The faery politician was not some violent street murderer skulking in London's alleys on fog-bound nights. One couldn't simply send the constable around to cart him off. He was Lord Chancellor to the Queen. He was wealthy and powerful, and if he wanted to he could grind Mr. Jelliby under his thumb like a louse. The Law would be no help to Mr. Jelliby. Not against a Sidhe.

But enough of that. Enough moping and wondering. He had a bird to catch. Only, he had no idea *how* to catch it. He sat down an a coffeehouse on the corner where the Strand runs into Trafalgar Square and wondered some more.

He could shoot the thing out of the sky, he supposed. An old hunting rifle hung above the mantel in his study. But the gun was a beast of a thing, and even if he somehow managed to smuggle it into the Westminster area, all London would hear it when it went off. Then there was the brace of Spanish pistols in the hall cabinet. And that little gun he had gotten for his fifteenth birthday. Its handle was mother-of-pearl and there were real rubies and opals all down its barrel and encrusting the trigger. He didn't know if it actually worked. Things so pretty seldom did.

A waiter in antiquated knee breeches and frock coat arrived at Mr. Jelliby's table, and he ordered one of those new tropical drinks that were said to be "sweet as sugar, cold as ice, bright as flowers, and twice as nice." London could be stiflingly hot in summer when the ash clouds closed like a lid overhead and not so much as a breeze stirred from the river. Even here, where the arteries of the city were wider than most, and the houses stood tall and straight on either side, the air was practically solid, rank with the smell of onions and chimneys and unwashed skin. The starched collar of Mr. Jelliby's shirt was already damp with sweat.

By the time the drink arrived it was no longer very cold. It looked like a cup of green paint, thick and syrupy and so sweet it set his teeth on edge. He took two sips and pushed it away, rubbing his eyes with the palms of his hands. What was he thinking? A *gun*? The bird would be shattered in midair. He had to knock it out of the sky and catch it with as little damage as possible. Not blow it to smithereens. Perhaps he should first see where the bird flew. He knew that clockwork things of that sort could only travel to and from a single point. Their whole being was constructed for one route, their wings the proper length, their cogs and insides the proper size for one stretch, and one stretch only. The newer ones, he knew, had tiny battery faeries to propel them. They were equipped with a sort of mechanical map that assured they did not run into church steeples or trestle bridges. The bird still had to be sent off from the correct place, from the correct height, and in the correct direction. Then it would simply fly until its spring wound down. That must be why Mr. Lickerish had launched it from the clerk's office high up in Westminster. Any lower and the bird would probably have crashed through someone's attic window.

A group of raggedy children came running up among the tables, all shouting and begging at once, trying to get some pennies before the waiters drove them off. One came up to Mr. Jelliby, hand outstretched, so dirty a little garden could have grown from it. Mr. Jelliby offered the urchin the green-paint drink, but the child just made a face and ran on.

He turned his attention back to the task at hand. All he had to do was find the bird's trajectory across London's rooftops. Then he could simply choose a point along its path and wait for it to arrive. He pictured himself balancing on a chimney somewhere, swinging wildly about with a butterfly net. It was not a nice thought. He hoped no one would be there to see it.

Leaning down from his chair, he poured the

sluggish green concoction into the gutter. Then he set off for home, drifting through the city streets at an aimless pace, eyes to the cobbles, hat pulled down low over his face. *Crimson lips, unmoving in a white face. Plum-colored skirts. The little top hat, casting a shadow over her eyes.* He was so deep in thought that he was already stepping up to the front door of his house on Belgrave Square before he realized it had begun to rain and he was soaked to the skin.

The next morning, after a good breakfast of sausage and buttered toast, Mr. Jelliby pedaled himself to Westminster on his bicycle and got off on the bridge in a place that gave him a view of the river-facing windows of the new palace. He leaned the bicycle up against a lamppost and crossed his arms on the railing, watching the rows of windows carefully. They barely ever opened. When they did, Mr. Jelliby would crane his neck and squint very determinedly, but the only things that came out of them were hot, flustered faces and once a gentleman's tailcoat. It fell into the river and was fished out by a boatman who put it on sopping wet.

The flower sellers next to Mr. Jelliby began shaking their heads at him. A police officer shot him ever more suspicious looks each time he stalked by. After six hours, Mr. Jelliby could take it no longer and cycled home, tired and humiliated, just as the flame faeries were beginning to flare in the streetlamps.

It took six days of this. Six days of watching the windows of Westminster like a madman before one finally opened, high up near the roof, and a little bead of clockwork and brass flittered out across the river.

The moment Mr. Jelliby saw it he set off running. He left his bicycle, he left his hat, he left the flower sellers hooting and twirling their fingers next to their ears, and he tore away across the bridge.

Just as before, the bird was flying straight toward the forest of garrets and chimney pots on London's east bank. Mr. Jelliby careened into the traffic on Lambeth Road, ignoring the blaring horns and angry shouts. A steam carriage whizzed past inches from his nose, but he barely flinched. He mustn't lose sight of the bird. Not now.

Fortunately for him it was not a real sparrow. Its metal wings made it heavy and slow no matter how frantically they flapped, and it didn't swoop after worms and insects lodged in the stonework the way regular flesh-and-feathers birds did. Mr. Jelliby could very nearly keep pace with it when he ran his fastest.

Unfortunately, his fastest was not overly impressive. He hadn't run properly since a fox hunt several years ago at Lord Peskinborough's country estate; Mr. Jelliby had disagreed with his horse over which direction to take, and the horse had left him to go whichever direction he pleased.

He sped into a side street, feet jarring against the cobblestones. His chin was pointed skyward, eyes blind to everything but the metal bird high above. Someone quite literally bounced off him as he ran, and he heard that someone thump against a shop window. People began shouting after him, laughing and jeering. A rough-looking man with metal teeth grabbed his arm and spun him around. Mr. Jelliby shook him off, only to collide violently with a plump lady holding a parasol. The lady screeched. The bundle he had taken to be a muff revealed a mouth and yelped, and a shower of colorfully wrapped packages tumbled around him. He didn't stop.

"Excuse me! I must get through! Do forgive me!" he cried, swatting a soot-blackened chimney sweep out of his way.

There it was. A glimpse of brass and clockwork, as the bird shot across the slit of sky between two roofs, and then it was gone again.

He had to get on different street. *Blast it, this one was leading him in the wrong direction!*

He spotted an alley, sinuous and dark, leading into a thicket of buildings, and hurled himself down it. Washing, sour with lye, lashed his face. Street children scattered shrieking before him, disappearing into various recesses like so many beetles before a broom. A fallen piece of gutter very nearly ended his chase then and there, but he leaped over it and burst out into the brightness of a wider street.

The bird! Where is the bird? He stopped, panting, whirling to scan the rooftops.

There. He was ahead of it. It was flying along the tops of the houses toward him, leisurely as could be. He dove into the cool shadow of an archway, sending a legless faery scrabbling for safety, and burst through a door. Up some stairs, down a hallway, up some more stairs that were so rickety he felt they might collapse under him at any moment. *Third floor, fourth floor* . . . He had to get to the top of the house, find a window, and snatch the bird right out of the air. It was the only way.

The stair ended at a low crooked door, painted with now-peeling whitewash. He hammered on it, and it was shaken off its bolt. It yawned open. A pretty room lay beyond. A tiny room under a sloping roof, clean and neat, with china in the cabinet and a snowy cloth on the table. An elderly woman sat in it, bent over an embroidery hoop. She looked up languidly when he burst in, as if his intrusion were the dullest thing in the world.

"Do forgive me, madam, I'll be along in a moment,

this is most embarrassing, just one moment, may I open your window?"

He didn't wait for her answer. In two strides he had crossed the room and was flinging the window wide. Its panes shivered in the frame as it knocked against the wall of the gable. He thrust his head out.

There was the bird. It was coming, coming up the street. In three seconds it would be past, fluttering on over the smoking city. But he *could* reach it. If he leaned all the way out and stretched his fingers as far as they went, the bird would fly straight into his hands.

He flailed out over the sill, over the street below. Fifty feet down, people stopped and pointed. Someone screamed. Mr. Jelliby saw the bird approaching—it looked suddenly rather frightening up close—and then . . . *Ow!* It was strong. The wafer-thin metal of its feathers chopped at his fingers as the wings continued to flap. He jerked it toward him, throwing himself back into the old woman's garret. The bird wrenched itself from his grasp and flew across the room, harsh and foreign in the lavender softness of the flat. It smashed against the wall, was hurled to the floor, and there it lay, skittering frantically.

Mr. Jelliby watched it, wide-eyed, his breath scraping in his throat.

"Herald?" The old woman was at his side, her hand on his sleeve. "Herald, deary, you're very late," she said. "It's time for tea."

She led Mr. Jelliby to the table. He didn't resist. The tea things were all there, laid out and waiting—two cups, two saucers, a creamer, a sugar bowl, and a gooseberry tart, as if he had been expected all along.

And so they drank tea, side by side, watching silently as the metal bird convulsed to pieces at their feet.

When it could flap no more, it gave a pitiful mew, and its beak opened and it coughed up a drop of golden light that sputtered and spun, before winking out like a star being covered up.

"Oh." The old lady said, setting down her cup. "It's dead now. Herald, be a sweet and take it outside in the dustpan. I'd want it didn't go bad on the rose-print rug."

CHAPTER IX
In Ashes

CROUCHED on the floor of his ruined sanctuary, Bartholomew Kettle made up his mind. That night he would catch his rebel faery. He would confront the little beast and whether it be good or bad, *force* it to do what he had called it to do. It didn't *want* to be his friend, and there was nothing he could do about that, but it thought it could play tricks on him. It thought it could break his treasures, and frighten Hettie, and Bartholomew wasn't going to stand for that anymore. At nightfall, when it came slipping in with the shadows and the moonlight, he would be ready.

But someone else came first that evening, and Bartholomew was forced to postpone his plans. Heavy boots shuffled in the stairwell, a lantern lit the edge of the door, and Agnes Skinner from the house down the way dropped in for a cup of tea. Bartholomew and Hettie were shooed into the tiny room Bartholomew slept in, and the door was locked behind them.

Settling against the clammy wall, Bartholomew waited for the voices in the kitchen to become louder. He dreaded company. He thought it was foolish, letting people in, like letting a wolf into a room full of birds. But wolves could be interesting, too. Sometimes he would hear a fragment, or a single word, and he would think about it for days. Sometimes he wished *he* could sit in the kitchen, listening and drinking tea.

As long as the wolf doesn't ask questions.

Only a few people knew of Betsy Kettle's two children, and Agnes Skinner was one of them. *Don't get yourself noticed, and you won't get yourself hanged.* It wouldn't take much to get noticed—a glimpse of too-white skin, or bad luck and a goose that didn't lay. Then people would stop bidding Mother good morning in the passage. They would creep past the Kettles' door like it was cursed. *And then . . .*

Hettie was the worrisome one. It hurt her when Mother tried to clip the branches from her head, and nothing short of a blindfold could hide her black-glass stare. Mother had sewn her a deep green hood so that she could go into the courtyard to scratch for sand, but she was never allowed to speak to anyone, never allowed up the stairs or into the street.

It was a delicate balance Mother had to strike, and Bartholomew felt a little bit proud when he thought how well she managed it. Too open, and they would be discovered; too secret and people would start to talk, filling in all the things they didn't know with their own ugly suspicions. So she kept a few friends, gossiped with the neighbors, and brought violets to folks when there was a death in the family. Agnes Skinner was one of her oldest friends. She was a widow and a thief, with a hard staccato voice that pried and poked into everything. She did ask about the children now and then, sometimes so pointedly Bartholomew wondered if she suspected. And every time she came he sat in the dark and worried, a little bird, and the wolf just beyond the door.

The kitchen filled with talk as the women pattered about. The kettle began to whistle, and Bartholomew smelled brewed tea leaves. He heard a cork being pulled free with a wet *plop*.

That would be the spirits. A tall, cut-glass bottle of blackberry cordial sat on a high shelf in the kitchen. It was a relic from the time when Bartholomew's father still lived with them. He had gone away often, without warning, sometimes for months at a time, and then the door would open and he would be back. Sometimes he came back dirty and travel-stained, sometimes clean and polished, with lace at his cuffs. He always brought something when he returned. One time it was ribbons, one time cabbages. Once he had brought a ham and a string of pearls stuffed inside his shirt. The blackberry cordial was one of those fleeting gifts, the only one Mother hadn't sold or traded. Bartholomew didn't know why she kept it. Still, the only reasonable excuse to use it was for company, and so she had the habit of lacing the tea with it.

It was not very long before the two women were quite merry in the other room. Every so often, a burst of giggling would erupt, and the voices would become so loud that Bartholomew could hear every word.

"Did you see she's planted roses?" Mother was saying, and he heard wood straining as one of them leaned back in her chair. "Roses, Aggy! As if she wants to make that ugly yard all *beautified*." She laughed, a trifle bitterly. "They won't grow, you know. The dirt's rotten out here with the factories going day and night, and even if it weren't, roses won't help that wretched house a bit. Not that one. She'd have been better off making jam out of the hips if she insists on buying such frivolousnesses in the first place. Or tea." Her voice became wistful. "Rose-hip tea does taste lovely. . . ."

Mrs. Skinner made an incoherent sound of consolation. "I wouldn't know, Betsy, but I wager it doesn't even compare to yours. Why, it warms my bones, it does. Every time."

Bartholomew could almost see Mother preening at the words, trying to be dainty, trying to be prim, flapping her work-worn hands as if they were the soft white fingers of a gentlewoman. "Nonsense, Aggy. But do have some more, won't you? There now, mind you don't snort it up when I tell you what Mr. Trimwick did last—"

The voices dropped low again. Bartholomew could hear nothing but a murmur through the wall. He sank to his knees and scooted silently across the floor, feeling in the dark for Hettie. He found her at the far end of the room. She was crouched under the window, playing silently with her doll. Its name was Pumpkin and it had a checkered handkerchief for a dress. It had a checkered handkerchief for a head, too, and handkerchief hands and feet. It was really nothing but checkered handkerchief.

"How does he look, Hettie?" Bartholomew's voice was the tiniest whisper. Mrs. Skinner mustn't hear them. Mother had probably told her they were asleep.

"Hettie, what's the raggedy man like?"

"Raggedy," she said, and danced her handkerchief into a different corner. Apparently she was not about to forgive him for leaving her under the stairs.

"*Shhh.* Keep quiet, will you? Look, Het, I'm sorry. I already said I was, and I shouldn't have run off like that. Please tell me?"

She eyed him from under her branches. He could practically hear the cogs whirring inside her head, debating whether to ignore him and give him what he deserved, or to enjoy the satisfaction of telling him something he desperately wanted to know.

"He doesn't stand straight," she said after a while. "He's all crooked and dark, and he's got a hat on his head with a popped top. I can never see much of him, and it sounds like he has bugs in his throat when he breathes, and . . ." She was having trouble putting it into words. "And the shadows—they follow him about."

No petal wings, then. Not nice at all. What a fool he'd been. "Oh. All right. Did he tell you anything? What are his songs about?"

Even in the dark Bartholomew could see her gaze go hard and flat. "I'm not going to talk about those," she said. She turned away again and hugged her doll to her cheek, rocking it like a baby.

Bartholomew felt a horrible guilt at that. This was his fault. The faery and all its tricks. And Hettie was the one suffering for it, more than him. The guilt turned to anger.

"Well, did he tell you who he was? Did the little beast tell you anything at all?"

Too late he realized he had said it louder than he had wanted to. It was quiet on the other side of the door. He heard Mother clear her throat.

Mrs. Skinner spoke. "How *are* your children, Betsy?" Was Bartholomew imagining it, or did her voice hold an unpleasant edge? "Mary says your boy's been up in the attic an awful lot lately. And nobody's seen nothin' of the girl all summer."

"They've been ill," Mother said sharply. For a long moment no one spoke. Then the cork popped again and there was a trickling sound, and Bartholomew could tell from Mother's voice that she was smiling.

"But it's naught to fret about. They'll be up and running in no time. Now, let's hear about you. Business has been right fair lately, if I'm not mistaken?"

Bartholomew let his breath out slowly. He hadn't even realized he'd been holding it. *That was good,* he thought. Agnes Skinner loved nothing more than to talk about her "business."

"Ah, one can't complain is all I say. Though there was a tender morsel slipped right through my fingers a few weeks back." Mrs. Skinner sighed. "All in purple velvets she was, and weighted half to the ground with gemstones. I wanted to bag her on her way out, but she never came. I s'pose someone else got her first."

Mother must have answered with something funny because the two women started laughing. Then the conversation was flowing again, drowning out all other sounds.

Hettie touched his arm. "He asked me a heap-load of questions," she whispered. "The raggedy man did. About you and me and Mummy, and who our father was. And when I didn't want to answer him anymore and pretended to be asleep, he just stood there and watched me. He stands so still in the dark. He just stands and stands until I can't bear it."

"And Het, he is a faery, isn't he?"

"Well, what d'you suppose he is! Mummy locks the door every night, and the hobgoblin downstairs bolts the door to the alley, but the raggedy man still gets in. He puts his finger into the keyholes, see, and the locks spring open, just like that." Hettie wasn't playing with her doll anymore. She was sitting very still, staring at Bartholomew. "I don't like him, Barthy. I don't like the way he watches me, all bent over, and I don't like his songs. Last night I fell asleep while he sang, and I had the most frightfullest dream." Her black eyes were glistening, wet.

"It's all right," Bartholomew said gently, crawling next to her and putting his arm around her. "It was only a nightmare. You know I won't let anything happen to you."

Hettie buried her head in his shirt. "It didn't feel like a nightmare, Barthy. It felt *real.* I dreamed I was lying all alone in the passage outside our door, and someone had nailed my branches to the floorboards. I called and called for Mummy and you, but no one heard. The house was empty. And then I saw that all the spiders were scurrying out of the walls, and the birds and bats were flying out, too. I couldn't see what they were running from, but I heard it, coming up through the house toward me with such an awful squeaking and chattering. I turned my head and asked a beetle that was racing by what everyone was running from. The beetle said, 'The Rat King. The Rat King is coming.' And then it ran on and left me there." Hettie took a breath. "You know the raggedy man goes to your room afterward. After he's sang to me."

Bartholomew shivered. He hadn't known that. He waited for her to say more, but she only closed her eyes and nestled against him. He sat looking down at her for a few minutes. Then he too curled up, and pulling his old blanket around them both, tried to sleep.

It was very late by the time the sounds of departure came from the other room. The voices became firm and businesslike in farewell, the flat door slammed, and the treads groaned as Mrs. Skinner tramped back downstairs. For a few minutes Bartholomew was afraid Mother would forget to unlock the door and he would have to wait even longer to put his plan into action. But once Mrs. Skinner's footsteps had echoed down Old Crow Alley and another door had slammed in the night, Mother came and looked in on them.

Hettie had fallen asleep in Bartholomew's lap. She was rolled up in a ball. Her twiggy hair was all that showed, and it looked as if a clump of shrubbery had sprouted out of her clothes. Bartholomew pretended to be asleep, too. He heard Mother take a few steps into the room. He made his breathing low and regular, and wondered what sort of expression was on her face.

After a moment she lifted Hettie up in her arms and carried her out.

No sooner had the door closed than Bartholomew was moving, crouching on the cold floor next to the wall. He mustn't drift off. He mustn't be too comfortable. He had a faery to catch. Wrapping his arms around his knees, he waited for everything to go quiet in the other room.

It took an age. The bells of Bath tolled five minutes after five minutes, shouts echoed in the alleys nearby, and still he heard Mother in the kitchen, creaking over the floorboards, stowing the blackberry cordial in its cobwebby corner, wiping the tea mugs, and crushing leaves and flower petals for tomorrow's washing. Sometime later he heard her blow out the lamp. Then her first soft snores. Bartholomew pulled himself up and crept into the kitchen.

The weather was good, but Mother still had to build fires in the potbellied stove to boil water for washing. There was always a good heap of ashes in the coal scuttle. Bartholomew tiptoed across the room and heaved up the scuttle, careful not to make a sound. It was too heavy for him. He only managed a few steps before he had to set it down again. He took a handful of the fine ash and began tossing it on the floor. He put a lot in front of Hettie's cupboard. Then he wrestled the scuttle back to his room and did the same around his own cot. When there was a heavy layer of ash on the floor, he filled the dipper from the drinking bucket, and walking backward, dribbled water over it all. He heard it splash in the darkness, and trickle, and when he leaned down to touch the mixture it stuck firmly to his fingers. That would do. Leaving the dipper by the door so that he would not have to disturb the carpet of sludge, he climbed into bed.

He was fast asleep when the lock to the flat clicked open.

The light from the windows was dull as an old pot when Bartholomew woke. The house was quiet.

He sat up straight. *The ash.* If Mother saw the mess it would mean more than just a box to the ears. It would mean an immediate trip to the hack doctor in the court behind the Bag o' Nails public house, and any number of prods and nasty ingestions. There mustn't be a flake left by the time she woke up.

He threw off his blanket and leaned over the edge of the bed, squinting. The water and the ash had dried together overnight, mixing into a sort of gray caked mud. And all through it, pockmarking it like scatterings of acorns, were tracks.

Now I've got you, Bartholomew thought. The tracks were small, two-pronged, with a cleft in the middle. They were all around his bed, all over the floor, hundreds of them going this way and that. They led away in a dirty trail under the door.

Bartholomew was a city boy through and through. He had never climbed a tree or run in a field. He had never seen a farm, besides the ones on the coffee tins. But Mother had taken him to markets when he was small, and he knew the bottom of an animal's foot. These were the tracks of a goat. Hooves.

He saw the sheets again, curling across the Buddelbinsters' yard, the sky turning to iron, and the faery mother's face gaping against the attic window.

You won't hear a thing, she had cried, and her voice echoed inside his head, aching, heart-rending. *The cloven hooves on the floorboards. The voices in the dark. It'll come for you and you won't hear a thing.*

Trembling, he got up and followed the tracks into the other room.

CHAPTER X
The Mechanicalchemist

"AH, Melusine, Melusine." Aunt Dorcas shook her head, clasped her hands over the cheap pewter brooch at her bosom, and looked ever so wistful and pitying. She spoke the name of the mysterious lady as if referring to the dearest of old friends.

Ophelia looked up from the dining room table where she was sorting through the bolts of cloth that Aunt Dorcas had brought with her in the steam-carriage. It was not so far to walk from Curzon Street to Belgrave Square, and the draper always supplied runners for larger purchases, but as Aunt Dorcas had said, "It is so terribly low to go by foot." Never mind that she'd had to beg the fare from the Jellibys' cook.

Mr. Jelliby, who up until this point had been slumped glumly in his paisley armchair, sat up straight. *Aunt Dorcas knew. She knew of the lady in plum.*

He cleared his throat. He fiddled with his shirt cuffs. Trying not to sound too interested, he asked, "And? Aunty, who is she?"

"Yes, who is she?" Ophelia echoed, a hint of sarcasm in her voice.

Aunt Dorcas smiled benevolently. "Melusine Aiofe O Baollagh," she said, flapping her fan at her red cheeks. The fan was supposed to look like that stylish sort where a tiny pisky is mounted on a stick and forced to stir the air with its gossamer wings. But hers was not alive. It was a poor copy made from sculpted wax and cotton, and one would have to be somewhat blind to mistake it for a live faery. Aunt Dorcas didn't seem to realize it, though, and no one could ever be so hard-hearted as to tell her. "From Ireland," she added quickly, noticing their blank looks. "The poor dear. I mean, she *was* only a merchant's daughter—tradespeople, you know—but such a *wealthy* merchant!"

Mr. Jelliby blinked. "Was?"

"She has fallen from favor." Aunt Dorcas sighed. "It was because of her sweetheart, I think. He was the most handsome person in all the world, if the stories are to be believed. They were engaged to be married. But there was an incident. Very mysterious. No one knows any details. At any rate the family grew suspicious of him, and the two little dears eloped! She was disowned, and they were never heard from again. It's just terribly romantic."

"Yes, terribly . . . ," Mr. Jelliby said, leaning back in his chair thoughtfully.

Ophelia set aside a particularly fine bolt of Venetian lace, and asked, "Might I ask where you know this passionate creature from, Arthur?"

"Oh, I don't *know* her," Mr. Jelliby said, shrugging somewhat sheepishly. "I've just *heard* of her. From some gentlemen at Westminster. Aunty, how long ago did all this happen?"

"Oh, not long. Let me see." She bowed her head and closed her eyes. Two seconds later they popped open

again and she said, "Last month! Last month I over-
heard Lady Swinton speaking about it whilst I was hem-
ming up her pettico— that is, while I was visiting. " She
stole a sharp look at them both. "And then again two
weeks ago from Madam Claremont, and last Tuesday
at the Baroness d'Erezaby's. It's been all over the place,
really. I can't imagine you haven't heard of it."

"Yes, how strange. Well, thank you, Aunty." Mr.
Jelliby got up and bowed to her, then turned and did
the same to his wife. "And good day, my dears. I'm
afraid I must be off."

With that, he hurried out of the room.

The other day, as soon as the old woman had sent
Mr. Jelliby on his way with the mechanical bird held
gingerly in a dustpan and his wounded hand well
bound in a piece of Herald's pajamas, he had hurried straight back to the coffeehouse on the corner of
Trafalgar Square.

Tossing the waiter a shilling so that he could sit
without having to order any more unnaturally colored drinks, he laid the broken creature on the

wobbly wrought-iron table and looked it over. A spring popped out from between its breastplates as it touched the tabletop. Mr. Jelliby swore silently. The bird was in ruins. Its wings hung in shards, and the black eyes, only a few hours before so keen and watchful, were now dull as coal. Shooting it out of the sky might have been an improvement.

He unclipped the capsule from around its leg and twirled it in his fingers. *There would be a hidden clasp here somewhere. . . .* He ran his nail across the surface, found it. The capsule clicked open and a loop of paper popped out. It was crisp, fine quality, an even unblemished white. He unrolled it carefully.

Send it to the Moon, it read, in fine spidery lettering. And then, spattered with ink and underlined with a vicious slash:

Child Number Ten is coming.

Mr. Jelliby blinked at it. He read it again. He flipped it over and looked on the back side. The words were odd and unsettling, but they didn't really tell him anything. No address. No "to so-and-so with regards from such-and-such." Nothing about the lady in plum. All that work for ten short words that may as well have been written in some Old Country faery dialect for all the sense they made to him. Why did someone have to send something to the moon? He didn't suppose the Royal Mail delivered there. And Child Number Ten? Who was—

An icy shiver trickled down Mr. Jelliby's spine despite the warmth of the day. The sounds of the Strand—the clop of horses' hooves, the shouts of the vendors, and peels of the bells of St. Martin-in-the-Fields—were all suddenly echoey and far away.

There have only been nine. . . . Those were the faery gentleman's words; the ones he had spoken to the lady while Mr. Jelliby listened from the darkness of the cabinet. Child Number Ten was a changeling. Mr. Lickerish was going to kill another one.

Mr. Jelliby glanced around him. It was late afternoon, and the coffeehouse was well attended. Several couples sat at the street-side tables, a handful of single gentlemen as well, and one of those modern, radical women who wear bloomers and go to cafés all by themselves. And they were all staring at him.

Discreetly, they thought, from behind raised fans and newspapers, over the tops of sun spectacles, and under the brims of flowered hats. But staring nonetheless. Just to see what the handsome man with the dustpan would do next.

Slowly, he turned back to the bird. For a second he wanted to run. To leave the bird and the coffeehouse, take a carriage back to Belgrave Square and drink brandy as if nothing had ever happened. Those people didn't know. Nobody knew what he knew, and nobody would care if he didn't do anything.

But somewhere in the faery slums a child was waiting to die. He couldn't drink brandy knowing that. It would make him gag. It would taste of blood and bones, and if his carriage should crash off a bridge the very next day, he didn't suppose he would feel very sorry for himself lying in the black depths of the river. He was the only one who knew what was going to happen. And so he was the only one who could do anything to stop it.

Taking a lacquered box from his coat pocket, he fitted a pair of reading glasses to his nose. He leaned down to study the bird more closely. Somewhere it should say where it was built. If he could only find it. . . . He squinted, turning the machine over in his hands. The bird felt very frail. He could feel the machinery shifting minutely under his fingertips, and for a second he was struck with the childish urge to crush it in his fist and feel how the springs and metal plates squelched out between his fingers. He didn't, of course. He had gone through far too much trouble just to smash the bird. Besides, there were words on it. He saw them now. Tiny, tiny writing etched with a red-hot stylus into the bottom of one of the metal feathers.

Mchn. Alch. it read.

And then, in tinier letters still: *X.Y.Z.*

The *Mchn. Alch.* part stood for mechanicalchemist. That much Mr. Jelliby knew. And X.Y.Z? Perhaps the initials of the shop, or the fabricator himself. But what strange initials they were. Mr. Jelliby would have to look them up in a directory when he got home. He hoped it was a manufacturer who advertised. A black-market mechanicalchemist toiling away in some hole in Limehouse would never be found, even if Mr. Jelliby searched a hundred years.

Leaving the coffeehouse, he headed up Regent Street toward Mayfair, keeping his eyes peeled for a newspost. They tended to have shop listings nailed to them, somewhere among the layers and layers of handbills that fluttered endlessly like the petals of a dirty flower—handbills for music halls and circuses, pantomimes, operas, and phantasmagorias. But when he came to one, he found only two leaflets concerning mechanicalchemists and they were both frightfully prestigious ones in Grosvenor Street without a single X, Y, or Z between them.

Mr. Jelliby took a cab back to Belgrave Square and tiptoed past the open door to the parlor. Ophelia was sitting in her favorite armchair, reading with rapt attention the latest issue of *Spidersilk and Dewdrops: A Journal of Faerie Magic*. She noticed him right away, but she didn't stop him, and he went upstairs, locked himself in his study, and fell to scouring the adverts of his gentlemen's newspapers with feverish haste. It took him all the rest of the day and much of the next morning to find what he was looking for. He forgot to come down to breakfast, forgot even to shave, and when he finally did find what he was looking for, it was something of a disappointment. The advertisement was small and plain, standing out starkly against the lavish illustrations of wigs and sardines and mechanical chambermaids. Three black lines declaring—still grandly enough for their humble looks—*Mr. Zerubbabel's Mechanical Marvels! Everything you can possibly dream of and a great many things you can't, wrought in brass and clockwork, handmade, one-of-a-kind. Long-lasting faery batteries for flawless performance. Commissions only. Fair rates.* And then the address: Fifth floor, Number 19, Stovepipe Road, Clerkenwell.

Clerkenwell? Mr. Jelliby set down the newspaper. Clerkenwell was not a very fashionable neighborhood. In fact, it was downright inferior. And he had certainly never heard of an establishment called "Mr. Zerubbabel's Mechanical Marvels." One would think a gentleman of Mr. Lickerish's standing would go to the finest mechanicalchemists in London for his wares. Not *Clerkenwell.* Unless the faery did not want the finest. Unless he wanted the quietest, the quickest, and the most secret.

It was then that the doorbell had rung, Aunt Dorcas had sailed into the house, Ophelia had called him down to greet her and be polite, and he had asked his questions concerning Melusine.

But he had escaped now. He went into the hall, snatching up his coat and hat from where they sat waiting to be brushed. Then he was out, hurrying across the rain-slick cobbles.

Clerkenwell was a good distance from Belgrave Square. It would be easiest to climb the endless corkscrew stair to the elevated steam engine, he decided, and ride across London's rooftops. Better, at least, than trying to find his way through the streets. He rarely ventured into the city north of Waterloo Bridge, never beyond Ludgate Hill, and to navigate the many dirty, dangerous neighborhoods that lay between his home and Clerkenwell was not something he wanted to do that day.

When Mr. Jelliby arrived, breathless, at the top of the stair, an automaton that had no legs or eyes, that looked nothing at all like a human and yet was equipped with a curled brass moustache and top hat, held out a pincer hand to him. Mr. Jelliby put a shilling in it. The pincer hand and shilling were snatched back, folding into some hidden part of the automaton's body. Then a brass bell *tinged* inside its belly and Mr. Jelliby was handed a green stub of ticket. The automaton waved him silently onto the platform.

The steam train arrived in due time, and Mr. Jelliby sat himself down in one of the dark-paneled compartments of its passenger carriage. The train began to move. Smoke and weathervanes whirled past his window. Despite the brightness of the day, gas lamps fizzled on the walls, sucking the oxygen from the compartment. By the time he got out at King's Cross station he had a splitting headache.

Descending the stairs into the smoky, cavernous streets of Clerkenwell did little to help it. The air beneath the ramshackle tenements was vile. It filled his lungs like a bottle being stuffed with black cotton, made him gasp. At least the population looked less dangerous than the air. It was mostly women, and gnomes, and hollow-cheeked children. *No doubt the thieves and hooligans are hard at work in more prosperous parts of the city*, Mr. Jelliby thought.

Stovepipe Road, Stovepipe Road. Heavens, were there no street signs in Clerkenwell? His eyes searched the filthy bricks, the peeling shop signs, and doorposts. He did find one, cracked and rusted, clinging by a shred of wire to the head of a lamppost, but he couldn't make out what it said. Someone had painted over it in dripping red letters: *Faeryland.*

He hurried up the street, saw nothing that looked like a mechanicalchemist's, turned back when he thought no one was looking, and hurried *down* the street instead. He did this several times over before finally gathering the courage to ask directions from a toothless woman in scarlet petticoats. She pointed him to a dark alley that wormed into a mass of dilapidated buildings. He had passed that same alley at least five times already, and each time he had thought it far too suspicious-looking to risk entering.

He stepped into it. The air was close here, viscous like tar. He looked up at the houses tilting overhead, and a great drop of sooty water splashed down toward him. He stepped aside, and it slapped the ground, echoing among the buildings. There were no signs in this alley either, not even shop-boards or tavern banners. Just leaning night-black houses and broken windows. Halfway down the alley, he spotted a gin-soaked hobgoblin sprawled across a doorstep and asked for directions a second time.

The goblin scowled out at him from under leafy eyebrows. "Right up there," he rasped, waving a claw in the direction of a tall, thin house near the end of the alley. The building was just as dilapidated as the others. Certainly not a place Mr. Jelliby could imagine the Lord Chancellor visiting. Him, with his extravagant costumes and perfect white skin.

Mr. Jelliby thanked the hobgoblin and approached the house uneasily. Looking up, he saw that it ended in a massive knot of chimneys and roiling fumes, like a head of wild black hair. He entered through a low door and began climbing some stairs, up and up, past leery-eyed lodgers and foul chambers until at last he came to the fifth floor. There he found a small hand-painted sign pointing to small hand-painted door on which was written quite simply *Mr. Zerubbabel.* No mechanical marvels.

A collection of rusty bells jangled over the door as Mr. Jelliby entered. The room beyond was dark, low-ceilinged, and cramped, its actual shape difficult to make out for all the shelves and stacks of machinery towering throughout it. The metal skeletons of half-built automata sat slouched on crates, staring at nothing with dead eyes. Wires crisscrossed the ceiling, and on them, wheeling to and fro with soft creaking noises, were dozens of little tin men on monocycles, carrying in their hands screwdrivers and hammers and spouted cans of glistening oil.

A metallic *ting* sounded from the far corner of the room, and Mr. Jelliby turned to see an old man hunched over a desk, adjusting the treads on a clockwork snail.

Mr. Jelliby took a step toward him. "Sir?" he said. The word fell like a furry ball to the floor. The old man looked up. Wrinkling his nose, he peered at Mr. Jelliby through half-moon spectacles.

"Yes, please?" he said, setting the snail down on

the desk. It gave a contented whir and began turning circles around a mug of black grease.

"Ah—do I have the pleasure of addressing Mr. Zerubbabel?"

"I am Mr. Zerubbabel, though whether you derive any pleasure from addressing me is entirely up to you." The old man's voice was clipped, educated, completely at odds with his jumbled little shop. On his head he wore a very tiny black hat. "Xerxes Yardley Zerubbabel, at your service."

Mr. Jelliby smiled gratefully. "I have a damaged piece of mechanics here that was constructed at your shop. It—it crashed through my attic window." He had practiced what he was going to say all through breakfast while pretending to read the *Times*. It had been nothing like what he had just said. "If you would be so kind as to tell me where it was headed, I will be along right away to give it back to its owner."

"Oh, not necessary, I assure you. Not necessary at all. I have all my customers written up. Show me the machine, please."

Mr. Jelliby set to work extracting the bird from his

pocket. A metal talon snagged on his trouser and tore off with a *twang.* The old man winced. While Mr. Jelliby struggled to undo the feathers from the stitchery on his waistcoat, the old man said, "Oh! The Sidhe's bird. Thank you, I will see that it is returned to him myself."

"Oh . . ." Mr. Jelliby looked unhappy. "Well, would you tell me where it was flying anyway?"

The little man's brow darkened. When he spoke, his voice was wary. "No. No, I don't suppose that I would."

Mr. Jelliby's mouth twitched. He flicked at one of the bird's springs. He shuffled his feet. Then he said, "All right, look here. I'm with the police, see, and the creature who bought this bird from you is a heinous criminal."

"He is a politician," the old man said flatly.

"But he is also a murderer! He's been all around London and Bath killing poor innocents and leaving them hollow like dead trees, and *you,* as an upright Englishman, are required by *honor* to help me."

Mr. Zerubbabel grunted. "Firstly, I am not an Englishman. Secondly, that's the dottiest tale I've ever heard. With the police, indeed. I don't believe a word of it. And even if I did . . ." He sniffed and, eyebrows raised, set back to fiddling with the clock-work snail. "It's none of my business."

Mr. Jelliby threw up his hands in exaspera-tion. "How can you—what in—have you no . . .?" He dropped his hands. He opened his wallet and fished out two gleaming sovereigns, waving them under the old man's nose. "Can I make it your business?"

The old man eyed the coins. Snatching one, he bit it. Then he looked hard at Mr. Jelliby, stood on his tiptoes to look out the window in the shop door, and said gruffly, "Let me get my records."

Like an old rat, Mr. Zerubbabel retreated into a hole between two drooping shelves. Mr. Jelliby could see nothing inside but blackness. Some oaths issued from within, followed by a heavy crash that shook the towering house to its roots. A cascade of clockwork mosquitoes tumbled from a jar nearby. The old man popped his head out. "It has been eaten. One moment, if you please." He disappeared back into the hole.

There was another crash, what sounded like claws tapping, and fierce whispers, and the old man emerged again, this time with a map in his hands.

"Now then!" he said, puffing. "Let's see what we've got here, shall we?" He unfurled the map across a pile of debris and began poring over it, eyes darting like flies. Long lines had been drawn across it in red ink. Mr. Zerubbabel traced them with a wizened finger. "I have a captive faery-of-the-air to travel the distances and calculate safe routes, et cetera," he explained. "It finds obstacles, measures the height from which my contraptions must launch." He cast Mr. Jelliby a sideways glance. "So that they don't crash through attic windows, you know."

Mr. Jelliby nodded wisely.

Mr. Zerubbabel turned back to the map, frowning. He rapped his finger three times, in different places on the map. "Here are the points he gave me. Three birds. Each bird has its own route. Three birds for three routes. And all starting from different spots in London." Mr. Zerubbabel looked thoughtful for a moment. "The one you picked up travels from Westminster Palace, it seems, on its way North. Yorkshire. It is launched toward the east to bypass the factory ash. The second one flies between Bath and a house on Blackfriars Bridge. And the third I never could understand. He had me calibrate it to fly in an upward line from a garret in Islington, three hundred feet into open sky. And when I sent Boniface—that's my faery-of-the-air—up to see what was what, he found nothing. Just clouds and sky."

Mr. Jelliby wasn't listening anymore. He had what he needed. "Thank you, sir, thank you so very much. Might you give me the marks, though? The longitudinal lines or whatever they're called." He held up another sovereign. "I'd be terribly grateful."

The old man pocketed the coin and scribbled a series of numbers on a yellowing scrap of paper. He passed it to Mr. Jelliby. "I don't know what you're up to. Trying to ruin the fellow like as not. Maybe a bit of blackmail? You are so alike really, you English and the faeries. So desperately far on either side that you can't see anything in between. Ah, well. I'll not talk. This part of London, nobody talks but the face on the coin, and as I said, it's none of my business."

Mr. Jelliby thought that was not a very nice thing

to say out loud. He was about to bid the man a cool farewell, when the bells above the door jangled again, and in ducked another customer.

And who should it be but the Lord Chancellor John Wednesday Lickerish's faery butler.

Mr. Jelliby's hand tightened around the bird. Slowly, slowly he began slipping it up his sleeve. The claw snagged his cuff. *It wouldn't go.* Quite out of nowhere it struck him how very like a praying mantis the faery butler looked, like a deathly pale insect, with those long arms and fingers. The faery had to bend his head to the side in an odd way to keep it from knocking against the ceiling. The brass machinery around his face was stiff, unmoving.

One step. One step to the right and Mr. Jelliby would be hidden behind the rivet-studded tentacles of a mechanical octopus. But it was too late. The faery butler turned, saw him.

"Ooh!" he whined, lenses clicking across his one green eye as it focused on the bird in Mr. Jelliby's hand. "Fancy seeing you here. . . ."

CHAPTER XI
Child Number Ten

THE goat tracks looped across the kitchen floor, from the door to the table to the beds and the potbellied stove under the drying herbs. Mother's bulk rose and fell gently in sleep, the old bed creaking with each breath. Inside her cupboard, Hettie shifted a little, and sighed.

Bartholomew let his breath out slowly. *What has the faery come for? What does it want?*

If only he hadn't invited it. If only he had listened to Mother and heeded her warnings. She had told him what might happen. She had practically begged him not to do it. But he had wanted a friend so badly.

He wanted something to protect him, and talk with him, something that would make him feel he wasn't just strange and ugly. Only it wasn't going to *be* his friend. It wasn't going to protect him, and it wasn't going to wind up the wash-wringer either. All it did was slither about in the night and put nightmares in Hettie's head. The number ten on the paper in the attic was another of its pranks, like as not. It was probably snickering into its sleeve right that very moment.

Bartholomew bit his lip and followed the tracks to the flat door. It was still locked. *He puts his finger into the keyholes, see, and the locks spring open, just like that.* And spring closed again, too, it seemed. Slipping the key down off its peg, he unlocked the door. Then, careful not to make a sound, he tiptoed out into the passageway.

The house was cool and dark. The floorboards, worn smooth by the years, gleamed dully in the feeble light from the window.

The trail of ash led upstairs. It became fainter as he followed it, whispering away until it was only breaths against the wood. By the time Bartholomew reached the third floor it had almost disappeared. It didn't matter. He knew where the faery had gone.

Silent as the moon, he slipped up through the trapdoor and into the attic. Ducking under the first crossbeam, he crept forward, eyes darting, searching for a hint of where the faery might be hiding. He would kill it if he found it. The thought came to him with sudden violence. If he found the little monster, he would wring its neck. Wring it before it wrung Hettie's, and Mother's, and his.

A sound stopped him dead—voices, muttering, muffled under the roof.

"Oh, yes. That one's a Peculiar if ever I saw one." The voice that was speaking was hushed, but Bartholomew recognized it at once. *Hollow, earthy. The singing voice.* Only this time its owner took great wheezing breaths every few words, sucked in between its teeth. "The leetle half-blood builds a house, see? A downright inferior house to catch himself a faery with. I found it whiles I was exploring the place. Kicked it to pieces, I did! Ha-ha! All in leetle pieces." There was a giggle.

Bartholomew dug his fingers into his palms and flattened himself against the sloping roof. The voice was coming from the place under the gable. His place.

"And the stupid changeling still thinks it worked. It thinks I'm its faery slave." A wheeze. "It asked me questions, it did. It wrotes me a letter, with words, all fancy like, and asked me what something meant in the language o' the faery lords and"—another wheeze—"now this is the strangest part of all. It was—"

"I don't care," a second voice interrupted. It was also very low, but in an entirely different way. It was a harsh, dangerous low, and so cold. "Is the changeling what I need, or is it not? I cannot afford any more mistakes. Not from you, not from anyone. I hire you to make sure the changelings are usable, to make sure they are what the Lord Chancellor needs." The voice rose in anger. "And nine times in a row you give me *rubbish!* It will be taken from my neck if the child is again unsuitable."

"Well, you got so many necks it wouldn't hardly make a—"

There was an angry hiss and Bartholomew saw a shadow lash out across the beam. "*Shut up.* Shut up, I tell you. Too much is at stake now. Did you make certain with the list my master sent you? Did you even *get* the list? There have been . . . interruptions of late with the Lord Chancellor's messenger birds. He could not be certain it had arrived."

"Yeh, I gots the bird. Came just as it always does."

Bartholomew edged closer. Through the gap between the beams he could just make out a figure. Bartholomew's breath caught in his throat. It was the raggedy man. There could be no doubt. The creature matched Hettie's description exactly. It was small and misshapen, standing very still with its chin against its neck. A broken stovepipe hat was pulled low over its face. A waistcoat and tattered jacket were its only clothes. It wore no trousers. Bartholomew saw why right away. From the waist down the creature was not a raggedy man but a raggedy goat. The fur on its haunches was thick and black, matted with dirt and blood. Two chipped hooves peeped out from under its shaggy fetlocks. The raggedy man was a faun.

"Very well," the cold voice said. "I will believe you. I haven't the time, or I would investigate these matters myself." Bartholomew couldn't see who had spoken those words. Whoever it was, he was hidden around the corner of the gable, and Bartholomew didn't dare go any closer for a better look.

The voice went on, just barely a whisper. "I warn you, *sluagh*. If the Lord Chancellor is again displeased with the delivery—if the changeling is again a failure—I will knock more from your head than just a few teeth."

The raggedy man shuffled its hooves and said nothing.

"Is that clear?" The voice was ice.

Bartholomew didn't wait to hear the rest. Sliding backward, he made for the trapdoor. Everything was different now. Everything had changed. This wasn't just about some silly house faery anymore. He didn't want to think what these creatures would do to him if they caught him listening. He climbed down into the third-story passage and hurried toward the stair.

His head was reeling. *It never worked, then. The invitation.*

The pitiful house with the cherries twisted into its walls. It has all been for nothing. The raggedy man wasn't his faery. The raggedy man had been hired. To spy. To make sure Bartholomew would *do*, be suitable, not a failure like the other nine. *Nine.* The Buddelbinster boy was one of those. He must be. And now Bartholomew was number ten. *The paper in the attic.* He pulled up his sleeve and examined the markings on his arms. Bloodred tens in the faery language. At least the raggedy man had told the truth about that.

He broke into a run, down the stairs, wood splinters pricking his hand from the rickety banister. He didn't know what they wanted him for. He didn't know whether he should hide, or tell Mother, or wait quietly until they came for him. The creature—the one he hadn't seen—had said it was working for the Lord Chancellor. Wasn't that good? Weren't only the kindest and wisest people allowed to be Lord Chancellors? *But why would a Lord Chancellor employ faeries that sounded like winter and knocked people's teeth out?* Bartholomew didn't know what to think anymore. He was terrified and excited, both at once, and it felt like a whole cloud of moths were beating their wings inside his stomach. An image flared up in his mind of grand people, of dukes and generals encrusted with medals, of ermine cloaks dragging across marble, and great halls ablaze with candles. A knife tapped, silvery, against a wineglass. A cheer went up. And Bartholomew realized they were cheering for him. Barthy Kettle. Child Number Ten, of Old Crow Alley, seventh faery district, Bath. It was a ridiculous thought. A happy, hopeful, ridiculous thought that had a million cracks running through it.

He was almost to the flat door when something caught his eye through the passage window. Something was out in the alley, an extra shadow where no shadow belonged. He retraced his steps and brought his face up close against the round leaded panes.

It was the lady in plum. She was back again in Old Crow Alley, sitting still as death on a rough-hewn bench against the wall of the place known as moss-bucket house. The moldering eaves hung low over her, drowning her in gloom. She was slumped against the wall, her hands in her lap, her chin resting against her neck.

Bartholomew raised his hand to the glass. The image of the candlelit halls, ermine cloaks, and admiring faces became brighter than ever. Why shouldn't the lady take him away? Someone—no, not just someone—the Lord Chancellor himself, had gone through a great deal of trouble to find him. That meant he was important. In the faery slums he wasn't important. In the faery slums he was just another ugly thing to be hidden away and never spoken of. He would die here. Sooner or later.

But the dreadful faeries in the attic, a voice cried, clanging in his head like a fire-engine bell. *The Buddelbinster mother's warning, that ugly face on the back of the lady's head, and the hooves, and the voices—* Bartholomew silenced it. It didn't matter. What did any of that matter when all they were doing was taking him to a better place? A place where he belonged. It would be better for everyone if he were gone. It would mean one less mouth to feed for Mother, one less changeling for her to worry about. Hettie would cry, and he would miss her awfully, but surely he could visit. And if the room he had traveled to through the mushroom ring was anything like the place he was going, he knew he wouldn't mind living there. He could just scrape bits of gilt off the furniture and Mother and Hettie would have pies and duck to eat for months.

By the time he turned away from the window he had made up his mind. Somewhere in London people were waiting for him, glorious people with clockwork birds, fine rooms, and fireplaces. He was leaving Old Crow Alley behind.

He laid his head against the door to the flat and whispered, "Good-bye, Mother. Good-bye, Hettie." He waited several heartbeats, as if listening for a reply. Then he went downstairs. The goblin was asleep on his stool. The face in the door stared out sightlessly, gray wooden eyes over gray wooden cheeks. Silently, Bartholomew said good-bye to them, too. Then he slipped out into the narrow confines of the alley.

The houses all around were black spikes against the sky. The sun was just starting to rise, and only the early morning red gave the alley any light. Somewhere several streets away, a cart was rattling over the cobbles, echoing.

Bartholomew crossed the alley and approached the lady cautiously, scraping himself along the wall toward her. She looked even larger up close, even darker and more forbidding, as if the shadows from the recesses and deep doorways were being drawn to her, soaking into her skirts. The last time Bartholomew had seen her he had been in the attic, behind glass. Now he could see her every detail. She was young. Not a great lady at all, but a girl no more than twenty. Her hat still sat askew atop her head, but the jewels were no longer around her throat and one of her night-hued gloves was torn, crisp with something like dried blood. Her red lip paint was somewhat smeared. Bartholomew thought she was the most marvelous and frightening thing he had ever seen.

He came within three steps of her and then stopped. She sat so still. So very, very still in the shadow of the eaves. He contemplated reaching out and touching her hand. It didn't seem wise at all.

He was just about to slip back inside and lie shivering against the door until he could think of something to say, when the lady moved. Her eyelids fluttered open and she said ever so softly, "Oh! Hello, sweet child."

Her voice was airy, dreamy, half between waking and sleeping.

Bartholomew flinched. For a moment he wasn't sure she had been speaking to him, since she hadn't turned her head or even really looked at him. But the alley was empty. He and the lady were the only ones in it.

"Did Father send you?" she asked. "Are you the new valet?"

Bartholomew stood, mouth open, unsure of how to answer. *Is this some sort of test? Oh, no. I mustn't muddle it. Something clever, something clever so she will be impressed.* This was still the sorceress who had taken his friend, still the lady with the secret, twisted face. But her eyes were so kind. And she had such a lovely voice. He couldn't even remember that second face anymore. Perhaps it had belonged to someone else.

"Tell him I will not relent," she continued. "Never as long as the hills are green. Jack will be mine, and nothing shall ever come between us. But I am so tired. . . . What is this hard chair I sit on? Where are my pillows? Where is Mirabel with *pêches et crème*? Sweet child, where am—"

Suddenly her eyes snapped wide. Her pupils focused on Bartholomew and she sat bolt upright, snatching both his hands. "Oh, no," she whispered, and her voice shivered at the edges. Desperation wrote itself across her face, and her eyes shone, fearful-bright. "No, no. You must run. Sweet child, they are here to *take* you. Don't let them. Run. Run with the wind and never look back."

All at once there came a sound, a tapping that drifted down into the alley. It was coming from the rooftops. Bartholomew looked up just in time to see the small round window of his little gable burst outward, shooting a cloud of glass into the air. A shape flew out, a writhing mass of blackness. It plummeted, glass glinting around it, and landed in the alley with a dreadful scuttling sound.

Bartholomew's heart lurched. The lady gasped and dropped his hands.

Everything seemed to move very slowly then. The glass from the window rained down, tinkling like diamonds into the gutter. The writhing shape hurtled toward them over the cobblestones. And the lady's head turned to Bartholomew, her eyes full of tears.

"Tell Daddy I'm sorry," she whispered. "Tell Daddy I'm sorry." And then the dark shape slammed into her and she doubled over, the breath knocked from her lungs.

When she raised her head again, her eyes were sharp and black. Faery eyes.

Bartholomew ran.

"*Vekistra takeshi! Vekistra!*" the lady in plum shrieked from behind him. "Take the tenth child!"

It was the voice of the creature from the attic. The hidden one that Bartholomew hadn't been able to see. And it wasn't quiet and cold anymore. It was shrill, desperate.

Bartholomew burst into the house. The instant

before the door slammed shut, he saw the lady in plum swoop down to the pavement, bottle in hand, dribbling black liquid onto the cobbles. Then the door smashed into its frame and he was running up the stairs and into the flat. He pushed that door closed, fingers slipping on the bolt. *Footsteps.* Someone was in the stairwell, feet booming in the silence. Bartholomew reached for the key, rammed it into the lock. *Where can I go?* The scream of *"Take the tenth child"* was still ringing in his ears, awful and final. The lady in plum was not going to lead him gently away, as she had the Buddelbinster boy. She was not whisking him off to some enchanted halls of light and finery. She was going to kidnap him.

"Hettie?" Bartholomew cried, racing to her bed. "Hettie, wake up. Wake up! They're going to come in!" He threw open the cupboard door, poking and jabbing at the sheets to wake her.

Hettie was not there.

He let out a wail and ran to his mother's bed. He shook her, beating his fists against her back. "Mother!" he cried, desperate tears biting his eyes.

"*Mother, wake* up!" She didn't even stir.

The footsteps had reached the passage. They were approaching the door, slowly, deliberately. *Why won't she wake?*

He would open the window. He would throw it wide and yell until the entire faery district was startled from their beds. But it was too late. A tiny *click* sounded from the door. The lock. Someone had opened it.

Bartholomew edged away from his mother's motionless form. His fingers closed around the iron handle of the coal scuttle. He drew it up, hugging it to himself. It was so heavy. If he had to, he could dash the faery's brains out with it. Flattening himself against the wall behind the potbellied stove, he waited.

The door to the flat yawned open. Slowly, slowly, it revealed a figure silhouetted against the dim light from the passage. The figure had goat legs and a ruined hat. Two hot-coal eyes glowed under its brim. They slid across the room, back and forth, back and forth. They paused. They turned back to the potbellied stove. *It can't know, it can't know....*

"Hello, leetle boy."

With a great raging sob, Bartholomew leaped from behind the stove, brandishing the coal scuttle as high as he could lift it. The raggedy man grinned. A savage bright flash flew from his eyes, sizzled across the room, and struck Bartholomew in some tender spot deep inside his skull. His vision stuttered out. He felt himself standing, blind and clumsy, in the middle of the floor. Somewhere far away he heard wings flapping, dark wings whirling, and the growl of icy wind. His body was so heavy, pulling him down. *Hettie,* he thought, before he collapsed. *Hettie was the one they wanted. And Hettie is gone.*

The scuttle slipped from his hand. It clanged against the floor like a thunderclap. But no one in the whole house woke.

CHAPTER XII
The House and the Anger

MR. Jelliby was not the sort of man to make hasty decisions. In fact, he wasn't really the sort of man to make decisions at all. But when the mechanical eye of the faery butler hissed and locked itself onto the bird in Mr. Jelliby's hand, and when the faery smiled that hungry smile at him and said, "Oh! Fancy seeing you here," as if they were the oldest of friends, Mr. Jelliby made a very hasty, very rash decision. He ran.

Plunging the bird into his trouser pocket, he dashed out of the shop and down the narrow corridor toward the stairs. Shouts rang out behind him. The bells above the shop door began to jangle violently. Down the stairs he leaped, four at a time, barely avoiding the decrepit old man who was making his way upward.

When Mr. Jelliby burst out into the swirling air of Stovepipe Road, he stopped dead.

Oh, no. A massive black carriage, still as a coffin, was parked across the mouth of the street, blocking his escape. Two mechanical horses stood at its front and pawed the cobblestones. Sparks flew from their metal hooves.

Mr. Jelliby ran the other direction, hurtling down a lane and into an alley. He made his way through a warren of tiny streets, sleeve-over-mouth to keep from gagging on the fumes, and as soon as he could, doubled back toward the wider thoroughfare. He arrived just as the seven o' clock bells were tolling the end of a workday. Laborers from the foundries and breweries were pouring out of doorways, clogging the streets. He fought his way through them, up the stairs toward the elevated railway station.

A steam engine was just pulling away as he mounted the platform, its whistle blowing. He swung onto the wrought-iron porch of the final wagon and collapsed, breathless, against the railing. Sweat dripped into his eyes, but he blinked it away. The streets below were packed, row upon row of weary, grimy bodies trudging toward lodgings or public houses, eyes hooked to the ooze beneath their boots. There was no faery, pale as death and cypress-slender, moving among them.

The last wagon had just begun to rumble around a bend when Mr. Jelliby caught sight of the black carriage, parting the crowds like a lustrous boat in dirty water. It paused briefly at a crossroad. Then it slid away, disappearing into the city.

Mr. Jelliby took a long, slow breath. Then another, and another, but nothing could loosen the panic that had fastened itself to his lungs. The faery butler had seen him. He had seen him with Mr. Lickerish's messenger bird in his hands, no doubt the very bird the faery butler had been sent to inquire about. If they had thought he was a spy before, they would be sure he was now. And a thief, too. And something occurred to Mr. Jelliby, then, that made him feel very ill: He had already decided to save Melusine, and stop the faery politician's murderous ways, and deliver England from whatever dastardly plans were under way. But he hadn't wanted to be noticed while he did it. He hadn't wanted to be frowned at, or laughed at, and he most certainly hadn't wanted to seem any different from the other gentlemen of Westminster. Only that was not the way things worked. He saw that now. Westminster gentlemen did not chase clockwork birds through city streets. They did not hunt down killers, or help people. Mr. Jelliby had. And there could be no turning back now.

The faery butler would tell Mr. Lickerish what he had seen. Mr. Lickerish would understand instantly. He would see that Mr. Jelliby knew things no human was supposed to know. He would see that Mr. Jelliby was intent on meddling. And what would he do? Oh, what would that stone-hearted faery do? Mr. Jelliby shivered and hunched into the ash-riddled wind.

He arrived back at Belgrave Square just before nightfall, bedraggled and besmirched with all the grime that comes from riding at thirty miles per hour among London's chimneys. Slamming the front door behind him, he barred it, chained it, searched out the key from inside the shade of a gas lamp and locked it. Then he leaned against it and shouted, "Brahms! Brahms! Close the shutters all the way up! And move all the furniture over the windows. Do it now! Ophelia?"

No one answered.

"Ophelia!"

A wide-eyed maid appeared at the top of the stairs. "Good evenin', sir," she mumbled. "Cook kept your dinner warm and they've got a—"

Mr. Jelliby spun on her.

"Jane? Or is it Margaret. No matter. Fetch all the guns from over the mantelpieces, and all the swords and the carving knives, and perhaps a frying pan or two, and anything else that can be used as a weapon, and then lock up the door to the back garden. And tell Cook to go out and buy a good supply of crackers and salted pork, and lock up the attic windows in case they come in through the roof, and don't forget the guns!"

The maid stood unmoving, her face a picture of confusion.

"Well? What's the matter? Do as I say!"

She stammered something and began backing away down the upstairs hall. Then she turned and ran, polished heels pounding the carpet. A door slammed. Not a minute later, Ophelia arrived at the head of the stairs, the maid peeking from behind her.

"Arthur? Darling, whatever is the matter?"

"You don't suppose we should knock him out," the maid whispered. "I hear folks get possessed by faeries an' start acting all strange, an' then you have to get a club, see, or that candlestick there will do, and—"

"That's enough, Phoebe," Ophelia said, without moving her gaze from Mr. Jelliby's face. "You may go sweep up the tea leaves in the sitting room. I'm sure they've collected a boatload of dust by now."

The maid bowed her head and hurried down the stairs. She inched past Mr. Jelliby, casting him the most despairing look, and sped on toward the sitting room. Ophelia waited until she heard the door click. Then she hurried down herself.

She pulled Mr. Jelliby away from the front door, her pretty face crinkling with worry. "Arthur, what's wrong? What's happened?"

Mr. Jelliby cast a fearful look around him and then led his wife to a chair, whispering, "We're in trouble, Ophelia. Terrible, terrible trouble. Oh, what's going to happen to us? What will happen?"

"Well, if you will tell me what *has* happened, then perhaps I can tell you what *will* happen," Ophelia said gently.

Mr. Jelliby buried his head in his hands. "I can't tell you what's happened. You can't know. You mustn't know. Oh, I stole something, all right? From someone rather important. And now they know. They *know* I stole it!"

"Arthur, you didn't! Oh, you couldn't have! With your inheritance?"

"People are being murdered, Ophelia. Children. I had to."

"You ought to have called the police. Stealing

money helps nothing in these cases."

Mr. Jelliby made a complicated sound of annoyance. "I didn't steal any money, won't you listen? I stole a bird. A pisky-cursed mechanical bird."

"A bird? From who? Mr. Lickerish? Darling, was it Mr. Lickerish?" She bit her nail. "Arthur, do you know what I suspect? I suspect you are reading crimes into his actions. Now, you will put your coat away—oh, it is sooty! Did you not have it brushed?—and sit down by the fire and drink some chamomile tea. Then you will take a hot bath and go to sleep, and tomorrow we shall see what must be done. Perhaps it won't be necessary to rearrange the furnishings after all."

That sounded sensible enough. Mr. Jelliby was in the safety of his front hall now. The window looked out on an emptying Belgrave Square, on carriages and people, shadowy in the dusk. The evening light was just touching the rooftops with copper and rose. What could Mr. Lickerish possibly do to him here? Out in the wilds of the city he could chase a million horrors onto Mr. Jelliby's back. He could have him pushed from a bridge, or under a steam carriage, or order all the spiders in Pimlico to drag him to the roofs and spin him to a chimney. But here in Mr. Jelliby's own home? The worst Mr. Lickerish could do was murder him in his sleep. And what were the chances of that . . . ?

Mr. Jelliby took off his coat and went to drink some chamomile tea.

Fog slunk among the headstones of St. Mary, Queen of Martyrs, that night. It smelled of charcoal and rot, and spread in slow shapes down the sloping grave-yard. Above, clouds drifted, snuffing out the moon. Somewhere in the maze of streets beyond the wall a dog barked.

The watchman sat in his hut against the side of the church, fast asleep in the wavering glow of a lantern. Grave robbers had come and gone, finished their business hours ago and were well on their way to the physicians in Harley Street, and to certain faeries of delicate diet. No one heard the sudden shriek of wind, or saw the pillar of wings take shape out of the dark. No one saw the lady who stepped from among them. She looked around her, head snapping about like a bird's. Then she turned and made for the gate, plum-colored skirts dragging over the damp soil.

The lady led a small child. It was a changeling girl, thin, with branches for hair. It was Hettie. She seemed to be falling asleep as they walked, stumbling over roots and sunken gravestones. Her head slumped to one side now and then, as if she didn't know she was in a foggy graveyard, as if she thought she might nestle into her pillow and go to sleep.

"Stop dawdling, ugly thing," the lady snapped, pulling her along. "We're almost done."

Her lips did not move as she spoke. The fog swallowed all sound, but even so the lady's voice was distant, as if it were coming from behind layers of fabric. "One more little thing I must take care of tonight, and then you can sleep until your fingernails grow halfway to Gloucester for all I care."

Hettie rubbed her eyes with her free hand and mumbled something about rats and houses.

"And hold your tongue." The lady stepped

through the gate of the graveyard, into Bellyache Street. She sniffed the air. Then she strode on over the cobblestones. Hettie could scarcely keep up, but the lady paid no attention. She dragged Hettie down Bellyache Street, into Belgrave Square. They hurried out across it, silent in the lamp-lit expanse.

They stopped in front of a tall house with a bicycle bolted to its fence. The house loomed, blacker than the night sky, not a single light tracing any of its windows. The lady eyed it a moment. Then she pulled Hettie toward the nearest lamppost and planted her under it, pointing up at the flame faery behind the glass and saying, "Do you see that? See how it presses its little orange hands against the panes and looks back at you? Now don't move. I'll return for you in seven breaths." She whirled away, leaving Hettie transfixed under the streetlamp.

At the top of the steps, the lady paused and took from the folds of her dress a heavy metal cylinder. It was ancient, green with verdigris and forged with heathenish symbols. A smiling face, all fat cheeks and twinkling eyes, was etched on its lid.

The lady twisted the lid, winding it like a clock, and suddenly the face began to change. As it turned upside down it became angry, and its eyes began to darken, and its mouth drooped into a bitter frown. The cylinder sprang open.

"Arthur Jelliby," the lady whispered, and smiled as something flew from the cylinder through the keyhole and into the plush darkness of the house. When there was nothing left inside the cylinder she tucked it back into her skirts, and collecting Hettie up off the curb, swept back toward St. Mary's and the graveyard.

It was not a sound that woke Mr. Jelliby. Rather, it was the combined effects of being too cold, lying half out of his blankets, and feeling an uncomfortable lump in his mattress at the small of his back, like a broken spring poking out.

He sat up and felt about in the dark, trying to find the source of this discomfort. He was so tired. Had a man in pointed shoes appeared right then and asked him to sign his name in blood inside a black book, he would have done it just to be allowed to fall back into his pillows and sleep.

His fingers touched on something smooth and cold among the bedsheets. It wasn't a bedspring. *What on earth?* It wasn't even metal.

With a groan, he heaved himself up and lit the lamp on the nightstand. He held it over the bed, surveying the wrinkled sheets. The thing that had woken him was a piece of wood. It was well polished and seemed to have grown from under the bed, piercing mattress and feather comforters until it had finally jabbed into his back.

Mr. Jelliby stared at it, his sleep-fogged mind stumbling, not understanding. Clumsily, he dropped to one knee and looked under the bed. It was a great old four-poster, built of dark wood and carved to look like a grove of weeping willows, their branches entwined to form a canopy. Now that he thought of it, the wood among the sheets looked very much—

He stiffened. Something was wrapping itself around his ankle. With a muffled yelp he jerked his leg around, whirling to see what it was. A brittle snap, like the breaking of a match. He looked down, and there at his feet was another piece of branch, lying still.

"Ophelia?" he whispered into the dark. "Ophelia, I believe you should have a look at this—"

But even as he spoke, another branch rose up behind him and snaked itself silently around his neck. With one swift movement, it drew itself tight. The lamp fell from Mr. Jelliby's hands. It smashed to the floor and went out. His eyes bulged. He reached for his throat, gagging.

"Ophelia!" he croaked, snapping the wood from his neck. The branches were coming quicker now, left and right, crackling from the woodwork of the bed and slithering toward him. *"Ophelia!"*

All of a sudden, the carpet under his feet gave a violent lurch and streaked out from under him. He struck the floor like a ten-ton stone. The carpet turned, flew back at him, and began wrapping itself around him, winding and knotting. With a cry, he kicked it off and started crawling desperately toward the door.

He managed to get out into the hall and would have lain there had not the floorboards begun flipping up, slamming him in the back, in the arm. He scooted down the front stairs and stood, trembling. This was a dream, surely. He *must* be dreaming.

He glanced around the hall. Everything was quiet.

He went into the library and took up the decanter of brandy. *In a few hours I will wake up again. Carpets and willow beds will be precisely what they are supposed to be, and I can—*

The creak of wood sounded behind him. He spun, just in time to see a claw-foot table bounding across the room toward him. It launched itself into the air. It caught him square in the chest. He was hurled back—decanter and all—against the far wall. The decanter burst, leaving a dripping blot on the wallpaper. Mr. Jelliby wrestled with the table, gasping, too stunned even to shout.

He saw the cutlass seconds before it struck. It came from the coat of arms above the fireplace, whizzing point-first toward him. He dragged the table up like a shield, but the cutlass sliced through it, singing past Mr. Jelliby's cheek and burying itself in the wall barely an inch from his left eye.

"Brahms!" he screamed. "Ophelia? Wake up! *Wake up!*" He ducked under the table, leaving it to thrash against the cutlass, and half limped, half crawled toward the front hall. A door banged upstairs. Voices called to each other and hurrying feet beat the floor.

By the time Mr. Jelliby arrived at the front door it was already moving. The mahogany lions carved into its frame snapped at him, straining against the edge of the beams. He gripped the door handle, but it squirmed in his hand. He let go with a cry. A brass lizard launched itself at his face, and its tail caught him on the cheek, leaving a bloody streak. From the ceiling, a plaster vine spiraled into his mouth. He bit down hard, cracking it in two.

At the top of the stairs a light appeared. Brahms stood there in his nightcap, a great kerosene lamp held aloft. It illuminated a circle of ghostly faces, all peering down in fear and wonderment at the battle raging below.

"Ophelia?" Mr. Jelliby shouted up. "Is Ophelia all right?" The hall carpet was alive, too, panthers and wildcats moving fluidly through the weave toward him.

His wife pushed through the huddle of servants, nightgown flaring white in the darkness. "I'm well, Arthur, we all are, but—"

Mr. Jelliby stamped his foot, mashing a red-eyed cat into the writhing stitches of the carpet. "It's Mr. Lickerish! He's sent someone. Something to—"

Another cat tore free. He felt it on his leg, a biting pain, as if the threads were sewing themselves into his skin. He clawed at it.

"Arthur, we're coming," Ophelia cried. Brahms made a move to descend, but the stairs folded up like an accordion, leaving the poor footman flailing sixteen feet above the floor. The others caught him and pulled him back, shouting in fear.

"Arthur, *what's happening?*"

He had to get out. None of the others would be safe until he was gone. And if the front door wouldn't let him leave, he would find another way. He hobbled down the hallway toward the library and the back garden.

Things were flying at him from all directions now. Nails ripped themselves from the floorboards, plant stands and chairs skittered after him out of the corners. The paintings on the walls let loose their inhabitants, and old men in powdered wigs suddenly attacked, clawing and whispering. A beak-nosed lady grabbed a handful of his hair and wrenched his head against her canvas.

"Did you not see?" she hissed into his ear. "Did you not see that common little maid scratch me with her hairpin? And you did *nothing*!"

He could smell her painted hand, turpentine and dust, the brushstrokes of her fingers scraping over his face, searching for his eyes. With a yell, he rent her canvas top to bottom and flung himself away from the wall of portraits. An umbrella closed around his leg. He tried to kick it off, staggered into a bust of some king. It spat a lump of marble straight into his eye.

"My nose does *not* look like that!" the bust cried. Mr. Jelliby backed away, felt the stained-glass door that led into the back garden. His hand found the knob. He rattled it. Locked. Grasping the bust by the neck, he hurled it with all his strength through the door. The door smashed. He leaped through it.

Everything became quiet.

Side tables and teakettles clattered to a halt on the threshold. The bust rolled away into the bushes.

Mr. Jelliby fell to the grass, lungs heaving, half expecting the plants to rise up and devour him, but the garden was silent. No complaining voices. No carnivorous roses or hideous wood spirits. He pushed himself up, the dew and earth cold under his bare feet. And then he heard it. A noise from the knot of rhododendrons that grew in the far corner of the garden. The sound of stone grinding against stone.

Something was moving through the branches. Several things. The leaves began to rustle. A moment later a gargoyle slid out of the shadows, dragging its stone wings behind it. An apple-cheeked elf followed, brandishing a dainty ax. A lunatic grin was fixed across its face. Stone fauns, nymphs, and a great brass frog all emerged from the foliage, each one complaining of its own particular woes.

"There you are," a Venus whispered, and the voice that came from her throat was eerie and grating. "Why do I not have arms? What sort of *imbecile* carves a goddess without arms? It is your good luck, I suppose, or I would surely strangle you with them."

Slowly, steadily, the creatures advanced, feet whispering in the grass. Behind him, in the house, Mr. Jelliby heard the furniture, the tap of wood and marble, and tinny rattling. In a few moments he would be completely surrounded.

Taking a deep breath, he ran straight at the statues. The gargoyle reared, teeth bared. Mr. Jelliby leaped. His foot caught the gargoyle in its mouth and he vaulted over it, through the air and onto the grass beyond. The gargoyle let out a grating roar, but it was too heavy to turn with any speed. Mr. Jelliby struck the garden wall at a run. He began to climb. His toes found a trellis, his hands buried themselves in the ancient ivy, and he scrambled up onto the top.

He turned, looking down into the garden.

They were watching him. After a moment the

Venus detached herself from the others and came to the base of the wall. She stared dolefully up at him with flat stone eyes.

"This is your home," she said. "You will have to come back someday. And when you do, we will kill you for all the wrongs you have done us."

"I didn't do anything!" Mr. Jelliby cried. "I didn't carve you without arms. I didn't hammer the nails into the floorboards or paint the pictures wrong!" But the Venus wasn't listening to him. It simply stared, its voice droning on about all the wicked things it was convinced he had done.

Mr. Jelliby swore and dropped down onto the other side of the wall. A narrow alley ran along it, a crooked chasm between the other garden walls. It was deserted. Wrought-iron gates and doors in peeling greens and yellows opened into it at regular intervals. Rain had fallen, and the moon shone down brightly on the slick pavement, turning it into a path of cold silver. Drips of water fell, echoing, from branches and drainpipes.

Mr. Jelliby looked back at his house, dark and

waiting behind the garden wall. A lamp bloomed in an upstairs window. Then voices, muffled behind the glass. The police would arrive soon, bells clanging. They wouldn't find anything. Nothing but a willow bed, slashed portraits, and stabbed tables, all still as could be.

Pulling his dressing gown tightly around him, Mr. Jelliby hurried off into the night.

CHAPTER XIII
Out of the Alley

BARTHOLOMEW didn't wake up because he had never truly gone to sleep. He had felt the coal scuttle slip from his hand, heard it fall and bounce, one long clear note going on and on inside his skull. He had fallen, too. Dull pain had stabbed his arm, and something inside his eyes had gone on, and he was able to see again, blurry and indistinct. The raggedy man stood at the window, a smudge against the light, waving out. Then the window had gone black, and the wings had filled the alley outside. But it had all seemed so far away. It had been as if Bartholomew were curled up, deep inside his stiff and hurting body, and what happened out in the world did not really concern him anymore.

It felt like he lay there for years. He imagined dust settling over him, and Old Crow Alley descending into ruins around him. But eventually he did feel himself drifting up, filling his body like a puddle spreading through a rut. It was bright outside. Sunlight fell through the grimy panes of the kitchen window and stung his eyes. He sat up and wiped his nose with the back of his hand.

Hettie is gone. It was a slow, hollow thought. *The lady in plum has come and stolen her away, just like the nine others before her. Just like my friend. I wasn't the one they wanted. I am just a silly little boy who didn't realize the danger until it was too late, who thought it was all about me, and going to London, and being important. And now Hettie is gone.*

Bartholomew pulled himself off the floor with the help of a table leg. His clothes were scaly with ash, but he didn't notice. He went to his mother's bed. She was just as he had left her, fast asleep, her breathing regular, peaceful. Sometimes she would smile a little, or snort, or roll over the way she did when she was normally sleeping. Only she wouldn't wake up.

Bartholomew grasped her shoulder. "Mother?" he wanted to say, but only a cracking sound came from his throat.

In a daze, he wandered out of the flat, listening at the neighbor's doors as he passed them. All was quiet. No crying children, no footfalls on the bare old boards, not even the smell of turnips. He went upstairs, downstairs, through the whole house, and everywhere it was the same. All he heard were snores now and then, what sounded like the creak of a bed-spring. Even the hobgoblin who kept the door to Old Crow Alley was asleep on his little stool, a string of spit glistening on his chin.

"Hello," Bartholomew said. "Hello?" A little louder this time. The word flittered up the staircase, through silent passages and squares of sunlight. It echoed back to him, *"Low, low, low . . ."*

Everyone was asleep. Every soul under the roof but him. The bells of Bath were ringing twelve o' clock noon. He went outside and stood in the alley, numb and staring, wondering what to do.

Clouds were drawing in, but it was still bright. He felt the sun on his skin, but it didn't warm him. A ring of mushrooms had grown up among the cobbles. They were few and far between, and when Bartholomew walked into their middle, the air didn't even stir. He stamped on them, one by one, and smeared the black liquid across the ground.

After a while he caught sight of a man working his way up the alley. The man wore a dirty white suit with a blue collar. Bartholomew thought he must be a sailor. He was only a few steps away when he noticed Bartholomew. His eyes went wide and he crossed himself as he passed, scraping himself along the wall and hurrying on around the corner. Bartholomew watched him go, a dull, cold expression on his face.

Stupid, stupid person. Suddenly Bartholomew hated him. *Why should he cross himself and stare? He isn't better than me. He's just a stupid, dirty sailor, and he probably can't even read. I can read.* Bartholomew's teeth began to ache, and he realized he was clenching them. His hand knotted into a fist at his side. In his mind he was hitting the man over and over again, punching his face until when he looked down it was no longer a face at all but a round broken pot with red stew dripping from it.

"Oi! You there!" a rough voice said behind him. A hand grabbed Bartholomew's shoulder and spun him violently about.

He found himself looking into a round, pock-marked face like an old pancake. The face belonged to a thick, small man practically bursting out of his tattered military coat. A peddler's backpack was on his back, but all the hooks where the spoons and pans and dollies should have been were empty.

"What d'you think you're doing, eh? Whispering enchantments at people's backs? What kind of witchcraft are you up to, boy?" The little man drew Bartholomew up by the collar until he was only inches from his dirty, stubbly face.

"Ah, a devil's child, are we," he wheezed. "A Peculiar. Tell me, devil boy, did your ma raise you on dog's blood instead of milk?"

"N-no," Bartholomew rasped. His mind was no longer dragging. It was blunt and quick with fear. *Don't get yourself noticed, and you won't get yourself hanged.*

Don't get— He had gotten himself noticed.

"Your lot is being murdered right now, did you hear 'bout that? Oh, yes! Being fished out of the river, all dripping and cold. I hear they have red marks up their arms, on their skin. And they're just . . . empty, floating like cloth in the swill." The little man laughed gleefully. "No guts! Ha-ha! No guts! Whada you think 'bout that, hmm? Do you have red lines up your arms, all a dancin' and a whirlin'?" He tore at one of Bartholomew's sleeves. His piggy eyes went wide, then narrowed slowly. When he spoke again his voice was low and dangerous.

"You're goina be dead soon, devil boy. You're marked. You know the last boy who died? He was right from around here, looked like you. Binsterbull or Biddelbummer or sommet like that. And they just fished him out o' the Thames, they did. In London. And he had just the same marks as that. Oh, yes. Just the same." The man's breath stank of gin and decaying teeth. Bartholomew began to feel sick. "Watcha been up to, eh, devil boy?" the man whined in his face. "Why they gonna kill you?

Maybe I should kill you first and save them the tr—"

Behind them, someone cleared his throat. "Excuse me," a polite voice said.

Without loosening his grip on Bartholomew's collar, the peddler whipped around. He snorted.

"Whada you want?"

"I want you to unhand the young man," the voice said.

"You best start runnin', mister. Run away, or I'll finish you next."

The man didn't move. "Release him or I'll shoot you dead."

Bartholomew craned his neck, trying to catch a glimpse of his benefactor. He found himself looking down the barrel of a gun. It was a tiny silver gun with mother-of-pearl on its handle and rubies and opals all down its sides.

The peddler only spat. "You? You couldn't shoot a kitten if it bit your nose."

The man shot. A fine round pearl rolled lazily down the barrel of the gun and plopped out, falling to the cobblestones and bouncing away.

"Drat," the man with the gun said. "Look, leave the boy alone, won't you? You can have the pistol. It's worth a great deal, I suppose. And I assure you there's no more. My money is all in named bills so you'll never be able to cash them, and I don't even have a watch chain, so you needn't bother robbing me." He held out the bejewelled pistol. "Now do unhand the child."

The man with the pancake face dropped Bartholomew unceremoniously to the cobbles. He snatched the pistol. "All right," he said, squinting warily at the stranger. "But this ain't no child. This is one o' them changelings, it is, and it's marked. It's gonna be dead soon."

Then he was gone, scrambling away down the alley.

Bartholomew got up off the ground and looked his rescuer over.

The man was a gentleman. His shoes gleamed black, and his collar was starched, and he smelled terribly clean, like soap and fresh-pumped water. He was rather tall, too, with broad shoulders and square features, and blond stubble pricked up along his jaw so that it looked like he hadn't shaved in several days. His face wore an expression of mild inquiry. Bartholomew disliked him right away.

"Hello," the gentleman said quietly. "Are you Child Number Ten?"

"Mi Sathir? There is a problem."

The lady in plum stood with her back to Mr. Lickerish. Her arms were at her sides, and her elegant fingers were moving ever so slightly, picking at the velvet of her skirts. Her lips remained motionless.

"Mi Sathir," the voice said again. Mr. Lickerish did not look up. He was busy scribbling away on a scrap of paper with a curling black feather, fierce concentration etched into his fine-boned features.

The lady and the faery were in a beautiful room. Books lined the walls and lamps cast halos around them. A low humming filled the air. Two metal birds were perched on the desk where Mr. Lickerish sat, their eyes dark and keen. In one corner of the room, a chalk circle had been drawn carefully on the floorboards. One section of the circle looked newer than the rest, crisper and whiter, as if it'd had to be redrawn.

"A *problem, Sathir.*"

Mr. Lickerish threw down the quill. "Yes, there are many problems, Jack Box, and one of them is you, and one is Arthur Jelliby, and one is old Mr. Zerubbabel and his crooked, slow fingers. How long does it take to build another bird out of metal? He has the plans and the route and . . . Speaking of which, did you kill him? Arthur Jelliby?"

"I did. He's dead by now. Most likely strangled by his bedsheets because they did not like being put under sizzling irons and drowned in suds. You know, it's almost a shame wasting the *Malundis Lavriel* spell so late at night. There's no one about to appreciate it. Now, on a crowded street, in the heat of the day, the result can be quite spectacular but . . . But I digress. We have a problem." The lady in plum stepped aside, revealing a little girl curled up on the floor. The lady extended a jet-black toe from under her skirts and dug it into the child's ribs. "Wake up, ugly thing. Wake up!"

Hettie raised her head sleepily. For half an instant her eyes were blank, as if she thought she was still at home, safe. Then she sat up. Her mouth pinched, and she glared at the lady and Mr. Lickerish, each in turn.

"Pull up your sleeves, half-blood. Show him."

She did as she was told, but she didn't stop glaring. The dirty fabric was rolled up, revealing a pattern of lines, red tendrils twisting around her thin white arms.

"Well?" the faery politician demanded. "What is it? She looks very nearly as wretched as the other nine."

A tongue clicked in annoyance. It was not the lady's tongue, not the tongue behind the vivid red lips. It was a long, rough, barbed tongue, scraping over teeth. "Read it," the voice growled.

The faery politician leaned across the desk. He paused. One perfect eyebrow arched. "Eleven? Why is she marked eleven?"

"*That* is the problem. I don't know. I set up the spell just as you ordered, *Skasrit Sylphii* to brand each of the changelings as they traveled through the wings and to open their skin to the magic. This one ought to have been marked number ten."

Mr. Lickerish snapped his fingers and settled back into his chair. "Well then. It counted incorrectly. Magic is only as clever as its user, and you are not nearly as clever as you suppose."

"My magic is quite sound, *Sathir*. And at least *I* can still do such things. You know nothing of the old ways. You buy all your spells and potions like a regular spoilt toff." The voice ought to have stopped there, but it went on, goading. "Or else you dispense with it altogether. Mechanics are so much more practical, after all. Clockwork birds and iron horses." There was a snicker. "Just like a proper *human*."

"Hold your tongue," Mr. Lickerish spat. "I am the one who is going to save you. Save us all from this cage of a country. And you will do your part just as I do mine. Now," he said, suddenly calm again. "If the spell is still functioning, what could have happened?"

"I see only one way: someone else came through the faery ring."

The room went deathly still. Only the gentle humming could be heard, throbbing somewhere in the walls.

The lady's fingers began to twitch, little jerks like a spider's legs when it's just been crushed.

"Someone," the voice said again, "after number nine and before this one. The magic fades slowly. If someone stepped in by accident, I suppose it's . . . No. No, it couldn't be. The sylphs would have devoured him in an instant, gnawed him to the bone. Oh, it makes no sense! Only a changeling would have been marked!"

Mr. Lickerish stared at the back of the lady's head. His eyes were hard and black.

The voice went on, hurrying, stumbling. "It is the only way. The magic did not count incorrectly. The spell is quite sound. Eleven changelings have traveled to this room. Nine have met their deaths. One— this one, I assure you"—the lady's hands were moving furiously now, scratching at the fabric like claws— "will be the means to a glorious end, and the other one is . . ."—the hands went limp—". . . still about."

"Still about," the faery politician enunciated slowly. "Still *about*? A changeling slipped into my private chambers, saw needle-knows-what, and is now marching lively as firelight through England?" Mr. Lickerish picked up a china figurine and hurled it across the room. *"Find it!"* he screamed. "Find it at once and kill it."

The lady in plum turned to face Mr. Lickerish. Her expression was blank, her lips slack. She slumped forward in a clumsy bow, and the voice said, "Yes, *Mi Sathir.* It will be the simplest thing in the world to track it down."

Hettie had crawled to where the figurine lay smashed. She was picking up the pieces one by one, staring at them in dismay. Mr. Lickerish turned on her.

"And take that one to the preparation room. Beg the rain and stones she is everything we need her to be, or you and your sweetheart can stumble off in your present state, secure in the knowledge that *nothing* will ever happen to change it. She is becoming more and more unbecoming, by the way. Your sweetheart."

The faery gentleman flicked his long fingers in the direction of the lady in plum. "You might have her change out of that horrid dress."

Mr. Jelliby had spent the night on a bench in Hyde Park. The moment the dreary London sky was light enough to see by, he'd set off to his bank in nothing but his dressing gown and had rung the bell frantically until a sleepy-eyed clerk had let him in. He demanded his jeweled pistol and a great deal of money from the family safe box, and when he had gotten them, he took a cab to Saville Row, woke the tailor, and paid double so that he could leave with the Baron d'Erezaby's new coat and waistcoat, a satin cravat, and a top hat. An urgent telegraph to his house on Belgrave Square told Ophelia that he was safe, that she must leave for Cardiff that very day if she could and not speak to anyone about it. By eight o'clock in the morning he was on his way to Bath.

It was a comfortable journey despite the damp and the chill that pervaded everything. The great black steam engine sped across the countryside, dragging its fumes in a plume behind it, and leaving only a watercolor blur of greens and grays painted on Mr. Jelliby's window. He arrived at the train station in New Bath just before noon.

He had decided right away there was no point in going anywhere else. The London coordinates made no sense at all to him, and the other address on Mr. Zerubbabel's scrap of paper was up north in Yorkshire. Besides, Bath was where the changelings were. If Mr. Jelliby was going to do anything to save them, it would be here.

He climbed down from the railway carriage, into the swirling steam of the platform. He had heard about this vertical, filthy city, but he had never been to it before. It was not the sort of place people went if they could help it. The train station had been built close to the city's foundations, under a rusting iron-and-glass dome. The platforms were almost deserted. Station masters and conductors rushed from wagon to wagon, hopping up onto the steps as soon as they could as if the ground were poison. No faeries waited here. Very few humans, either. One look at the rabbit-hole streets and drooping houses surrounding him, and Mr. Jelliby was convinced to go in search of a cab.

A few dingy transports stood at the edge of the train station—a wolf-drawn carriage, two huge snails with tents atop their shells, and twelve bottles of potion that were more likely to leave you knocked out and penniless than take you where you wanted to go. Mr. Jelliby chose a towering blue troll with a palanquin strapped to its back and put a guinea into the box on its belt. Even on his toes, he could barely reach it. The guinea struck the bottom of the box with a *clunk*. There were no other coins inside.

The troll grunted and flared its nostrils, and Mr. Jelliby was certain it would lift him up into the palanquin. It didn't. He waited. Then he saw the wooden footholds attached to the outer part of the troll's leg, and he climbed into the palanquin himself.

The troll heaved into motion. Mr. Jelliby settled into a heap of pungent-smelling cushions and studiously avoided looking at the faery city as they traveled down through it.

At the base of the city, the troll stopped abruptly. Mr. Jelliby leaned out to complain, but one look at the creature's storm-dark eyes and he closed his mouth with a clap. He climbed down the blue leg and watched the troll loaf back into the shadows of New Bath. Then he waved down a proper steam cab and gave the driver the Bath address that Mr. Zerubbabel had written down for him.

The cab had driven no more than five minutes before it stopped, too. Mr. Jelliby wanted to scream. He thrust his head out the window.

"What is it *now*?"

"That's a faery slum, through there," the coachman said, pointing his whip toward an ivy-strangled arch between two tall stone buildings. "You'll have to go on foot the rest of the way."

With an oath, Mr. Jelliby climbed out and walked under the arch. He went down first one foul street, then another. He asked directions several times, got lost, was stared at and cackled at and had his hat stolen off his head. But eventually he turned into a cramped, crooked little street called Old Crow

Alley, and there came upon a child in the process of being murdered.

"Well, are you?" Mr. Jelliby asked, trying to make his voice as kind as possible. "Are you Child Number Ten?" He wasn't in any mood to be kind. His eyes kept returning to the boy's pointed ears, his sharp, hungry face. *So this is what a changeling looks like.* Ugly, partway between a starving street child and a goat. But not really something to make a fuss about. Half of England's faery population was uglier, and no one buried *them* under elderberry bushes. The boy didn't look like he could cast curses on people, either. All he looked was sad and banged up. Mr. Jelliby was not sure what to make of that.

"I don't know," the boy mumbled. "Mother's asleep and she won't wake up."

"I beg your pardon?"

"She won't wake up," the boy repeated. For an instant his dark eyes had looked Mr. Jelliby over, read his face, read his clothes. Now they refused to look at him.

"Oh. Well—She must be very tired. Perhaps you know of a lady in a plum-colored dress? She wears a little hat on her head with a flower in it. And blue gloves. I am quite determined to find her."

A flicker passed behind the boy's eyes, and Mr. Jelliby could not tell if it was recognition or fear or something else entirely.

For a moment the boy just stood there, staring at his feet. Then, very quietly, he asked, "How do you know about her?"

"I met her once." Impatience was plucking at Mr. Jelliby's brows, pulling them into a frown, but he forced himself to remain calm. He mustn't scare the child off. "She appears to be in some peril, is associating unwillingly with a murderer, and is beset with troubles concerning her beau. Also, I believe she—"

The boy wasn't listening. He was looking past him, through him, his eyes piercing. "She's been here," he said. Mr. Jelliby could barely hear him. "Twice now. She took my friend and then my sister. She steals changelings out of the faery slums and . . ."

〜〜〜

Bartholomew went cold all over. *Fished out of the river, all dripping and cold. Empty, floating like cloth in the swill. No guts! Ha-ha! No guts!*

The changelings were dead. His friend, and . . . *No.* No, not Hettie. Hettie couldn't be dead.

Panic gripped his neck with bony fingers. "Please, sir," he whispered, looking Mr. Jelliby in the eye for the first time since their meeting. "The lady took my sister."

Mr. Jelliby looked uncomfortable. "I'm sure I'm very sorry," he said.

"I have to get her back. There's still time. She wouldn't have killed her yet, would she?" It was a plea, really, more than a question.

"Well—well, I don't know!" Mr. Jelliby was becoming flustered. He had come too late. The lady had been and gone, and there was nothing to do now but go to the next of Mr. Zerubbabel's coordinates and hope he would find *something.* He didn't want to hear the grief of the child's brother. He didn't want to know how much his failure had cost.

"It was only a few hours ago," the boy was saying.

"She might still be close. Have you seen her?"

Somewhere in Mr. Jelliby's mind a little bell rang. *The coffeehouse on the corner of Trafalgar Square. A glinting brass capsule and a note dashed with ink.* "Send it to the Moon," it had read.

"Your sister is on the moon," he said. "Whatever that means. Good luck. I need to go now." He began to walk.

Bartholomew kept pace with him. "She's not dead then?"

"I don't *know!*" Mr. Jelliby walked faster.

"Will you help me find her? Will you take me with you?"

Mr. Jelliby stopped. He wheeled around to face Bartholomew.

"Look, boy. I'm very sorry. I'm sorry for your loss, and all your troubles, but I can't be bothered with them now. Evil machinations are under way and I fear I have very little time to stop them. Finding the lady is the only way I know how. Now, if you know where she is staying, do not hesitate to tell me. Otherwise kindly leave me alone."

Bartholomew wasn't listening. "I'd be hardly any trouble at all. I could walk behind you, and half the time you wouldn't even know I was there, and then when we find Hettie—"

Mr. Jelliby began to turn away, a look of apology on his face.

Horrid, aching panic seized Bartholomew when he saw it. "You can't go," he cried, grasping at Mr. Jelliby's sleeve. "She's *with* the lady in plum! If we find her we'll find my sister! Please, sir, *please* take me with you!"

Mr. Jelliby stared at Bartholomew in alarm. He couldn't take a changeling with him.

"Your mother," he said. "Your mother will never allow it."

"I told you. She's asleep. I don't know when she'll wake up. But if she does and I'm here and Hettie's not, she could never bear it."

Mr. Jelliby didn't like the way the child spoke. There was something tired and sad and old about it. "Well, surely you have lessons," he said, somewhat more sharply than he had intended. "Lessons are very important, you know. You must attend to them diligently."

Bartholomew gave Mr. Jelliby a look that said he thought him very stupid. "I don't have lessons. I don't go to school. Now will you let me come with you?"

Mr. Jelliby made a face. He pinched the bridge of his nose. He looked up at the sky and over his shoulder. Finally he said, "You will have to disguise yourself."

Bartholomew was gone in an instant. Three minutes later he was back, wearing a shabby woolen cloak and hood of forest green. It was a hobgoblin's cloak, taken from the cupboard of the sleeping doorkeeper. On Bartholomew's feet was a pair of knob-toed boots, much too big for him. He had wrapped a strip of cotton around his face, over and over again, until only a narrow slit was left for him to look through.

Mr. Jelliby thought he looked like a leprous dwarf. He sighed.

"Let's be on our way, then." The faery slums had wasted enough of his time already. Even by rail, the next of Mr. Zerubbabel's coordinates lay many hours' journey from Bath.

He set off down the alley, and Bartholomew clumped after him.

They had barely gone seven steps when something caught Bartholomew's eye. He paused, looking up. The sky between the roofs was the color of pewter. A single black feather was drifting down, down. . . . It looked like a flake of dark snow, falling from the angry clouds above. Slowly, it spiraled toward him.

He turned to Mr. Jelliby. "Run," he said. And a moment later the alley was filled with wings.

CHAPTER XIV
The Ugliest Thing

THEY ran, fighting their way out of the shrieking wings and pounding down the alley. Bartholomew threw a glance back over his shoulder just in time to see the tall form of the lady in plum sweeping out of the blackness. Her face, half hidden in the shadow of her hat, turned toward him. Then he was around the corner, running with all his might after Mr. Jelliby.

"Why are we running?" Mr. Jelliby yelled as they dashed across a little court, under the branches of a gnarled old tree. "Changeling, what were those wings? What is *happening*?"

"The lady," Bartholomew gasped, trying to keep

up. "The lady in plum! She's back, and she wouldn't come for noth—"

I know you're here, a dark voice said, sliding silken into his head. *Child Number Ten, I can feel you.*

A searing pain exploded in Bartholomew's arms, tracing like the tip of a knife along his skin. He almost collapsed in his tracks.

"The lady in plum?" demanded Mr. Jelliby, stopping short.

Bartholomew collided with his back. Wrenching up a sleeve of his cloak, he saw that the red lines were swollen, raised, pulsating with a ruddy light.

You are running, half-blood, the voice said, mildly surprised. *Why do you run? Are you afraid of something?* A snicker echoed in Bartholomew's skull. *Surely you don't have something to hide from me.*

"But that's excellent!" Mr. Jelliby was saying. "I've been searching for her for *weeks*! And your sister is with her, you said! I must speak to her at once." He gave a resolute stamp and turned on his heel.

Bartholomew ran full force at Mr. Jelliby, shoving him into a doorway. "You don't understand," he said, gritting his teeth against the pain in his arms. "She's not the same all the time. She does dreadful things. Don't you see, *she's* the murderer!"

Mr. Jelliby frowned down at him. "She asked for my help," he said. Then he shook Bartholomew off and began walking back the way he had come, shouting, "Miss! Oh, miss!"

"You can't *do this*!" Bartholomew cried frantically, running after him. But it was too late.

A gust of black wings filled the mouth of the street and there was the lady in plum, velvet skirts swirling around her. Something twitched under her skin when she caught sight of Mr. Jelliby. Something like a tiny snake wriggling through bone and sinew.

"You," the voice said, and this time it was not only in Bartholomew's head. It slithered up among the houses, prickled in his ears. The lady began to move.

"Miss!" Mr. Jelliby called. "Miss, I must speak with you on a matter of great urgency! You asked for my help, remember? In Westminster? I was in the cupboard and you—"

The lady did not slow down. Lifting one

blue-gloved finger, she slashed it viciously through the air in front of her. Mr. Jelliby was swept off his feet and hurled against the wall. Bartholomew spun back into the doorway just as something like a swarm of invisible birds rushed past his face.

"How did you survive?" the voice spat at Mr. Jelliby. The lady's finger was still pointing at him, pinning him to the wall. His feet dangled several strides above the cobblestones. "Why are you still alive? No one has *ever* survived that magic before!" Mr. Jelliby began to gag, his hands clawing at his collar.

Quickly and stealthily, Bartholomew crept out of the doorway and pried a loose cobblestone out of the street. Then he moved toward the lady's back, weapon raised.

There was a warning cry. The lady reached behind her head and parted her hair. Mr. Jelliby crumpled to the ground. Bartholomew froze.

The other face, the tiny leathery one, was looking straight at him, its eyes glittering points inside the folds of flesh. Thick brown tentacles writhed through the lady's hair. It opened its mouth in a sneer.

"Child Number Ten," it said. "The boy in the window." Bartholomew hurled the cobblestone.

A howl of pain tore through the alley, so loud it sent a flock of jackdaws wheeling into the sky. The lady raised three fingers, no doubt to finish them both off, once and for all, but Bartholomew was already running, skidding around the corner at Mr. Jelliby's heels.

The next alley was wider. Bartholomew had the briefest impression of people stopping their business to stare at them, a casement banging open, a butcher shop with offal running black into the gutter. Then they were out in the open again, out among the rattling trams and the crowds. Washing blew in the breeze overhead. The air was full of smoke and voices. Bartholomew thought he smelled boiled turnips, just like in the upstairs of their house in Old Crow Alley.

"We have to get to the train station!" Mr. Jelliby shouted, shoving his way between a peppermint-water seller and a faery with mouths where its eyes should have been. "Keep watch for a rickshaw, boy.

There should be a blue chap somewhere hereabouts."

Bartholomew peered out from between the strips of fabric. All around he saw nothing but legs. Legs in suits, legs in rags, legs in cotton, gray and dove colors, hurrying in every direction. *So many people.* The thought was accompanied by a stab of panic. *Don't get yourself noticed. Don't let them see.* They were all around, fingers and eyes so close and dangerous. And then, among the legs, he spotted a flicker of purple; plum-colored velvet clutched in a midnight-blue hand.

"She's here," Bartholomew hissed to Mr. Jelliby.

Mr. Jelliby stole a glance over his shoulder. Sure enough, there was the lady in plum, advancing steadily through the crowds. She stood a head above the endless flow of drab coats and hats, her shadowed face fixed. Stiff as a marionette she walked, no more than twenty paces behind them, and the gap was closing swiftly.

Without a word Bartholomew and Mr. Jelliby slipped into a doorway and down a gray stone passage that looked out over a vegetable garden. The passage led into a bustling kitchen and then out again into a narrow shop-lined street. They paused to get their bearings.

"Why does she want to kill me?" Mr. Jelliby said, halfway between a whisper and a shout. He was turning circles on the cobbles, running his fingers through his hair. "She asked for my help! My *help*, for goodness' sake! And now that I've finally found her she very well near murders me!"

Birds croaked along the roof gutter. Bartholomew was trying to find a way to lace up his boots.

"She asked for your help, did she?"

It was not Bartholomew who had spoken. Mr. Jelliby spun. There, not six steps away, stood the lady in plum, lips unmoving in her face. Slowly, she began to turn. The second face came into view, leering out at them through a curtain of hair. Black liquid dribbled down its chin from a horrid gash across its mouth.

"Melusine, you little traitor." The voice was sickly sweet, but it shook, a razor thread close to snapping.

Mr. Jelliby gaped at the face. It stared back, cracked lips trembling, little black eyes twitching like beetles.

Bartholomew saw his chance. Sidestepping into the kitchen, he began to run again.

Mr. Jelliby watched him go, and his heart sank. *There's the gratitude for my charity,* he thought bitterly. *The little devil boy's abandoned me.* And then the lady in plum lifted a dainty finger, and Mr. Jelliby was swept off his feet and hurled across the street.

He smashed through a shoemaker's window into the closed-up shop behind it. For an instant he floated in the center of the room, surrounded by boots and darkness. Then he was dragged out again, back across the street, smashing into a door so hard the metal studs split his skin.

Something snagged the fabric of his coat and rent it side to side. A shard of glass caught him in the hand. He saw the droplets of blood fly down through the air, ruby-red and glistening.

This was the end, then. The thought came to him idly as his head rapped against a painted signboard. This was the end. He would die now.

But something was happening in the street below. He heard commotion, a flurry of feet on the cobbles, followed by the desperate shout of, "There she is! Help him! Help him, she's going to murder him!"

Boy? He forced himself to open his eyes. He was about eight feet above the ground, tangled in the metalwork of a blacksmith's sign. Below, two uniformed officers stood, looking from him to the lady in plum and back again with the most befuddled expressions on their mustached faces. Their confusion seemed to last an eternity. Then they ran at the lady, arms outstretched, prepared to snatch her up like a child.

The lady in plum did not even flinch. Still holding Mr. Jelliby suspended with one hand, she swept the other one about and pointed it, palm outward, at one of the policemen. His face flattened, as if against glass, and he reeled back, clutching his nose. The other one was almost upon her when he too stopped short. He began marching like a wind-up soldier and walked straight into a wall.

Mr. Jelliby was airborne again. Something had pulled him from the sign, and he was flying, the howl of wings and wind filling his ears. He was dragged as high as the rooftops, then dropped, then snatched up again inches before he smashed to the cobbles. He swooped past the lady. His fingers brushed hair and shriveled skin.

He had only a split second. A split second to think and even less to strike, but he did. His fist caught the little face in the mouth. The lady in plum went reeling forward, and suddenly nothing was holding Mr. Jelliby anymore and he plummeted.

A frightful, pain-filled wheezing filled the alley. Mr. Jelliby collapsed into the gutter, and the wheezing went on and on, scratching at the inside of his bones. The lady began to whirl like a dancer on a stage. The edges of her skirt and the tips of her fingers were turning to black feathers, glistening and sparkling in the light. Then the officer with the bloody nose leaped toward her and seized her. The two figures struggled, black wings pouring around them. The lady shrieked and thrashed, but it was no use. The flapping weakened. And all in an instant it was over. The wings were gone. The rushing wind as well. The street became utterly still.

Bartholomew, the lady, the officers, all stood as if turned to stone. Then the noise of the city enveloped them. Shouts and steam horns—warm, familiar sounds.

The police were the first to move. They clapped metal cuffs across the lady's wrists, and one of them began leading her away.

Mr. Jelliby crawled out of the gutter, aching and winded. Bartholomew made a move to disappear down the stone passageway, back into the close-packed crowds of the wider street, but the other officer caught him by the hood of his cloak.

"We're not finished with you, hobgoblin. And I'm afraid with you neither, sir. It looks like we'll all be taking a pleasant jaunt down to the station."

The Bath Police of precinct eight were established in a squat brick building directly below the smoke and falling sparks of an iron bridge that vaulted up into the new city. The windows were sooty, the floors unswept, and everything from the file cabinets to the lampshades smelled strongly of opium.

Bartholomew and Mr. Jelliby were made to sit down in a cold little office, in the presence of an incessantly scowling secretary. Mr. Jelliby's head flopped about now and again, and Bartholomew was afraid he might tip forward onto the floor. After a long while, a young woman in a red-and-white cap came in and bound up all Mr. Jelliby's various wounds in clean gauze. She was cheerful enough to him, but she looked at Bartholomew nervously and always pulled her apron a little tighter around herself when she moved within reach, as if she were afraid Bartholomew was going to pluck at it. After a time, she left again. They waited another age. The secretary scowled at them. An old metal clock hung on the wall, and its clacking hands seemed to slow time down rather than count it.

Bartholomew's foot tapped the floor. He wanted to move, to get out of the building and run until he found Hettie. *How much time do I have?* Not long. Not long before she was like the other changelings, quiet and dead. He saw her in the water suddenly. *A white shape bobbing in the dark. Her branches wilted, limp in the currents. Hettie.* Bartholomew pinched his eyes shut.

"Thank you for coming back for me," Mr. Jelliby said suddenly, and Bartholomew jumped a little. The man hadn't raised his head. His eyes were still shut. Bartholomew didn't know what to say. For a long moment he just sat there, trying to think of something, anything at all. Then the door burst open and an inspector came in, and Bartholomew wished he could sink into the shadows of his cloak and never be seen.

The inspector began asking Mr. Jelliby a great many questions. Mr. Jelliby was tempted to tell him everything. All about Mr. Lickerish, and the changeling murders, and the clockwork birds. Then *they* could handle it. *They* could do all this. But he knew it wouldn't do any good. Mr. Zerubbabel hadn't believed him. Not even Ophelia had believed him.

Once the inspector had convinced himself that Mr. Jelliby knew very little about anything at all, he too left and was replaced by a small bearded man in a tweed coat. The man was very plain. His face was plain, his bald head was plain, and his wrinkled necktie was plain. All but his eyes, which were a star-tling, frigid blue, like glacier water. It looked as if he wanted to eat you up with them.

"Good day," he said. His voice was soft. "I am Dr. Harrow, head of Sidhe studies at Bradford College. The lady who attacked you today is possessed by one. A faery, that is, not a college. Now. If you would be so kind as to recount to me every detail you can remember of her actions, her *re*-actions, the sound of her voice, and the character of her thaumaturgic abilities, I would be much obliged."

Mr. Jelliby nodded glumly from under his ban-dages and began a lengthy description of being attacked and pursued and thrown about alleyways. Then, when he thought he might dare, he asked, "Might I be allowed to speak with her? Is it safe? I'm sure I'd only need a moment."

Dr. Harrow looked doubtful. "You say you do not know her at all?"

"Oh, I don't," Mr. Jelliby assured him hurriedly. "I'd . . . just like to ask her something, if that's all right."

"And that is a gnome?" the doctor asked, pointing

a thumb toward Bartholomew. "He will have to stay out. They are likely to plot together by magic."

Mr. Jelliby hadn't thought of that. "Very well," he said. "I'll be back shortly, boy."

Dr. Harrow motioned for Mr. Jelliby to follow, and the two of them went out into a corridor and down a flight of metal stairs. At the foot of the stairs was another corridor, but this one was low and vaulted, with whitewashed walls and a green tile floor. Thick iron doors lined both sides. The smell of lye soap and carbolic soda hung in the air, so strong it burned in Mr. Jelliby's nostrils, and yet even that wasn't able to cover the stench of filthy humans and faeries.

The doctor led him to one of the doors and motioned the guard who sat at the far end of the passage to unlock it.

They were shown into a stark white room. It had no windows, no comforts at all. Its only furnishing was a plain wooden chair in the center of the floor. And seated on it, dark and still, was the lady in plum.

The gloves had been pulled from her hands so that her fingerprints could be taken. Parts of her dress had been cut away. Her hat was still in place, though, hiding her eyes.

"The faery inhabiting her is some sort of leeching faery," the doctor explained, circling her. "A parasite. Such cases are extraordinary. Usually the parasite will take over the consciousness of an animal or a tree. That it should attach itself in such a way to a human is almost unheard of. According to Spense, once the parasite has infiltrated its host, it begins to slowly consume it. The leeching faery takes over the mind, worms into flesh and sinew. . . ." He pulled aside the locks of hair at the back of her head, revealing the twisted, mangled face underneath. "Only the voice box is said to be impossible to control. So beware, should you ever cross paths with a silent cow." The doctor tittered at his own joke.

The face beneath the hair was the ugliest thing Mr. Jelliby had ever seen. Not human, barely fay, a sagging mass of teeth and tentacles and wrinkled skin. Its mouth hung open. Its eyes were shut, almost hidden under the swelling wound from Bartholomew's cobblestone.

"The faery is under a powerful sedative," Dr. Harrow said, letting the hair fall back. "By the looks of things it has been inhabiting the lady for many months. It is rooted very deeply. Anything it eats or feels will to some extent affect her as well. She will be drowsy. I doubt she will be able to tell you anything useful."

Mr. Jelliby nodded. Kneeling down so that he could see under her hat, he said, "Miss? Miss, can you hear me?"

There was no response. She sat there, a dark statue upon the chair, and did not stir.

Mr. Jelliby looked over his shoulder at the doctor. "Consumed her, you say? Will she live? Can't the faery be . . . extricated somehow?"

"Surgically perhaps," Dr. Harrow answered coolly. "But I do not know if she will ever fully recover, if her mind will ever work on its own again, or her limbs follow her own directions. It is very doubtful."

Mr. Jelliby turned back to the lady, his face grave. "Melusine?" he said quietly.

This time her eyelids flickered open. The eyes

underneath were dead-black, glistening.

He breathed in sharply. "Melusine, you asked for my help, do you remember?" The words came quickly and quietly. "I don't know if I have helped you at all. I hope you will be safe here. But in truth I am the one in desperate need of your help. Do you remember anything of the past few months? Where you were? What you did? Melusine?"

She continued to stare straight ahead.

"I need you to remember," he whispered. "Could you try?" Behind him the doctor was frowning, one hand on the alarm bell. "Anything! Anything at all!"

Something shifted in her eyes then, a change behind the mask of her face. Her mouth opened. She sighed a long, drowsy sigh.

"There was a hallway," she said. It was so sudden it made Mr. Jelliby start. "A hallway into the Moon."

Out of the corner of his eye, Mr. Jelliby thought he saw something. A mass of dark, swarming along the white wall.

"I was hurrying down it," the lady went on. "Searching for something. And there was someone behind me . . . standing . . . staring after me."

Mr. Jelliby glanced at the wall. *Nothing there.* He stood, turning his back on the lady. "That was me in the hallway," he said quietly. "In Nonsuch House. It was not the moon." Her mind was quite gone. She would be no help to him.

"I'll be going now," he said, addressing Dr. Harrow. "My utmost gratitude for your time."

The bearded man gave a small bow. "Oh, not at all," he said, and his blue eyes gleamed with a strange light. "Not . . . at . . . all." With a flourish, he opened the door to the cell and held it for Mr. Jelliby to step through.

Mr. Jelliby smiled weakly. He walked toward the door. But just as he was crossing the threshold, he spun. His fist flew up and he struck the doctor square between the eyes. Then he bolted down the corridor.

"Boy?" he cried, knocking aside the guard and hurtling up the stairs. *"Boy, get out of here!"*

Dr. Harrow's lips: they hadn't moved.

CHAPTER XV
Goblin Market

BARTHOLOMEW thought he heard something in the depths of the building, a faint banging vibrating up through the water pipes and the walls. He looked over at the scowling secretary. The man was busy hammering away at a typewriter. He didn't seem to have noticed anything.

The noise was getting louder. Bartholomew could hear it even above the clatter of the keys. A heavy clang, like a metal door slamming. Then running feet, pounding somewhere in the depths of the building. *Shouts.* Someone was shouting at the top of his lungs, but Bartholomew couldn't hear the words.

The secretary's fingers froze, hovering above the keys. He looked up sharply, black eyebrows bristling.

The shouting came closer. Bartholomew didn't dare move, but his ears were straining, trying to make out the cries. Just a little bit closer. . . .

Both Bartholomew and the secretary caught the words at the same time. "Run, boy!" Mr. Jelliby was screaming. *"Get out!"*

The secretary leaped. Sheaves of papers went sailing into the air as he scrambled across his desk, but Bartholomew was too quick. He ran out the door, slamming it behind him. He turned just in time to see Mr. Jelliby stumbling up out of a stairwell, eyes wild and frightened.

"Run for the street! We'll find each other outside!"

The hallway of the police station was lined with dozens of walnut doors and all those doors seemed to open at once, revealing ruddy, curious faces and loose ties. A few officers ran out, struggling with the buckles on their weapons. Mr. Jelliby barged past them. Bartholomew wormed under them, and soon they were both out in the open again, limping and stumbling among the supports of the iron bridge.

Mr. Jelliby glanced back over his shoulder. Dr. Harrow had reached the steps of the police station. He was walking jerkily, blood running from his nose where Mr. Jelliby had struck him. Behind him, police officers shouted and pushed, staring in confusion after the fleeing figures. Two blew their whistles and gave chase, but they were soon lost in the evening crowds as Bartholomew and Mr. Jelliby hurried deeper into the city.

Mr. Jelliby guessed right away why the police did not try harder to catch him. They knew who he was. A member of the Privy Council with a penchant for spying and violent outbreaks could not very well disappear. They would be wiring London right this very minute, telling the constabulary to send a patrol to the house on Belgrave Square, with orders to have him arrested as soon as he arrived.

But Mr. Jelliby had no intention of returning to London. Not yet. There were two more addresses on that scrap of paper. Two lives he could possibly save. *As long as Ophelia isn't in London.* . . . He hoped she had gone to Cardiff. It would break her heart if she were in Belgrave Square when the police came.

When they had slowed enough that they could breathe again, Bartholomew scurried forward.

"What happened?" he asked, dodging a heap of wicker-bound casks to keep at Mr. Jelliby's side. He didn't really want to know. It would probably make him angry. They had wasted so many hours in there, and it was likely because the gentleman had done something foolish again and gotten in trouble for it. But Bartholomew thought he should try to say *something* to make up for being silent when the man had thanked him.

"Melusine was a pawn," Mr. Jelliby said, not even glancing at Bartholomew. He raised his hand, hailing a passing cab drawn by two giant wolves. The cab didn't stop. The wolves loped on, yellow eyes dull and unseeing. Mr. Jelliby scowled after them. "It makes a bit of sense now, I suppose. The lady was controlled by a faery. Like a puppet on a string. And I'd wager my little finger that faery works for the Lord Chancellor. It's why she tried to kill me, and now that she's locked up with the Bath police the faery's gone into the bearded chap. He looked a bit unsteady on his feet, though. It'll buy us some time, I hope, before he's after us again."

Mr. Jelliby hailed another cab. This one stopped, coal smoke belching from every seam, but it clacked away noisily when he told the driver where they wanted to go.

Mr. Jelliby cursed and set off again, crossing a stone bridge that spanned a frothing little river. "We'll need to buy provisions. Weapons, perhaps, and I want a hat. I have no idea what is waiting for us at the other coordinates, but I *will* be prepared."

"What coordinates?" Bartholomew asked. "I need to find my sister. Where are we going?"

"North. I can't tell you where your sister is, but I know where John Lickerish's birds flew, and if she's anywhere, she's there. We must get to the faery city and find a train to Yorkshire. We're going north."

Not fifteen minutes after they had fled the police station, they were both collapsed behind the red curtain of a rickshaw, jolting up the road into New Bath. The rickshaw was of the conventional sort, helmed by a large-wheeled bicycle and pedaled by a very tiny spryte, who gasped and strained against the pedals with all his might.

The interior was dark. Mr. Jelliby sat sprawled across the bench, holding his aching head and moaning. Bartholomew had pressed himself into the farthest corner.

When he was certain the gentleman wasn't paying attention, he parted the curtain an inch and looked out in awe at the vertical city unfolding around him. Never in all his life had he entered New Bath. It was barely half a mile of narrow streets away from Old Crow Alley, but in Bartholomew's world that was an impenetrable forest. You didn't simply go places. It was unwise to leave the house, dangerous to go into the street, but it was mind-bogglingly fool-ish to venture out of the faery slums. Bartholomew had not needed to be mind-bogglingly foolish until very recently. Besides, Mother didn't like New Bath. She had always told him it was a wicked, deadly place, even worse than the faery districts of the old city. New Bath, she had said, was where the Sidhe ran rampant, where the fay lived in all the wildness and lawlessness of their own country, and where not even the long arm of the Royal Police could reach. When Bartholomew was very small, she had gathered him into her lap and told him a tale about how New Bath was a living, breathing creature, and that one day it would grow legs and open its cloud-gray eyes and stalk away into the countryside, leaving the city behind it.

Staring out from behind the curtain, Bartholomew almost believed Mother's story. The rickshaw was creaking up a steep road made of stone and seemingly held aloft by the branches of a massive tree. Evening was approaching, and little yellow lights were springing up all about, lining the street and sprinkling the mass of odd buildings with droplets of gold.

Bartholomew pulled his cloak tighter around him. It was all so very different from Old Bath. Everything was quieter, the shadows somehow deeper. Now and then he thought he heard a sad passage of music flitting in and out on the breeze, brushing against his ears like moth wings. He imagined it was the city's thoughts escaping from its brain and dancing away through the air. There were no steam creatures here either, he noticed. No street trolleys, or automatons. No technology of any sort. Perhaps that was why it seemed so silent. The only engines in the whole place were those rattling in and out of the New Bath Train Terminal far below, near the roots of the city, and that was a relic from an age past, when the government had tried to connect the faery city with the rest of England. It was the *only* thing that connected the two. Those iron tracks. Nothing else.

Spluttering and heaving, the poor spryte at the helm of the rickshaw steered them up the wide thoroughfare, past towers and hovels and houses hanging from chains, until they came to the edge of a vast open space at the heart of the city. *It's not so much like a monster,* Bartholomew thought. *It's more like an apple. A huge, black, rotten apple with the core pulled out.* The space extended from the structures on the ground, all the way to the clouds far above. Walkways wrapped

around it, crisscrossing it on all the many levels—
bridges and ladders and gangplanks trussed up with
ropes, dangling, creaking, swaying. Thousands of
small shops lined them, shacks, and carts, giant silk
cocoons of the sort butterflies slip from, and color-
ful tents with fluttering awnings. Lanterns shone
from every post and railing, turning the walkways
into blazing ribbons.

"We've arrived," the spryte panted, collapsing
against the handlebars. "The Goblin Market."

Mr. Jelliby pulled back the rickshaw's curtain
and stepped out, staring. Bartholomew followed
cautiously.

They stood at the end of the stone road, hundreds
of feet up, and faeries swarmed everywhere. More
faeries than he had ever seen in his life. Faeries of
all shapes and sizes, some small and pale like Mrs.
Buddelbinster, some brown and knobby like Mary
Cloud, some enormously tall. There were leaf-green
ones and silvery ones, ones that looked like they were
made entirely of mist, and graceful nut-colored ones
with dragonfly wings sprouting from their backs.

They moved in a constant stream along the walkways, spinning and turning upward and downward. And yet the whole enormous space was eerily quiet. There was a sound in the air, but it was not the cacophony of shouts and clattering machines that filled the alleyways of Old Bath below. It was a steady, unbroken whisper, like a thousand dead leaves all rustling at once.

Mr. Jelliby tossed the rickshaw driver a coin, and he and Bartholomew moved into the market. Dozens of black eyes turned to watch them as they passed. Voices, sharp and suspicious, poked at their backs. Bartholomew kept close behind Mr. Jelliby, head lowered, wishing his cloak was made of stone and brambles, wishing he could retreat into it as far as he liked. But the faeries weren't even glancing at him. He realized it with a start. The faeries were staring at the gentleman.

They pushed down the walkways for several minutes, and Bartholomew could tell by the way the man stuck out his chin and looked straight ahead that he was becoming nervous. Bartholomew felt an angry little glow in his chest. *That's what it's like,* he thought. *Now you know, too.* It was as if they had switched places going up the road in the rickshaw. Bartholomew almost belonged here in this strange place. He could do the same things everyone else did, and no one would drag him off for it. No one would even notice him. For once in his life it wasn't he who was peculiar.

Pushing back his hood, he peered in wonder at the shops surrounding him. One sold beautiful black bottles with labels like SORROW WINE or OCTOPUS INK or DISTILLATION OF HATE. Another sold coins, towers and heaps of them, but when Bartholomew passed close by and really looked at them, he saw only leaves and dirt. Another shop had row upon row of fat, bloodred flies stuck to a board with sewing pins.

He spotted a stand laid out with an array of smooth gray humps and approached it curiously. An ancient crone sat behind the wares, dozing under a crimson hood. Bartholomew took a cautious breath. He reached out and touched one. It was so soft, a lovely roll of perfect, silky fur. He wanted to bury his whole hand in it and—

"Scrumptious-looking mouseys, aren't they," the crone said suddenly. She hadn't been dozing. She had been watching him, eyes fixed on him from inside the darkness of her hood.

Bartholomew jerked his hand away and backed into a troll. It grunted angrily. Then the gentleman was at his side, pulling him along.

"Come on! No dilly-dallying. We don't want to spend any more time here than we absolutely must."

They crossed a rope bridge, went along another walkway, climbed a knotted ladder, and then Mr. Jelliby scrunched his eyes closed and in a very strained voice told Bartholomew to be so kind and ask for directions. Bartholomew's insides squirmed at that. The gentleman ought to do it himself. It wasn't as if the faeries didn't speak English. But Bartholomew didn't want the man to think him a coward, either, so he went up to a lithe, scaly creature with webbed hands and glassy eyes and asked very quietly where he might buy a brace of pistols.

The creature's diaphanous eyelids slid once across its gaze as it took in Bartholomew's small cloaked figure. Then it answered in the deepest, roughest English, "Right that way, past the fingernail seller and on seventy foot or so toward the Heartgivers' booths. Turn left at Nell Curlicue's candy shop. You'd 'ave to be blind to miss it."

Bartholomew nodded to the water faery and hurried after Mr. Jelliby, who had started walking at the words "fingernail seller." At a candy shop with flavors of "starlight" and "hemlock" and "icicles," they turned and eventually came to a garish little establishment with the word BAZAAR in colorfully painted letters above the door. Bartholomew waited until Mr. Jelliby had ducked in and then followed.

The shop called BAZAAR was far larger inside than it looked from the walkway. It seemed to sell everything that ever existed. The front part of the shop had regular things like barrels of crackers and pickles, but the farther back one went the more mysterious the objects for sale became. While Mr. Jelliby haggled awkwardly over the price of a compass, Bartholomew wandered down the aisles, trying to look at everything at once. There were puppets in red-and-black patchwork that blinked at him as he passed, seeds purported to grow into massive beanstalks, and intricate rings and brooches that scuttled on insect legs under bell jars. At the end of one particularly long aisle, he came upon a wire cage that held what looked like a black parrot, wrapped in its wings. The wings were powerful, dark oily feathers sprouting from thick bone. They rose to a point over the creature's head.

Penumbral Sylph, read a messy sign under the cage. *Semi-elemental. Rare & extremely magical. Even a single specimen is a much-desired treasure, can be used for near-instant errands + message deliveries, etc. Price: English: 40£ / Faery: no less than the equivalent of one arm and one leg.*

Bartholomew edged up to the cage. It was iron. He could feel it even without touching it, an elusive ache at the back of his head. The creature inside seemed to sense it was being watched. The wings folded back and a delicate white face looked out at Bartholomew. Its mouth was wide and blue-lipped.

They peered at each other in silence for a moment. The wings opened yet farther. Bartholomew saw the sylph's body, disproportionally small compared to its wings, twig-thin arms and legs almost lost among the feathers. Then the sylph's lips curled back over its teeth and it let out a hiss.

"*Changeling,*" it said quietly.

Bartholomew jerked his head back from the cage.

"Changeling," it said again, louder this time.

"Be quiet," Bartholomew whispered.

"Changeling, changeling, changeling." The sylph was pacing now, circling the cage, eyes locked on Bartholomew. Then it let out a shriek and threw itself against the wires, leaving sear marks on its flesh.

"*Changeling!*"

Bartholomew backed away, knocking a tray labeled LIES off a shelf. They fell to the floor and began to expand, blue and emerald bulbs growing bigger and bigger until they exploded in a shower of stinking gas. He turned to run, but a gnome was already bearing down on him from the other end of the aisle. Before Bartholomew had taken two steps, cold fingers took hold of him, digging at the strips of cloth that covered his face. The cloth unwound. The gnome leaped back as if he'd been bitten.

"Out," he said, and his voice was just a squeak. "Get out before the customers see you. Take your horridness away from here!"

Bartholomew ran, past the bean seeds and the puppets, holding his disguise around his face with his hands. He passed the gentleman at the door. The man's arms were full of pistols, a new hat, a compass, and a very large map. He started to say something, but Bartholomew didn't wait to hear it. He pushed past him, out of the bazaar, onto the swaying walkway. A troupe of dwarfish faeries in red pointed hats was coming up it. Behind him, Bartholomew heard wings skittering, the titter of voices. He spotted a dark gap between two shop tents and threw himself into it. There he collapsed and wrapped himself into a ball.

All those faeries thought I was a hobgoblin. That's why they hadn't stared. They thought I was like them. But he wasn't like them. He wasn't like anyone.

Mr. Jelliby found him ten minutes later. His head was in his arms. He was shivering a little.

"Boy?" Mr. Jelliby asked quietly. "What's the matter, boy? Why didn't you wait for me?"

Bartholomew sat up with a start. He wiped his nose on his hand. "Oh," he said. "Nothing. We should go."

Mr. Jelliby was looking at him curiously. Bartholomew didn't want to be looked at. He wanted to be left alone, and if nobody liked him he wished they would keep it to their own stupid selves. He got to his feet and began to walk away.

"I got the pistols!" Mr. Jelliby said, hurrying after him. "And a hat. Are you hungry?"

Bartholomew hadn't eaten since last night's supper, but he didn't say anything. He kept walking, hood pulled low, head down. He had to force himself not to peek over his shoulder to see if the man was following. For a while he simply walked, not really knowing where he was going. Then the gentleman appeared at his side, two crusty pies in his hand. He handed one to Bartholomew.

Bartholomew stared at it.

"Go on," Mr. Jelliby said. "Eat it!"

The pie was full of gristle, made with some horrid

street animal like as not, but Bartholomew gulped it down, bones and all, and licked the grease from his fingers. Mr. Jelliby picked the crust off his and then handed the rest to Bartholomew. He ate that, too. It made him think of the wax-drip soup and Hettie, and that made him want to start running again—anywhere—to find her.

They left the Goblin Market behind them, pressing onto a walkway that wound around the outermost side of the towering city. "The train station," Mr. Jelliby had said, "is near the ground." And that was where they were going.

They were still hundreds of feet up; Bartholomew could see for miles, all the way to the farm country beyond the city's edge. The sky was spread out before him, turning copper as the sun set, clouds rolling low and ominous along the arch of the world.

He paused, staring. There was something in the sky, something besides the endless dusk. A flashing. A burst of black, darker than the clouds, moving at incredible speeds away from the city.

Bartholomew leaned out across the rope railing.

"Look," he called, waving for Mr. Jelliby. "Look over there."

Mr. Jelliby came up beside him. His eyes narrowed. "What on earth . . ."

"It's the wings," Bartholomew said quietly. "They're leaving." *Oh Hettie,* he thought. *Please be safe.*

Mr. Jelliby saw the change in his face. "Come now," he said. "Don't worry. We'll get your sister. We'll get her back." He smiled then—not his wide, Westminster smile, but a real one. "Though if we're to go off adventuring together, I think we should know each other's names, don't you?" He held out his hand to Bartholomew. "I'm Arthur. Arthur Jelliby."

Bartholomew didn't move. He stared at Mr. Jelliby, then at his hand. Then, very cautiously, he took it, and they shook.

"Bartholomew," he said.

Together they turned and hurried down into the darkening city.

CHAPTER XVI
Greenwitch

THE train's pistons plunged, once, twice, and Mr. Jelliby was asleep.

Bartholomew had hoped he might say something, discuss their plans, or tell him more about the lady in plum, but he didn't. *Oh well.* The air was warm, and the seat was plush, and so Bartholomew snuggled into it and pressed his nose against the cold window. The city swam by below in a blue-dark blur, towers and rooftops gone so quick he barely saw them. They crossed the river, chugged among the soaring black flues of the cannon foundries. Then, in the blink of an eye, the city was behind them and they were slicing through the green fields of the country. In a few minutes Bath was only an inky stain on the horizon, growing smaller with every breath.

Bartholomew looked back and felt an odd ache grow in his chest. He was leaving. Leaving all the few things he had ever known. Going who-knew-where with a gentleman who didn't eat when there was food to be had and who shook hands with changelings. Somewhere back in that shrinking spot was Mother, asleep in an empty flat. And Hettie . . . Hettie was somewhere. Not there, but somewhere.

He turned his attention to their compartment in the No. 10 to Leeds. Mr. Jelliby had bought first-class tickets just as he always did, and Bartholomew was not so far out of sorts that he didn't notice how terribly swish everything was. Small framed paintings hung above the seats—happy, comfortable scenes of richly dressed people at tea, or outdoors, smiling vacantly into shop windows and fishponds. On the paneled walls, two lamps were mounted, each with a flame faery imprisoned inside. The one on Bartholomew's side tapped the glass to catch his attention and began pulling its glowing face into a parade of rude expressions. Bartholomew stared at it a while. When he turned back to the window, the faery set to pounding its fists against the inside of the lamp and spitting little angry bursts of flame. Bartholomew glanced back. It promptly resumed making faces at him.

Some time later Mr. Jelliby woke up. Bartholomew dropped his head against the window and pretended to be asleep, watching the gentleman through half-closed lids. Mr. Jelliby looked at him once. Then he began unfolding his newly acquired map, spreading it leaf by leaf throughout the compartment.

Arthur Jelliby's fingers ran across the thick white paper, bouncing as the train rumbled under him. The map was somewhat different from what he was used to. The English Isle was called "The Withering Place." London was labeled "The Great Stink-Pile," and North Yorkshire, "The Almost World," but he understood it well enough. The train would take them to Leeds in Yorkshire. The coordinates on Mr. Zerubbabel's scrap of paper were not in Leeds, though. In fact, as far as Mr. Jelliby could tell, they weren't anywhere in particular. The spot he had marked on the map was not a city, or a hamlet, or even a single farm. It was simply empty open country.

He frowned at the map, turned it upside down, folded it up, and reopened it. He read the coordinates again, recalculated longitude and latitude. It was all no use. The place refused to move anywhere sensible.

When the train stopped in Birmingham, an elderly lady in a silver fur pelisse entered their compartment to sit down. She took one look at Bartholomew's masked face and the pistols on Mr. Jelliby's belt and turned around in something of a flurry, sliding the door closed behind her. No one disturbed them for the rest of the journey.

It was well past midnight when they arrived in Leeds. At the loading docks, they were able to bribe a stagecoach driver to abandon his scheduled passengers and take them as close as he could to the point Mr. Jelliby had marked on the map. No roads led within five miles of it. They would have to do some walking that night.

They left the city by moonlight. The coach was drawn by a pair of unnaturally large grasshoppers, and they ran with reckless abandon, dragging it across stones and ruts until Mr. Jelliby was afraid it would jolt to pieces. A chill wind blew through the chinks in the sides of the coach. Branches tapped against the windowpanes. Soon Bartholomew and Mr. Jelliby were blue with bruises, and cold to the bone. After an hour, the stagecoach stopped. They climbed out blearily.

"Now then," the driver said, hunching into his greatcoat and peering out at them with glinting eyes. "Here's as close as I can get you. There's an inn about a mile back. The Marshlight. I'll wait for you there."

Mr. Jelliby nodded and glanced at the surrounding country, running his hatband around and around through his fingers. "Don't speak of us to anyone, will you? And if we're not back by dawn you may assume that . . . that we've found another way. Good night."

The driver grunted and cracked his whip. The grasshoppers broke into a run and the stagecoach thundered away down the road. Bartholomew watched it go, shivering.

Mr. Jelliby consulted his compass. Then they set out across a wet green field. A thin mist hovered over the grass, soaking their trousers to the knee. Before long it began to drizzle. Bartholomew's head buzzed with sleepiness and Mr. Jelliby was limping, but neither of them said anything. On and on they walked, through field after field, over hills and trickling brooks until there was not a muscle in their bodies that did not ache.

Mr. Jelliby heaved himself over a low stone wall, one eye still locked on the compass. "We ought to be getting there shortly," he said, and brushed the dirt from his knees. "Wherever 'there' is. . . ."

"There," as it turned out, was a knot of trees in the middle of a wide empty field. It was not a forest. It might have been a forest once, when there were still forests in these parts, but all its arms and legs had been cut down, and now it was simply a great clump of oak and elm rising out of the rolling grass. Mr. Jelliby paused at its edge, staring up into the vaulting branches. Then he walked in, Bartholomew close behind him.

The air under the trees was damp, but not like in the fields. It was a musty, living damp, heavy with the smell of bark and wet earth. Moss blanketed the ground, and although the trees grew very close together, it was not difficult to walk. After no more than twenty paces, they found themselves in a small clearing. The rain rustled down, and the grass grew tall here. A heap of charred sticks sizzled under the water droplets. And in the center of the clearing, cheery and welcoming as could be, stood a round-topped wooden wagon. It was painted red, with yellow daffodils and primroses on the door and round the spokes of the wheels. Smoke curled up from a tin funnel on its roof. A single window looked out of its side, and scarlet curtains were drawn across the inside of the panes. Warm light shown through them, casting glowing squares on the grass.

Bartholomew and Mr. Jelliby looked around them uncertainly. There were no monstrous contraptions here, no small graves, or black-winged sylphs whispering in the branches. *What could Mr. Lickerish possibly be interested in here, that his bird should fly all this way?* Bartholomew hoped, desperately hoped, that Hettie was in that painted wagon. He felt suddenly incredibly impatient.

Mr. Jelliby climbed the steps to the door at the back of the wagon and knocked twice. "Hullo!" he called, in what he hoped was a commanding voice. "Who lives here? We must speak with you!"

Something smashed inside. A quick, sharp smash, as if someone had just had a dreadful fright and let a cup or a bowl slip straight from her hands. "Oh, no. Oh no, oh no, oh no," a frail voice cried. "Please go away. Go away. I have no money. No money anywhere."

Mr. Jelliby glanced at Bartholomew, but he didn't look back. He was watching the door intently.

"Madam, I assure you we do not want any money," Mr. Jelliby said. "I received your address from one Xerxes Ya— From a mutual acquaintance. And I need to speak to you. Madam? Are you all right in there?"

A small shutter snapped open in the door, and a face appeared. Mr. Jelliby stumbled back. It was a gray, wrinkled face framed by a shower of wispy birch branches. An old faery woman.

"You're not from the Faery Bureau Inspectors, are you?" she asked. "Or the Court of Thorns? Or the *government*?"

"I'm—well, I'm from England," Mr. Jelliby answered stupidly.

The faery woman gave a nervous laugh and unbolted the door. "Oh. I'm not. Let's get you out of the rain, then, shall we? Unless you like the rain, of course. Some folks do. It's good for selkies, heals boils on nymphs, though I've never known it to do anything for— Oh!" Her hands went to her mouth when she saw Bartholomew. "Oh, the poor little Peculiar! He's thin as a fish bone!"

Bartholomew tried to peer around the faery, into her wagon. Then he looked at her. *Poor little Peculiar?* There was no disgust in her voice, none of the fright of the goblin in the bazaar, or the petty evil of the peddler in Old Crow Alley. She sounded more alarmed by his resemblance to a fish than the fact that he was a changeling.

Yes, well, we don't have to eat him with parsnips, now do we, Mr. Jelliby thought, as the faery woman ushered them into the wagon. It was tiny inside, cramped and warm, and cluttered with parchments and bottles in pretty colors. Bundles of herbs hung from the ceiling. Candles dripped in fantastical shapes down the shelves. The wagon was too small to hide anyone, and Hettie wasn't there.

The old faery busied herself with sweeping up the shards of a pottery bowl from the floor. "Oh, such a mess," she whined. "Don't get many visitors, I don't. Not good ones anyway." Her voice was creaky and old, a bit like the faery butler's. Friendlier, though. *Perhaps too friendly for one who has just had her far-off clearing invaded by strangers.*

"Madam, we've come on a matter of great importance," Mr. Jelliby said.

"Have you, at that?" She tipped the shards into a cat dish. It was full of milk. "And how comes it that an old greenwitch like me can help such good sirs as you? Are you sick? Has the cholera gotten one of you? I hear he is quite busy in London now."

Mr. Jelliby stamped the wet from his shoes and took off his hat. *He?* "No, not cholera. We need to speak to you about someone."

The faery straightened, joints popping, and hurried a teakettle to the stove in the corner. "Don't know many someones anymore. Who might it be?"

"The Lord Chancellor. John Lickerish."

The old faery almost dropped the kettle. She wheeled around to face them. "Oh," she whispered, eyes quivering. "Oh, I meant no harm. Whatever he's done, whatever he's doing, I meant no harm."

Mr. Jelliby's hand fell to the grip of his pistol. "We're not here to accuse you, madam," he said quietly. "We need your help. We have reasonable proof that you are connected to Mr. Lickerish, and we must know why. Please, we must know!"

The faery knotted her hands into her apron and began pacing to and fro, the floor of the wagon creaking with each step. "I don't know him. Barely at all. It's not my fault!" She stopped to face them. "You won't take me away, will you? Not to the cities and their horrid fumes? Oh, I would *perish!*"

"Please, madam, calm yourself. We're not taking you anywhere. We simply need you to tell us things. Everything."

The faery's eyes flicked to the pistols. She looked from Mr. Jelliby to them and back. Then she returned to the stove. Tea hissed as she poured it into blue china cups. "Everything . . ." she said. "You'd be dead of old age before I was halfway through." She brought the tea and slumped into her rocker.

Bartholomew didn't take his cup. *Hettie isn't here.* Nothing was here but a mad old faery. They should be leaving, running back across the fields to the coachman and Leeds. Not drinking tea. He tugged at Mr. Jelliby's sleeve, opened his mouth to say something, but the faery saw him and spoke first.

"Life's hard out here," she said, and her voice was petulant. "Folks in the cities, they work in factories, always among the engines and the church bells and the iron. And they lose their magic. I couldn't do that. Out here I can hold on to bits of it. Just little shreds. It's not like home. Not really. But it's almost there. It's as close as I can get." Bartholomew knew she was talking of her home in the Old Country. She must be very old indeed.

"And I need to live!" the faery woman wailed. "I'm just an old greenwitch and nobody wants my help anymore. Faeries come once in a while out of the big cities when their young 'uns cough blood, but they can't pay much. And I had to sell poor Dolly for glue, so there was no more traveling the circuits. I need to live, you know!" A strange spark came into her eyes. "The Lord Chancellor sends me gold."

"Does he," Mr. Jelliby said coldly. "And did you know he's been killing changelings? Or does he pay you so well that you don't care? I will thank you to tell us now what this is all about. In honest words. What is the Lord Chancellor planning?"

The greenwitch looked about to cry; Bartholomew suspected it was more because of the disapproval in Mr. Jelliby's voice than because of any of his actual words. "You don't know?" she said. "You're trying to stop him, aren't you? That's why you're here. And you don't even know *what* you're trying to stop?"

Mr. Jelliby gulped at his tea. He didn't know. All he had was fragments and pieces—the bird, the message, the conversation in Westminster—but they didn't really add up to anything.

The old faery scooted her chair a little closer to him. "He is going to open another faery door, of course."

Mr. Jelliby blinked at her from over the rim of his teacup. Bartholomew made a little sound in his throat, partway between a gasp and cough.

"You didn't know that?" She giggled, scraped even closer. "Yes. The faery door. He's going to open another one. Very soon, I think. Tomorrow. The last one happened by itself, see. A natural phenomenon brought about by a lot of unfortunate coincidences. There have always been cracks between the worlds. Things have always been slipping back and forth, and there are many tales of humans who have found themselves in the Old Country quite by accident. But this new door won't be a crack. It won't be an accident. John Lickerish is *engineering* it. Commanding it into existence. A massive gateway in the middle of London. In the middle of the night."

Mr. Jelliby set down his teacup sharply. "But it'll be carnage!" he exclaimed, aghast. "Ophelia, and Brahms, and— It'll be Bath all over again!"

"It'll be worse," the faery said, and her face split into a smile then, so bright and toothy it made Mr. Jelliby's skin crawl.

"It won't work," he said, looking studiously at a braid of garlic above the faery's head. "The bells. The bells will stop it. They're always ringing. Every five minutes. Mr. Lickerish won't be able to get a spell in edgewise."

"Ooh. The bells." The faery continued to grin. "Bath had bells. Bath had iron and salt, and not a few clocks and it was still blown six miles north of the moon. Bells don't help against magic like that. They might stop a pisky from giving you a wart or muddle a minor enchantment, but they won't keep a faery door from opening. Not a road to the Old Country."

"Then what do we *do*?" Mr. Jelliby almost shouted it. "We can't just sit here! How do we stop it?"

"*I* don't know." She was so close now. Mr. Jelliby was certain he could smell her—flowers and smoke and sour milk. "It's a complicated process, opening a faery door. I don't understand it. I don't *want* to understand it. All I know is that Mr. Lickerish needs a concoction. Plants and animal parts. I give it to him. It's a binding potion, that concoction is. It lures a sort of faery called the penumbral sylph, can pattern whole flocks of them and make them do what someone tells them to. But I don't know what he needs sylphs for. I'm just a tiny thread, see. A tiny thread in a great big spider's web." She made a scuttling motion with her fingers.

"He sends me his notes in a mechanical bird. A bird out of metal, did you ever hear of such a thing? And I do what they tell me. But those changelings . . ." Her grin fell from her face, and she shrank back into her chair. She looked suddenly frightened and sad again. "I don't know what they're for. Poor, poor creatures. I don't know why he's killing them. I've sent nine bottles to London. A lot of little ones as well. Little bottles. So little. And . . . and last I heard there had been nine deaths. You are from London, yes? I saw it from the dirt on your shoes. Perhaps he's been trying over and over again to open that door. Nine times over. Nine times you could have died in your bed and were spared." Her gaze turned to the window. "I didn't mean for anyone to get hurt. I didn't, truly. And when I heard about the changelings in the river, I knew right away it was him. But, oh, don't make me think about it. I couldn't do anything. What could I have done?" She asked it almost pleadingly.

Bartholomew looked up from his boots. He was glaring. "What d' you mean, what could you have done?" The greenwitch turned to him in surprise. He hadn't spoken in hours and his voice was rough. "You could have done *nothing*, that's what you could have done. You could have stopped helping him. He has my sister now, did you know that? She's next, and it's your fault. It's your fault as much as anybody's."

The old faery stared at him a moment. The firelight danced in her eyes. When she spoke her voice was soft. "It wasn't my fault. Oh, it wasn't. Mr. Lickerish was the one doing the killing. All I did was stir my little pot in my little clearing. Won't think about it. *Won't think about it!*"

Mr. Jelliby started to rise. The greenwitch jerked around to face him. She smiled again. "But in the end I suppose it is my fault, isn't it. Oh, I *am* sorry. Do you know? When I first learned of John Lickerish's plan, I thought, 'Why not?' Why should I care what happens to London? It's about time the faeries broke free, about time the English learned their lesson. But I changed my mind. Would you like some more tea? I decided that Mr. Lickerish was not doing it for the faeries. He's not doing it for anyone, really. No one but himself. He says he doesn't like walls and chains, but he really does. As long as *he* builds the walls and makes the chains. Because you see, when the faery door is opened he isn't just going to let it go. He's going to guard it like a great watchdog, and it will be his. It will always be open, but he'll decide what goes in and what comes out."

Bartholomew stared at her. *What is wrong with her?* It was as if her mind were twisting and shoving and telling itself lies. She kept gazing at Mr. Jelliby, little twitches under her eye and in her fingers, that ghastly smile on her face.

"A great many creatures will die when it opens," she said. "Humans and faeries, all dead in their beds. Twenty thousand perished in Bath. A hundred thousand in the aftermath. Do you remember the Smiling War? Tar Hill and the Drowning Days? Of course you don't. You're too young, and too well fed. But *I* remember. Years and years after the door opened, and there was still nothing but confusion and bloodshed. It'll all happen again. New faeries will come, and they'll be wild and free, and they'll dance in the guts of the people and the silly, tired, English faeries. Because the faeries who are already here won't know what to do. They don't remember how they once were. I think they'll all die, don't you? Die along with everyone else. And Mr. Lickerish will watch it all from some safe place." She looked at Mr. Jelliby adoringly. "But you'll stop him, won't you. . . ."

Mr. Jelliby pushed aside his teacup. "I don't know," he said shortly, and took from his waistcoat pocket the scrap of paper Mr. Zerubbabel had given him. "I have one more address from Mr. Lickerish's messenger bird. The address is in London somewhere. It's the place, isn't it? Has he told you? I believe the messenger birds connect Mr. Lickerish to all the points of his scheme—Bath and the changelings, you. Then back to London."

The old faery's smile turned sly. "Oh, you *are* clever. So clever and tall. How did you get your hands on the Lord Chancellor's messenger bird, hmm? If he ever finds out he'll have you killed."

He already tried, Mr. Jelliby thought, but he said, "Look madam, we haven't time for nonsense. Tell us what the door looks like and where we'll find it, and we'll leave you be."

"Oh, but I don't want you to leave me be! Don't go! I can't tell you those things. I can't, it would be bad, so bad. Or perhaps I could. Perhaps a little. My memories of the last one are very dim, that's all. So dim and faraway. I woke in my bed in the crown of a tree, and . . ." The greenwitch's eyes clouded over. "Mama. Mama was packing bags. She was telling us to hurry because there was a great wonder under way by the City of Black Laughter.

And I remember walking, walking. I was very young then. It seemed to me we walked a hundred nights, but it couldn't have been long at all. And then there was a door in the air. It was like a rip in the sky and its edges were black wings flapping. Feathers fell around us. We went through it, but I don't remember how it looked from the other side. I didn't look back, you see. Not once. Not until it was too late. The door could have been huge or it could have been tiny. Thousands of us fit through it at a time, but it was all magic, that door; it might have been no bigger than my nose." She wiggled her nose. "The London door could be anything. Anywhere. It could be a mouse hole or a cupboard. It could be the marble arch in Park Lane."

She smiled, wistful, her thumb rubbing the chip in the rim of her teacup. "I want to go back, you know. To the Old Country. Home." She looked at Bartholomew, her blue eyes faint and watery. Then she set down her cup and put her hands to her ears. "Best not to think of it. Best not. *Won't think about it!* Nothing good will come of Mr. Lickerish's plans. Not for me. Not for me, and not for anyone."

The wagon was silent for a minute. The fire crackled inside the little stove. Outside in the trees, an owl hooted mournfully.

Then Mr. Jelliby stood. "Indeed. We'll be leaving now. Thank you for the tea."

The greenwitch began to speak again, stumbling out of her chair, trying to keep them a little longer, but Mr. Jelliby was already unlatching the door. He stepped out into the night. Bartholomew followed, pulling his hood down low.

Out in the clearing, Mr. Jelliby took a deep breath. He turned to Bartholomew. "Cracked as an egg, that one. Let's be off then, if we're to save the world."

They trudged out of the circle of warmth from the wagon, out into the heavy damp of the wood.

"I don't care about the world," Bartholomew said under his breath. "All I want is Hettie."

The old faery climbed down from her wagon and watched them go, gazing after them until long after they had been swallowed by the night.

Hours passed. She stood so still she might almost

have been mistaken for a tree herself. Finally a clock-work sparrow swooped down into the clearing and alighted on the dewy grass by her feet. She scooped it up. Cradling it in her palm, she undid the brass capsule from its leg and took out a message.

Rejoice, sister, it read, in Mr. Lickerish's familiar, spidery handwriting. *Child Number Eleven is everything. Everything we hoped her to be. Prepare the potion. Make it your strongest yet and send it to the Moon. The door will not fail this time. In two days' time, when the sun rises, she will stand tall and proud over the ruins of London, a herald to our glorious new age.*

And a symbol of the fall of man.

The sun will not rise for them.

The Age of Smoke is over.

The old faery's face split into that wide, wide grin. Slowly, she rolled the note back into the capsule. Then she took a gun from under her apron. It was new, Goblin Market—bought, one of a pair. The other was in the wagon, hidden quickly behind the stove. She raised the gun, pointing it at the place where the two figures had disappeared into the woods.

Boom, she mouthed, and giggled a little.

CHAPTER XVII
The Cloud That Hides the Moon

"MI Sathir, *they have her!*" A small bearded man stood in front of Mr. Lickerish's desk. The man's nose was bandaged and his face was paper white, but he looked otherwise quite calm, completely at odds with the ragged, desperate voice that had spoken. "They have my Melusine!"

Mr. Lickerish did not answer at once. He had a game of chess laid out in front of him and was carefully touching black paint onto the ivory pieces with a little brush.

"Who?" he asked at length, barely glancing at the faery's new guise.

"The police. They caught us. We—"

"They caught her. You, apparently, have escaped. That is good. Is the other half-blood dead? Our little visitor?"

The faery inside Dr. Harrow's skull hesitated. For a full minute the only sound in the room was the ever-present thrumming noise and the faint *scritch-scritch* of Mr. Lickerish's brush bristles against the chess piece.

"No," he said at last. "No, Child Number Ten is still alive. And so is Arthur Jelliby."

Mr. Lickerish dropped the chess piece. It fell to the desktop with a sharp *clack* and rolled away, leaving a pattern of black paint across the wine-colored leather.

"What?" The word was uttered with startling force, a savage, guttural sound like the snarl of a wolf. Mr. Lickerish's face cracked into a mask of wrinkles and white lines and he stared at the bearded man, his eyes glittering, furious. "Turn around and look at me, you coward. What happened?"

The doctor turned slowly, revealing the dark

and shriveled face on the back of his bald head. "He escaped. I don't know how. I don't know how it could have happened, but it's not my fault. He survived the magic and escaped, and now Melusine—"

"Arthur Jelliby cannot *be* alive," Mr. Lickerish said, rising from his chair. His long white fingers were shaking, rattling like bones against the wood of the armrests. "He will compromise us! He knows too much. Too much. He cannot be alive," he said, as if trying to convince himself.

"It's not my fault!"

The faery politician spun on the bearded man. "Oh, Jack Box, believe me, it *is* your fault. You were to kill him. I told you to *kill him*!"

"I thought I had. I couldn't have known he would survive. *Sathir,* I did everything you asked of me. I brought you the new child, did I not? I cast the spell on the house on Belgrave Square, and went back for Child Number Ten. You must help me! Melusine *must* get out!"

"Melusine." Mr. Lickerish's voice was dark with contempt. "I don't care a bat's eye what happens to

Melusine. Whether she lives or dies will be entirely up to you. She will stay in prison. She will not go anywhere until you have done what I ordered you to do. And if it takes you a thousand years, she will rot there."

Jack Box took a trembling breath, and something very like tears sparkled in the corners of his eyes. "No," he said. "No, you can't leave her there. She won't survive without me. She's dying! Send a letter. Wire them. They will let her out the instant you say so!"

"But I won't say so."

Jack Box stared at Mr. Lickerish. Mr. Lickerish stared back coldly. Then he cocked an eyebrow and picked up the fallen chess piece with pale fingers.

"Child Number Ten. That is what you called our little visitor, was it not? You will find him. You will find them both, Arthur Jelliby and the half-blood. And since it appears you are an utterly useless and woebegone faery if ever I saw one, you will bring them to me alive. I will deal with them myself."

~ ⌄ ~

Much to Mr. Jelliby's bewilderment, London looked the same on the eve of its destruction as it always had. He had expected to see some change on its last day as the greatest city on earth. People running in the streets, perhaps, dragging their trunks and silver plate. Flames pouring out of windows. Panic in the air so thick you could taste it. But as Bartholomew and Mr. Jelliby rode along the Strand in a carriage, the only thing in the air was the oily black smoke pouring out of the eye socket of a badly rusted cross-sweeper, and as for running people, there weren't many of those, either. The sea of top hats bobbed along Fleet Street as unbroken as ever. Trams and omnibuses steamed just as grubbily toward the factories and quays. Coach-and-fours rumbled just as solemnly, letting off their well-dressed passengers just as steadily into the elegant cafés and shops. None of them knew how close it all was to ending, how soon the houses would be ruins, the streets empty, and the coaches on their sides, wheels turning in the wind.

Mr. Jelliby let the blind fall back over the window and slumped against the glossy leather headboard.

He and Bartholomew had arrived in Leeds early that morning, wet and cold and very miserable. They had caught the seven o'clock train to London, and pulled into the capital just as their socks were beginning to dry. A carriage had been secured on the bustling curb at Paddington Station. Mr. Jelliby had discovered his pistols were gone, but he had greater worries just then. He ordered the driver to take them to Belgrave Square at once.

He hadn't told Bartholomew where they were going, and he hadn't wanted to. He was relieved when the first slow breaths of sleep sounded from the corner of the carriage.

At the very edge of the square Mr. Jelliby signaled a stop. He peeked out again. There was his house—tall, grand, and white, only thirty feet away. The heavy winter drapes had been drawn across the windows. The first-floor shutters were closed. And parked at the gate for all the world to see was a shiny black steam carriage, its door emblazoned with the silver markings of the London police.

One of the curtains stirred in an upstairs window.

A face appeared at it—Ophelia's, looking out. Her skin was very pale. Her hand was at her throat. The last time Mr. Jelliby had seen her doing this was when the letter had come that told her her father was dead.

Mr. Jelliby swore and buried his head in his hands. She hadn't gone. She must be so angry at him, sick with worry and confused. Everyone in Belgrave Square would be making up their own reasons why the police were at the Jellibys' doorstep, and none of them would be right.

What do you suppose Mr. Jelliby has done this time, dear Jemima? I think he's probably murdered someone. With a knife.

Well, they could think of him what they wanted, but not Ophelia. He wanted to leap out of the carriage, run to the house and tell her that it was all lies, that she must flee the city, and that whatever the police had told her was not the case. The front door was only a short dash away. But they would catch him if he did. The house, or the police. And who was to say Ophelia would even believe him now, raving about murderous Lord Chancellors and magical portals and the doom of London? The officers would drag him away, perhaps to an asylum. Ophelia would watch him go with sad and serious eyes. No, Mr. Jelliby could not go home. Not until he found a way to stop Mr. Lickerish.

With a long sigh, Mr. Jelliby extended his hand out the coach window and waved the driver on. The carriage pulled away toward Bishopsgate and the river. They would go to the last of the coordinates now. Tomorrow no one would even care about gossip and scandal. Either he would expose Mr. Lickerish for what he truly was and become the hero of the age, or the faery door would open. And if the faery door opened, that meant Mr. Jelliby was dead. That meant Ophelia was dead, and Bartholomew was dead, and his little changeling sister as well. That meant most of London was dead.

Mr. Jelliby pushed those thoughts away and set to studying his map.

In the corner of the carriage, Bartholomew began to stir. His limbs felt heavy, solid like the boughs of a tree. He sat up and stole a look out the window.

London. His mother had told him about this city. That huge, faraway place where laws were made, and money was made, and where the most dazzling shows were, and the gaudiest music halls. It was the place where the roads were so wide and yet the people had to fly in balloons to get any air.

It was a very different sort of city than Bath, that much was clear, but Bartholomew didn't think it looked too jolly. Mother probably only liked it because there weren't so many faeries here. A few were about—the ones in the streetlamps, a goblin herding a flock of goats, and a handful of spriggan house-maids hurrying across the pavement with tired eyes and cloth-covered baskets. Bartholomew thought he saw one or two magical walking sticks of the sort that sing in sweet voices. But that was all. There were no dancing roots, or faces in the doors, and no trees. Not even any vines to climb up the sooty stone walls. The city seemed to be made entirely of smoke and clockwork.

"Will we be there soon?" he asked, turning to Mr. Jelliby. The map was spread out in front of the gentleman, taking up half the carriage. He was frowning at it, his brows pinching over his nose.

"Mr. Jelliby?" Bartholomew's voice was quiet, insistent. How much time did they have? The Lord Chancellor had Hettie, those black-winged sylphs, and probably the greenwitch's potion. They couldn't have much time at all.

Mr. Jelliby glanced up. "Oh. Good morning. I took a slight detour, but have no fear. We're on our way. All dead in their beds, the greenwitch said. Mr. Lickerish is going to open the door in the night and it's not gone four o'clock."

A detour? The door might only open in the night, but that doesn't mean Hettie is safe.

"Well, how long till we get there?"

"An hour. Perhaps two, depending on the traffic. And depending on whether I can understand this. So far I've been not at all successful." His frown deepened as he peered at the map. "Longitude and latitude would place our destination in Wapping, in the Docklands, but the altitude! Three hundred feet in the air! It makes no sense."

"Perhaps it's a tower," Bartholomew said, stretching his sore legs out slowly in front of him. "They build very tall towers nowadays."

He was beginning to feel dreadful. His joints ached, and he felt tired and very grubby. He wanted to be home again. Not the empty, sleeping place he had left, but the home from before all that. Mother would let him wash in the old laundry water while it was still warm. It always smelled of lavender, and since Hettie got it first, it would have pieces of bark and twigs floating in it. He used to set up such a fuss about that. It had made Hettie cry once, and she had hid her branchy hair under a sheet for a week. He had felt awful for that afterward, but he felt even worse now. Once he got back to Bath, back with Hettie and Mother, he would never make Hettie cry. He would never let anything bad happen to her again.

"But not three hundred feet tall," Mr. Jelliby said matter-of-factly. "Mr. Zerubbabel mentioned it, I believe. Something about the address being up in the air, and a faery named Boniface and . . . Oh, I can't remember!" He made an angry noise with his tongue and began folding up the map. "There's nothing to do but go to Wapping and see what's there."

Bartholomew looked over at him. "Hettie'll be there."

Mr. Jelliby paused crumpling with the map and looked back at him. He smiled. "Yes," he said. "Hettie'll be there." And that was all.

Bartholomew knew right away when they had entered the Docklands. The smell of fish and muddy water seeped into the carriage. The streets became wider to accommodate the colossal iron steam-mobiles that hauled the freight, and there were no longer houses on either side—only warehouses and forests of masts, their tips just peaking over the rooftops.

"Wapping," Mr. Jelliby said, and no sooner had the words left his mouth than the carriage came to a halt in front of a great stone building. It looked to Bartholomew like the huge train stations he had seen, like Paddington and the station in Leeds, only more desolate, without the din and the engines. It had large sooty windows and a low tin roof adorned with points and spires. It had a single wooden door some thirty feet across at its front. A thick metal cable extended up from the roof into the sky. His gaze followed it, up, up, up . . .

Next to him, Mr. Jelliby gave a low whistle.

There it was. The final address. Hovering three hundred feet above the quay like a brooding storm cloud was an airship. Its envelope was vast, sleek, blacker than smoke and crows, blacker than everything else in the gloomy sky. A trio of propellers whirred slowly under its cabin.

"Three hundred feet," Mr. Jelliby said quietly. "That's where he'll be safe when the door opens."

They climbed out of the carriage and approached the warehouse slowly, still staring at the airship high above. The warehouse stood in a very quiet, shadowy part of the quays. Rubbish lay in heaps against the foundation. Newspapers and handbills skittered across the cobblestones. No dockworkers were about. No one but a grizzled old sailor sitting on a barrel some ways down the street. He had a pipe in his mouth. He was watching them.

Mr. Jelliby waved the carriage away and walked along the front of the warehouse. Bartholomew followed, glancing around warily. They tried to look in at one of the windows, but it was impossible to see anything. The glass was completely dark, as if someone had painted over the inside with black paint.

"We'll have to break in," Mr. Jelliby said matter-of-factly. "This is where Mr. Lickerish will have his portal open. It has to be. Perhaps it's that door right there. The door to the warehouse."

Stationing Bartholomew at the corner of the building to keep watch, Mr. Jelliby slipped down the alley that ran along the warehouse's north wall. A hook lay on the ground some ways down it, half hidden under a heap of slimy, staring fish. He snatched it up and tapped it against a pane in one of the warehouse's windows. He tried to strike gently, without making much noise, but on the third tap the pane burst inward. Glass clattered in the space beyond. He threw a questioning glance back at Bartholomew. The boy nodded, signaling it was safe to proceed.

Mr. Jelliby peered in through the broken window. The interior was very dim. He could just make out wooden crates rising in cliffs and towers toward the roof. In the shaft of light from the hole in the window, he also saw that the floor was scarred black, as if from fire.

He hissed loudly for Bartholomew. "*Psst.* Bartholomew? Bartholomew! Come on!"

Bartholomew threw one last glance around the quay. Then he too came darting down the alley.

"We're going in," Mr. Jelliby said. He lifted the hook and began breaking more of the window, scraping the glass away with its tip. When there was a hole large enough to crawl through, he pushed Bartholomew up onto the ledge and then climbed up after him. They both dropped down into the warehouse.

Everything echoed inside. The space was vast and dark, and every shuffle, every breath flew up to the roof on metal wings. When they heard the sounds again, they were eerie and far away, as if other things were sliding through the trestles, whispering.

Bartholomew took a few steps forward. An odd smell tickled his nose. Hooks were faintly visible in the gloom above, pulleys and long chains. Somewhere at the far end of the warehouse he could hear water lapping against stone.

"It's a loading dock," Mr. Jelliby said. "The warehouse runs right into the Thames. The dead changelings . . . They must have been dumped into the river here."

Bartholomew shivered and stepped closer to Mr. Jelliby. *Hettie.* He looked around, straining to see something in the blackness. *Is she here somewhere? Is anything here?*

Suddenly he clutched Mr. Jelliby's arm, so tightly the man jumped.

"What in—!" he said, but Bartholomew didn't loosen his grip.

"Someone's here," he said in a small voice. He raised a finger, pointing toward a narrow gap that ran like a passageway into the wall of crates.

Someone *was* there. Far back in the shadows stood a plain wooden chair. A figure was reclining on it. It sat very still, slung across the chair. One hand hung down limply, fingertips brushing the ground.

Mr. Jelliby's heart skipped a beat. He tried to swallow, couldn't. He signaled for Bartholomew to stay where he was.

"Hello?" Mr. Jelliby called out, taking a step toward the figure. His voice tolled in the darkness, cold and hollow like a watery bell.

The figure in the chair remained motionless. He looked almost to be sleeping. His legs were stretched out in front of him. His head was thrown back over one shoulder.

Mr. Jelliby took several more steps and froze. It was the doctor from the prison in Bath. Dr. Harrow of Sidhe studies. His eyes were open, staring, but they were no longer blue. They were dull and sightless, gray as a sky of rain. Dr. Harrow was dead.

Mr. Jelliby backed away, horror and revulsion gripping his throat.

"Who is it?" Bartholomew whispered from behind him. "Mr. Jelliby, what's—"

Mr. Jelliby turned. He opened his mouth to say

something. Glass shattered on the floor. *The window we climbed through.* He spun toward it. The window was empty, but something had been there a moment ago. A few bits of glass tinkled to the floor.

"Bartholomew?" he hissed. "Bartholomew, what was that?"

"Something came in," Bartholomew whimpered. He was looking around frantically, trying to distinguish shapes in the shadows all around. *"Something's here."*

Just then, an orange glow lit the edge of a stack of crates. It grew steadily, spreading across the surface of the wood. Then a figure stepped into view. The glow came from a pipe. The pipe was pinched between the scabbed lips of the old sailor. He had followed them.

The sailor shuffled along slowly, head to the ground, the glow of his pipe flaring with every breath. Then he stopped.

Something shifted in the darkness behind him, and suddenly he went limp like a flag when the wind has died. A writhing mass of shadow mounted his shoulder, pin-prick eyes sparking out of the dark.

Child Number Ten, a voice said inside Bartholomew's head.

The pipe fell from the sailor's mouth, but not before Bartholomew caught a glimpse of the thing that had spoken. What he saw made his skin crawl. The parasite on the back of the lady's head, the shadow in the attic, the shape racing across the cobbles in Old Crow Alley—now it was a mass of rats. It had no feet other than the scuttling claws of rats, no hands but what it twisted together out of fat brown rats' tails. Its misshapen face seemed to be stretched across their matted hides like a mask.

Mr. Jelliby snatched Bartholomew's arm and pulled him down behind a huge iron winch, just as the creature's gaze swept toward them.

"Hide," Mr. Jelliby mouthed. Bartholomew nodded, and they both sidled back into the ravine of crates.

No use running, boy. I can feel you.

Bartholomew kept his eyes on the ground and walked. Whoever it was propped up on the chair at the end of the passage, he didn't want to know any-more. He could smell the death in the air and it ter-rified him.

Naughty boy with the iron coal scuttle. Should be out cold like the rest. Is Arthur Jelliby with you? It would save me much trouble if he were.

Bartholomew's arms began to throb. He looked down and saw red light bleeding through the thin fabric of his sleeves. The lines were glowing again.

Ahead of him, a crate stuck out further than the rest. He dashed around it and slid down, eyes shut. Mr. Jelliby tried to drag him back up, but Bartholomew shook his head.

"You have to go," he whispered. "It'll find me no matter where I hide. It's got me marked. Get my sister, Mr. Jelliby. Get her, and I'll try to find you later."

Do I hear whispers? Little lying whispers sneaking in the dark? Didn't your mummy ever tell you it's not nice to whisper behind other people's backs?

Mr. Jelliby looked at Bartholomew gravely. He nodded once. Then he patted Bartholomew on the shoulder, and with a final halfhearted smile, crawled toward the slouched shape of Dr. Harrow.

Oh, but of course, the voice rasped. *Your mummy is sleeping, isn't she. Don't worry, she will wake up in a few days' time, absolutely starving and practically dying of thirst. And she'll think she slept a thousand years, so changed will the world be. Her darling children. Children Ten and Eleven. How she'll miss them. Because they will be changed, too. Oh, yes. Quite changed.*

Bartholomew closed his eyes even tighter and pressed his cheek against the rough wood of the crate. *Mother won't miss us,* he thought. *She won't have to.* Claws rattled on stone somewhere close. *We'll go home, Hettie and me. We'll go home, we'll go home, we'll go home. . . .*

"No," the voice spat. It was no longer in his head. It was on the other side of the crate, sharp as nails. A hand, fingers of knotted rat tails, curled around the edge. Then a face appeared, teeth bared. "No, Bartholomew Kettle, you will not."

A little hunchbacked gnome stepped into Mr. Lickerish's study and bowed, sweeping so low his bulb-brown nose was only inches from the rich carpet.

"*Mi Sathir* will permit me to speak, yes? *Mi Sathir* will listen? A great black cat has been found in the warehouse below. It is a very strange cat with too many teeth. It has a bottle round its neck. We suppose it is from the greenwitch, yes?"

"Ah," said Mr. Lickerish, allowing a smile to creep across his features. "My lunatic little witch has been busy then. I was beginning to worry we would have to wait yet another day. Bring it to me. The bottle, I mean. Shoo the creature away."

Almost half an hour was counted by the brass hands of the clock before the gnome reappeared. His face and hands were traced with scratches. He was clutching a perfectly round glass bottle to his chest. The bottle was filled with a dark liquid. Eyes fastened to the ground, the gnome scuttled up to the desk, deposited the bottle, and without a word, backed out of the room.

Mr. Lickerish waited until the lock clicked. Then he picked up his handkerchief and began to polish the bottle with it, smoothing the thick glass until it shone. The liquid inside was very beautiful. It was not black or blue or purple but something in between. He held it up against the lamp to admire the colors. He peered closer. Something was floating inside the bottle, something barely visible at the center of the liquid.

His eyes went wide. It was a feather. A perfect metal feather, its quill still hung with the broken cogs of a clockwork sparrow.

Bartholomew and the rat faery were traveling up into the sky in a steam-engine elevator. It ran up the cable that anchored the airship to the warehouse, pistons banging. The elevator had no walls—only railings and a metal grille floor—and the higher it went the colder the air became. The wind flew through Bartholomew's hair, straight through his cloak and shirt, icy-cold against his skin. The rat faery's hand was coiled around his wrist. It was just as cold as the wind.

"You might have lived, you know," the faery said, drawing the tails so tight they pinched. "You escaped me in Old Crow Alley. You escaped me in Bath, and in the police station. And then you came all the way to London, all this way after your sister. Just to die."

I'm not going to die, Bartholomew thought. *And neither is Hettie.* But he didn't say anything. He shut out the rat faery's voice and pressed himself back from the railing. The elevator was so high up. He could see all of London laid out below him, a black smoldering carpet of roofs and chimneys, sprawling away for miles. In the distance, the spires of Westminster. A little closer, the great white dome of St. Paul's like the thumb of God.

Bartholomew looked up to where the airship was slowly looming. It was so vast, its black canvas swallowing the sky. A huge cabin hung below, grand as any house, two floors high with rows of mullioned windows reflecting the somber clouds. Written in curling silver letters on the prow of the cabin, beneath an ornate explosion of sculpted black wings, were the words *The Cloud That Hides the Moon.*

Bartholomew clenched his teeth to keep them from chattering. *What a silly name for an airship.* He closed his eyes. Mr. Lickerish had better be keeping Hettie up there.

By the time the elevator pulled into the belly of the airship, he could barely feel his fingers. The luxury of the place wrapped around him like a fur coat. The air turned warm. The wind was gone. Paneling and woodwork glimmered all around, gas lamps lending them a coppery sheen. Indian carpets covered the floor. On the ceiling, a great mural had been painted of a black bird—a raven or a crow, Bartholomew didn't know which. It held a bottle in its beak, and a child in its talons, and there was a little wooden door in its feathered breast. Bartholomew stared at it.

"Stop your gawping," the rat faery snapped, jabbing him up a sweeping staircase. "Don't act like you've never seen this place before."

The staircase brought them into a narrow corridor, brightly lit. The rat faery pushed Bartholomew down it. At the very last door they stopped. The faery knocked once and, without waiting to be invited, entered.

Bartholomew's eyes widened. It was *the* room. The beautiful room with the painted lampshades and the bookshelves, the ring of chalk on the floor, and the clockwork sparrows. The same one he had stumbled into from the whirling black wings. Only this time someone was sitting behind the desk. A wiry white faery dressed all in black, eating a brilliant red apple.

The faery looked up sharply as they entered. Juice ran down his chin, and flecks of the apple's red skin clung to his lips.

"I have him, Lickerish. Now what of Melusine?"

The Lord Chancellor said nothing. He touched a handkerchief to his lips and fixed his eyes on Bartholomew, watching him keenly.

The rat faery pushed Bartholomew toward the desk, dozens of tiny mouths nipping at his shoulders, the backs of his legs, compelling him on. Still the Lord Chancellor said nothing. He folded the hand-kerchief. He set it aside. He picked up a tiny metal feather and began twirling it slowly between thumb and forefinger.

When Bartholomew was only inches away, Mr. Lickerish stopped. "Ah," he said. "Here you are again."

Bartholomew gritted his teeth. "I want my sister,"

he said. "Give her back. Why can't you open your stupid door and leave Hettie be?"

The feather snapped in two. "Leave Hettie be?" The faery politician breathed. "Oh, I'm afraid I could never do that. Hettie is the most important part. Hettie *is* the door."

CHAPTER XVIII
The Peculiar

MR. Jelliby was pretending to be a corpse. He sat on the chair, drowned in shadows, not daring to move, not daring to breathe, waiting for Bartholomew and the rat faery to leave.

A minute later and he knew it had fallen for his trick. He lifted one eyelid. The faery's voice echoed in the vastness of the warehouse, then was lost in an explosion of mechanical clanks and hisses. Mr. Jelliby opened both eyes wide and stood up. Edging around one of Dr. Harrow's shoes, the scuffed and muddied tip of which just stuck out from a crack between two crates, Mr. Jelliby stole out of his hiding place.

He had not gone ten paces when a booming noise sounded above him. Dim light flooded the warehouse, as a great portion of the roof slid open, baring the sky and the airship hanging in it. Night was approaching. A gear-work elevator was rising, swinging gently on the anchor cable. The elevator was not closed in, and Mr. Jelliby could still see its two passengers clearly. The rat faery stood, arms and legs and appendages that had no name wrapped around the railing. Next to him, crouched on the floor, was Bartholomew.

Mr. Jelliby darted out from among the crates. He could see the inside of the warehouse clearly now, dank and dripping, the mountains of crates touched with moss, cranes and hooks hanging down over the dark water that lapped at the far end. At the center of the warehouse, a pair of leather shoes sat. They were small—children's shoes—and blackened. Scorch marks radiated from them like a charred sun. Their soles were nailed to the floor. Close by, the huge heap of the elevator's cable dwindled away, uncoiling into the sky. The elevator was already thirty feet above

Mr. Jelliby, and getting farther away by the second.

Rushing forward, he gripped the cable with both hands. *Just don't look down,* he thought. If the rat faery saw him, he didn't suppose it could do much. At least not until Mr. Jelliby arrived in the airship.

The cable pulled him into the air. The cold metal bit into his hands. He tried to support himself with his feet, but the tips of his shoes kept slipping and he had to claw with all his might to keep from falling.

Higher and higher he rose, through the open roof and into the sky. The warehouse shrank away beneath him. The wind growled, cold and fierce, swinging the cable. His fingers went from stiff to unfeeling. Above, the elevator whirred, and he caught snatches of the rat faery's voice jeering at Bartholomew.

He closed his eyes. He didn't dare look down at the city. But he didn't dare look up either. If he saw how much longer he had to endure before reaching the safety of the airship, he thought he might give up then and there. He pressed his forehead against the cable, feeling the sharp frost against his skin. *Safety.* There was nothing safe where he was going. Mr.

Lickerish was almost certainly up there, along with who-knew-how-many of his faery minions. Even if Mr. Jelliby survived the journey, he would only have gone from bad to worse.

The air became colder still as the dirigible cast its shadow across him. He opened his eyes. The airship was huge, filling everything, a giant black whale swimming in the sky. Mr. Jelliby had taken Ophelia on a pleasure flight in an air balloon once. He remembered how they had both stared at it in wonder as they approached it across Hampstead Heath. Its colors—the colors of a tropical bird—had been poison bright, brighter than the trees and the grass and the blue summer's day. So bright that it had been impossible to look at anything else. It could have fit inside this one's cabin.

Mr. Jelliby's arms felt ready to snap. He could feel every cord in them, every tendon and muscle straining against his bones. The cable pulled him higher, up and up. He could make out the vessel's name now, picked out in silver filigree on its prow.

The Cloud That Hides the Moon.

His shoulder gave a violent twitch. For a horrible moment he thought his arms would simply give way and he would fall down, down, down into Wapping. *Moon?* This was the moon? The moon in the sparrow's note. The moon Melusine had been speaking of. She hadn't been mad. It was an airship.

A hatch began to open in the underbelly of the cabin. Mr. Jelliby caught a glimpse of a hall, all aglow with warmth and yellow light. The elevator rose into it and came to a halt. The cable stopped too. Three hundred feet above London, Mr. Jelliby looked around him uncertainly.

God in heaven. His eyes swiveled up to the hall. The rat faery had dragged Bartholomew out of the elevator and disappeared. The hatch started to close.

"No," Mr. Jelliby gasped, and his lungs scraped as if coated with ice. "No! Stop!"

But even if someone in the airship had heard him, they were more likely to give the cable a sharp shake than to rescue him.

He began pulling himself upward, inch by inch. The hatch was closing slowly, but it seemed so far away, miles and miles up. He could barely feel the pain in his arms anymore. They just felt dead, solid. . . .

No. He set his jaw. He wasn't going to die up here. Not frozen to the cable like some foolish insect. Fifteen more feet, that was all. He could manage fifteen feet. For Ophelia. For Bartholomew and Hettie.

He struggled on, hands and legs and feet all trying to push him upward. The hatch continued to close. If it shut completely there would be nothing but a small hole where the elevator cable went into the hall. Not nearly large enough for a man. *Five more feet. Four more feet. Only a little longer.* . . . With a final surge of strength, Mr. Jelliby forced himself through the opening. The metal cut into his ankles, clamping. He jerked his feet up with a cry, scrambled away, lay shivering and gasping on the floor. The hatch clanged shut. Then all was still.

He would have liked to just lie there. The carpet was soft against his cheek. It smelled of lamp oil and tobacco, and the air was warm. He would have liked to just sleep there for hours and hours, and forget about everything else. But he willed himself to get up, and blowing on his chapped hands, hobbled toward the stairs.

Keeping himself pressed to the wall, he stumbled up them. A corridor was at the top. It was long and brightly lit, strangely familiar. He saw no one and heard nothing but the hum of the engines, and so he crept down it, pausing at each door to listen. He felt sure he had been here before. Sometime not so long ago. He came to the end of the corridor. The last door looked newer than the rest, smoother and more polished. And then he knew. Nonsuch House. The lady in plum flitting down the gaslit corridor. The faery butler's words when he had caught Mr. Jelliby. *"Come away from here this instant. Come back into the house."* The hallway was in the airship. That day of the ale meeting he had unwittingly wandered into Mr. Lickerish's secret place. Somehow they were connected, the old house on Blackfriar Bridge and the dirigible in the sky. Some faery magic had knitted them together.

Voices were coming from the other side of the door. The voice of Mr. Lickerish. The voice of

Bartholomew, quiet but firm. And then another door began to open some ways up the corridor.

Mr. Jelliby spun, fear welling in his chest. He was trapped. *No place to hide, no place to hide.* The hall was bare, just lamps and paneling. The doors were all locked. *All but one.* One had a key in its keyhole. He ran to it, twisted the key. A well-oiled bolt clicked open. He slipped in just as a small brown gnome emerged into the corridor.

The room in which he found himself was pitch black. Drapes had been pulled across the window and all he could see was a splinter of red light from the setting sun, bleeding in.

Someone else was in the room. He realized it suddenly, paralyzingly. He could hear breaths—small soft breaths close to the floor.

His hand reached for the pistols on his belt, and he cursed silently when he remembered they weren't there. He pressed his back to the door, fumbling for something to turn on the lights. His fingers found a porcelain dial and he turned it. Lamps flared to life along the walls.

He was in a small sitting room. It held a wardrobe, and a Turkish sofa, and a great many carpets and tasseled pillows strewn across the floor. And there was a girl. Curled up on a cushion of jade-green silk was a changeling. She had a sharp, pointed face. Branches grew from her head. She was asleep.

Mr. Jelliby's hand fell from the dial. "Hettie?" he whispered, taking a few steps toward her. "Is that your name, little girl? Are you Hettie?"

The child did not stir at his voice. But it was as if she could sense she was being watched, even in her dreams, and after a heartbeat or two she sat up with a start. She looked at Mr. Jelliby with wide black eyes.

"Don't worry," he said, going down on his haunches and smiling. "Bartholomew's here, too, and we've come to rescue you. You needn't be afraid."

Her face remained taut. For a moment she just stared at him. Then, in a small frantic whisper, she said, "Put out the lights. Quickly, sir, *put them out!*"

Mr. Jelliby looked at her, confused. Then he heard it, too. Footsteps snapping quickly along the corridor. Not the dancing footsteps of Mr. Lickerish, or the shuffling ones of the hunchbacked gnome. Something heavy and strong was out there, coming straight for the door to the sitting room.

Mr. Jelliby leaped up and wrenched the dial all the way around. The lamps fizzed out, and he flew across the room, plunging into the drapes that hid the window. Someone stopped outside the door. A hand was laid on the key. Then it was taken away again and there was a pause. The door banged open.

Mr. Jelliby could just see a figure come into the room before the door closed again. Whoever it was did not turn on the lights. But the figure had a lamp. A small green orb floated in the darkness. It made a ticking noise, *snick-snick-snick*, like a clock. It expanded slightly. Suddenly the lamps blazed again. There stood the faery butler, his mechanical eye fixed on the far side of the room, a slight frown creasing his brow.

"Little girl?" he asked, in his oozing, whining voice. "Little girl, tell me something. Can you walk through walls?"

Hettie didn't look at him. "No," she said, and burrowed into her pillow.

"Oh." The faery butler's frown darkened. "Then why was the door unlocked?"

Mr. Lickerish extended one long finger and touched it to Bartholomew's chin. Then he crooked his finger sharply, jerking Bartholomew's face up with it. Bartholomew gasped and bit his tongue to keep from crying out.

"Changelings are of both worlds, you see," Mr. Lickerish said. "A child of man with blood of the fay. A bridge. A door. Don't suppose I will explain my plans to you, though, because I shan't. You're far too stupid to understand them."

"Just tell me why it has to be Hettie," Bartholomew said, twisting against the rat faery's grasp. He knew this was the end. He would be lucky to leave the room alive. There was no point being timid anymore. "Why wasn't it one of the others? Why wasn't it the boy from across the way?"

"The boy from across the way? If you mean Child Number Nine then it was because he was a flawed, degenerate creature just like the eight before him.

Descendants of low faeries, the lot of them. Sons and daughters of goblins and gnomes and spriggans. The door did open for them. It did work. But it was such a small, weak door. And it opened inside them."

The fire crackled in the hearth. Mr. Lickerish laughed softly and released Bartholomew's chin, settling back into his chair. "Perhaps you heard that the changelings were hollow? Surely you did. The papers made such a fuss over it. What did they have to be shocked about, I wonder. Some faery, going about his business in the Old Country unsuspecting as you like, found himself suddenly confronted with a heap of steaming changeling innards. They were not enough, those other nine. They were too common. Too faerylike, or too human. But Child Number Eleven. Hettie. She is the daughter of a Sidhe. She is perfect."

Bartholomew swallowed. "I'm her brother. He's my father, too. I'll be the door."

"You?" The faery politician sounded as if he were about to laugh. But then he paused, and gazed at Bartholomew. Bartholomew thought he saw surprise in those black eyes. "You *want* to be the door?" the faery asked. "You want to die?"

"No," Bartholomew said quietly. "But I want Hettie to live. I want her to go home. Please, sir, I'll be the door, just let Hettie go."

Mr. Lickerish looked at him a long while. A smirk played at the corners of his mouth. Finally he said, "Oh. What a foolish thing to want." And then, turning to the rat faery, "Take him back down to the warehouse and dispose of him. I thought he might be dangerous. He is not dangerous. He is not even strong. He is simply peculiar."

The rat faery peered at Mr. Lickerish, rats slithering and squeaking. "Melusine," he said quietly. "What of Melusine?"

"The warehouse, Jack Box. Now."

The rat faery pushed Bartholomew toward the door.

"Where is Hettie?" Bartholomew shouted, struggling against the rat faery's grip. "Where's my sister?"

But Mr. Lickerish only took a great malicious bite out of his apple and gave no reply.

Mr. Jelliby remained perfectly still behind the drapes. The swaths of black velvet wrapped around him, stifling him, smothering him with their odor of old wax and withered petals. Sweat broke across his forehead and the drapes stuck to his face, hot and itching. He pressed himself farther back into the window well, all the way until he felt the cold panes against his cheek. *Drat.* The door had been locked from the outside. It was dead proof someone else was in the room.

On the other side of the drapes, the faery butler's green eye began to flick back and forth along the walls, clicking and buzzing as it focused on everything. The wrinkle in the carpet, the indents in the pillows, the fingerprints on the porcelain dial . . .

"Troutbelly? Are you here? Little girl, did that degenerate gnome come in?"

Hettie gave no answer, and the faery butler didn't wait for one. He strode across the room, looking into the wardrobe, opening drawers, kicking at the plump silk pillows.

"Jack Box? *Selenyo pekkal!* This is no time for games!"

The faery butler was directly in front of the drapes. Mr. Jelliby could hear his wheezing breaths, feel his presence like a weight on the other side of the velvet. The faery butler's green eye narrowed. He reached forward, ready to throw open the drapes. Mr. Jelliby had his hands in fists. One second more and he would leap out, swinging like a maniac. But then a speaking machine rang from the wall, shrilling and rattling like an angry bird.

The faery turned abruptly and picked up the mouthpiece.

"Mi Sathir?"

The rat faery was very quiet as it herded Bartholomew down the corridor. No taunting, no threats. Bartholomew had expected it to begin the moment they were out of earshot of the study, but Jack Box's mouth remained clamped shut.

They walked down the curving staircase, toward the hall of the airship. The rat faery moved behind

Bartholomew, claws scuttling, pinning his arm to his back.

"Mr. Lickerish isn't going to help you, you know." Bartholomew's voice was sharp. "I don't know why you think he will. I don't know what's wrong with the lady in plum, but Mr. Lickerish doesn't care. He just keeps you to do things for him."

"Shut up," the rat faery spat, and yellow teeth pinched into Bartholomew's back, his wrists, and shoulders. "Shut up, boy, you don't know—"

Bartholomew wanted to cry with the pain, but he didn't. "He's not going to help you, can't you see? You're going to die when that door opens. You're going to die just like everyone else. Mr. Lickerish doesn't care about you. He doesn't care about anyone but himself."

All at once the rat faery threw Bartholomew against the banister and collapsed, rolling and tumbling down the steps. Bartholomew watched it come to rest at the foot of the stairs, a wretched trembling mass.

He glanced back up the stairs. *Should I run?* Someone

might be watching. Some little pisky peeking down from the chandeliers, or a wooden face inside the wainscoting. *And where would I run to?*

Bartholomew approached the rat faery slowly.

"What is wrong with Melusine?" he asked. He tried to make his voice gentle. "If we stop Mr. Lickerish you can help her. That's the *only* way you can help her."

The rat faery looked up at Bartholomew. Its face twisted in surprise, then suspicion, then confusion. Bartholomew thought it would say something, but its mouth just opened and closed over its uneven teeth.

"Who is she?" Bartholomew asked, stooping down next to him. "Who is Melusine?"

There was an instant when some of the rat faery's hardness came back into its face. Bartholomew flinched, sure it was going to get up again and drag him on. But the hardness was gone again as quickly as it had come, replaced by something Bartholomew had never seen in a face so inhuman. A wistful look, sad and faraway.

"I met her in Dublin," it said, and its voice was

a rasp in its throat. "She was shopping for ribbons on Nassau Street, and she was so fair. So fair. And I so ugly, watching from the shadows. I cast a spell on myself, a powerful glamour that in a wink made me the most handsome creature in all the world. I strolled up beside her and told her how pretty the purple ribbons would look with her hair. We began to talk. She introduced me to her parents and I was invited to dine with them. . . .

"We were going to be married in May. But the stupid maid . . . Silly superstitious thing with an iron ring on her finger night and day. Or perhaps not so silly. She saw through my magic from the start. She saw me for what I was, a horrid knot of rats slinking at her mistress's side. For a while she thought she was mad. Then she confided in the footman. The footman told the cook, the cook told the housekeeper, and eventually the tale reached the ears of Melusine's father. He was always such a kind man, even to me, and he loved his daughter very much. The rumor disturbed him. A faery hunter was sent for from Arklow, to divine whether there was magical deception at work in the house, and Melusine's father called her to him, told her of his fear. But I had spoken to her first. I turned her mind against him. She called him a liar and a heartless monster, and we fled together into a gathering storm, taking the ponies across the hill."

There was a pause, and the airship went very still. The flames in the gas lamps flared and dimmed silently. Only the hum of the engines made any sound at all.

Bartholomew's mind was racing. *I don't have time for this. I need to find Mr. Jelliby, find Hettie before she is turned into some horrible door.* He wondered how strong the rat faery still was, what it would do if he tried to run. His fingers wrapped around a spindle in the banister. He could wrench it out, he thought, and beat the rats with it.

But then the faery was looking at him again, and its eyes were wet and deep and unbearably sad.

"We went to London," it said, not really to Bartholomew. Not really to anyone. "We sold her jewels for wine, and danced until our feet were sore.

I thought everything was going grandly, but not Melusine. Not my fair, fair Melusine. She missed her parents. She missed Ireland, and the high green hills. She is such a young thing, after all." Bartholomew let his hand slip from the spindle. "And I knew then that she would never really be mine while the deception lasted. She didn't love me. The thing she loved was an illusion and a lie, and so one day I shed my glamour. I showed her what I was."

The rat faery looked away. When it spoke again its voice was choked. "And she hated me. She hated me for my ugliness. She ran. Ran to the door, crying and screaming, but I couldn't let her go. I *couldn't*. I knew it would kill her. I knew the rats would eat into her and she would never be the same again, but how else was I to keep her with me? *I couldn't let her leave me!*" The rat faery jerked on the floor, as if all its many legs were hurtling in different directions. Then it curled around itself like a snail, hiding its head. "I met Mr. Lickerish then," it whispered. "In the street in the night. He told me of his plan, how he needed someone to fetch him changelings. If the faery door were opened, he said, all would be well again. Magic would be strong in England and I would be able to keep Melusine from dying. I would be able to cast a glamour so strong and deep that not even the maid's iron ring could help her see through it. And all this . . ." He raised a rat-tail hand, and waved it blindly. "All this would seem like an evil dream. And so I did it all. Everything he asked of me."

Bartholomew said nothing. He didn't like what he had heard. He wanted to find Hettie and he wanted to hate Jack Box. He wanted to think him a monster for all the pain he had caused. But a nasty voice had crept into Bartholomew's head and was saying, *A monster? But he's just like you. Just as ugly, just as selfish. You're no different from him. Wouldn't you kill a* million *people to save Hettie?*

Bartholomew closed his eyes. "But Melusine," he said, trying to sound calm. "She'll live now that you've left her. Bath is so far away. She'll be safe now."

"Safe." The faery's voice was a bare, rattling whisper. "Safe from me. Safe forever."

Bartholomew stared at him.

"No one helped her. Not the police, or Mr. Lickerish, even though I begged him and did everything he asked of me. One day, she lasted, perhaps two. And then she died, all alone on that chair, in that white room under the earth."

Mr. Lickerish spoke quickly into the brass speaking apparatus, excitement glimmering at the edge of his voice. "The greenwitch's elixir has arrived at last. Take Child Number Eleven down to the warehouse and give it to her. Make certain she drinks every drop. And then hurry. The sylphs will come quickly. You will have only minutes before the door begins to destroy the city. Hurry back to the *Moon*, and do not delay. I will need you in the world of tomorrow." He set down the mouthpiece, nibbling thoughtfully at the end of his silk watch ribbon.

"*Sathir?*" the faery butler's voice crackled through the device. "*Sathir*, are you there? Is there anything more you wish to say?"

Mr. Lickerish picked up the mouthpiece again. "Yes. Yes, I believe there is. Jack Box has become . . .

unstable. He is on his way down to the warehouse as we speak. Make sure he stays there." And without waiting for a reply he slammed the mouthpiece into its cradle.

The faery butler replaced the speaking apparatus slowly.

"Very well," he said to no one at all, and shooting one last suspicious look about the room, he took Hettie by the hand and pulled her toward the door.

"Come along, half-blood. Are you thirsty? I imagine you must be parched."

"I'm sorry she's dead," Bartholomew said softly. In an odd way he really was sorry. She had always seemed a phantom and a witch, a symbol of all the evil that had intruded into his life. She had started it, walking into the alley and whisking away the Buddelbinster boy. But it hadn't really been her at all. When he had edged up to her under the eaves of the house on Old Crow Alley, that was when he had met the true Melusine. He had heard her soft voice and silly notions of valets and peaches and cream. He would never forget the shining pain in her eyes when she had seen the rat faery, racing across the cobbles toward her. *Tell Daddy I'm sorry,* she had said. *Tell Daddy I'm sorry.*

If Bartholomew lived long enough, he would tell her father. He would find him and tell him how much Melusine had loved him in her last days, how much she had wanted to be home again.

Bartholomew knelt down next to Jack Box. He almost reached out and touched him. He couldn't bring himself to do it. He knotted his fist, and said, "You don't have to listen to Mr. Lickerish anymore. You don't have to hurt people. Do you know where my sister is? Could you take me to her? Please, sir. Please help me save her?"

For a moment Jack Box said nothing. His face was lost in the seething mass of hides and tails. The rats seemed to sense something was wrong. They were crawling over each other, eyes rolling back in their heads, yellow teeth chattering. For a moment Jack Box said nothing. Then, his voice muffled, "Why should I help you? Why should I help anyone now?"

Bartholomew dug his nails into his palms. "Because . . ." he stammered, but he didn't have an answer. Not then. All he could think of was Hettie, and her hand in his, and her stupid, unsnippable branches. "Just please help me? Please, please won't you help?"

A clank sounded in the hall and the hatch in the floor began to open, tearing a gaping hole in the warmth. Wind flew into the room, whistling around Bartholomew's ears. Then a door opened and closed in the corridor above. Footsteps beat the carpet.

Someone is coming. Bartholomew half rose, ready to run. *We have to leave. We have to leave* now.

But the rat faery only sat up a little and stared at Bartholomew, his black eyes pleading.

"You have to help me!" Bartholomew repeated desperately. "I don't know why, you just *have to*! My sister is going to die! Please won't you help?"

Jack Box looked away. The rats were stirring into a frenzy, but the faery's face had gone very still, almost calm.

"No," he said. The little word dropped like stone

from his mouth. And then, dragging himself to the edge of the hatch, he slipped over it into the night. Bartholomew did not watch him fall. He stopped his ears against the cries of the rats and turned his face to the wall.

Mr. Lickerish had finished his apple. He set the core down and began picking out the seeds, placing them in a neat row on top of his desk. When he had completed the task to his satisfaction, he rang a servant's bell and ordered a glass of milk from the hunch-backed gnome. The milk arrived in due time, but instead of drinking it, Mr. Lickerish swept the apple seeds into his palm and dropped them into the glass. Then he went to the window and looked out, black satin cuffs crossed behind his back.

A faint tinkling made him turn. The room was empty. A clockwork bird stared out at nothing with its beady eyes. In the cup, a film had formed on top of the milk the way it always does when milk is mildly fresh. As Mr. Lickerish watched, the film turned into a skin. The skin grew thicker. And all of a sudden the glass tipped over and a blue-white gobbet of milk plopped out onto the smooth top of the desk. It jiggled toward the edge. Mr. Lickerish caught it in his hand and held it up to his face. His mouth stretched across his sharp teeth in a gleaming smile. Faintly he could see the apple seeds in the center of the milk, little veins and lungs and a heart all sprouting out from them. Then two seeds popped forward as its eyes, and it tottered up on a pair of stemlike legs. It had a huge mouth that hung open, wide and bare and empty.

"Charming," Mr. Lickerish said, still smiling. "You will be my eyes for a little while, imp. Hurry down to the warehouse and keep watch. Whatever you see, I will see, and whatever I say, you are to say. Do you understand that?"

The gobbet of milk stared at Mr. Lickerish, its apple-seed eyes somewhat mournful. It nodded slowly. Then it hopped down from the faery's hand and wobbled off across the floorboards toward the door.

~ ⁓ ~

Mr. Jelliby found Bartholomew in the airship's hall, trying to hide himself under the carpets. The hatch was open. It was a clear, cold night, and the city spread away forever. The streets made a glowing spider's web, Mayfair and High Holborn bright with the fierce lights of flame faeries, while the poorer streets were only gaslit threads, dim and flickering, or not lit at all. The river cut it all in half, sluggish and black, broken only by the occasional lantern of a corpse boat.

"Bartholomew! What are you doing? Get away from the edge!" Mr. Jelliby hissed, tiptoeing across the hall. "The faery butler is with Mr. Lickerish as we speak. He has your sister, and he's getting the potion and he's going to take her down in the elevator."

Bartholomew sat bolt upright. "Hettie? You saw her?"

"Yes! With my own eyes! But we must hurry." He ran to the edge of the floor and reached out for the elevator, looking it over rapidly.

"There. See those metal bars underneath? We can squeeze down there, I think, and then leap out when the butler's alone in the warehouse. Quick now! In with you."

Without another word, Bartholomew scooted off the edge of the floor and onto the metal bars. The warmth of the hall was gone in an instant. Wind and frozen ash blew around him freely, but he barely noticed. *Mr. Jelliby has found her. She is here and she is alive.*

The space under the elevator was barely a foot high and utterly open. Only the widely set bars kept him from falling into the dark. *It's the luggage rack,* he thought. It was where the trunks and hatboxes would have been packed had the dirigible been used for anything ordinary.

Mr. Jelliby dragged at the cable, and the elevator sank a foot. The luggage rack dropped below the lip of the hatch, hidden. Then he, too, swung down.

Not a moment too soon. Mr. Jelliby barely had time to arrange his arms and legs before the first tread of feet sounded on the stairs.

"Come *on!*" the faery butler's whine drifted into the hall. "By stone, you are the most tiresome creature! The other nine weren't half as bad."

There was a scuffling sound as he pulled Hettie along and she hurried to match his pace.

Then the elevator swayed as they stepped aboard. Bartholomew could see a little through the metal grille of the floor. He could just make out the shadows of Hettie's bare feet, the great long soles of the faery butler's shoes. And there was something else, too. Something small and round that never stayed still, and made an odd sound like water in a jug.

Bartholomew held his breath. Hettie was so close. Inches above him. He wanted to climb up and grab her, and tell her that he had found her and they'd be going home soon. *Only a little longer....*

The elevator began to descend, creaking down through the night. The only light came from the faery butler's green eye. Mr. Jelliby prayed he wouldn't look down. He would see them instantly if he did, lying there under the floor. His mechanical eye would pierce metal and darkness and—

The faery lifted his nose and sniffed the air. Mr. Jelliby stiffened.

"I smell rain," the faery said, looking at Hettie curiously. "Rain and mud."

Hettie said nothing.

The faery butler tapped his fingers against the railing. "It has not rained in London for days."

For several heartbeats the only sound was the wind. Then, without warning, a jagged blade descended from the faery butler's sleeve, and he slashed it down through the air, driving it through the floor. Its tip came to a halt, ringing, inches from Bartholomew's eye. He screamed.

"Barthy?" Hettie cried, pressing her face to the grating.

Mr. Jelliby dragged himself off the bars and hung from them, legs flailing forty feet above the ground. "Get out! Get out, Bartholomew, he'll kill you!"

The blade came down again, over and over, slicing Bartholomew's arm, drawing blood. The elevator had reached the roof of the warehouse. The air turned warm as they sank into it.

"Now!" Mr. Jelliby shouted, from where he clung. "Let go! It's not far anymore!"

Bartholomew saw the blade hurtling down toward him, glimmering like a streak of rain. It would kill him this time. It would meet its mark, go clean through his heart. But just as its tip bit into his skin, he slipped between the bars and fell, down, down into the warehouse.

The impact smashed the breath from his lungs. His knees buckled under him and he rolled, over and over, until he came to rest against a wall of crates. He heard the elevator clang against the floor. Then the patter of Hettie's bare feet, the faery butler's heels ringing on stone. When he opened his eyes he half expected to see the creature standing over him, knife poised to snuff him out.

But the faery butler seemed to have lost all interest in him. Nor was he paying any attention to Mr. Jelliby, who had dragged himself into the sea of crates and sat crouched there, gasping. With quick, efficient movements, the faery forced Hettie's feet into the charred shoes and set to knotting the shoelaces, over and over, until there was not the slightest chance she could step out of them.

She tried to lift her feet, kick his hands away, but the shoes were hammered fast to the floor. His long fingers tugged at the knots, testing them. She scratched at his head, tried to pick at the laces herself, but the faery swatted her away.

Bartholomew began crawling toward her on hands and knees. Still the faery took no notice of him. The butler rose and took the greenwitch's elixir from his coat. He placed it to Hettie's lips, tipping up the bottle. She spluttered once, spat, but he clenched her little face in his hand and forced it skyward, and there was nothing she could do but cough the liquid down in great gulps.

When the bottle was empty the faery flung it aside. Without another word, he strode back toward the elevator.

Mr. Jelliby leaped out from among the crates, swinging a metal hook before him like a rapier. The faery didn't even flinch. He dodged it gracefully, sliding around it like a snake, and spinning, he struck Mr. Jelliby a vicious blow to the side of the head. Bartholomew watched Mr. Jelliby stagger and then scrabbled toward Hettie. *I'll get her to the window. We'll climb out while the faery butler's distracted and—*

He froze. The faery butler did, too. Mr. Jelliby dropped the hook.

A gentle breeze had sprung up out of nowhere, carrying on it the smell of snow. And something was happening to Hettie. A black line had begun to trace itself along her skin, starting at the top of her head and slithering down over her shoulders, down her arms and her legs.

"Barthy?" she said, her voice cracking with fear. The pale skin around her mouth was stained blackberry-dark. "Barthy, what's happening? What are you looking at?"

The instant the line reached the nailed-down shoes, they disintegrated, turning to delicate flakes that scudded over the floor. The breeze became a wind, stirring the branches of her hair. And suddenly there was no longer a wall behind her, or crates, or a warehouse, but a great, dark wood extending into the distance. Snow lay on the ground. The trees were black and leafless, older and taller than any English trees. Far back among them, Bartholomew could see a stone cottage. A light was burning in its window.

Hettie wrapped her arms around herself and looked at him, eyes wide.

"It's working," a voice lisped from the ceiling. Bartholomew glanced up, whirling, and saw a small white shape in the gloom, perched at the end of one of the dangling chains. It was staring at the woods, at Hettie. Its mouth was wide and empty, and somewhere inside its cold, wet voice was the echo of Mr. Lickerish's whispery one. "The door is opening."

Bartholomew spun back to Hettie. The door *was* opening. Slowly the black line expanded, stretching into a ring, like a black flaming hoop for a tiger to leap through. And as the door grew so did its frame, until it was no longer only a thread but a writhing chain of angry, flapping wings. They looked like the wings that flew around Jack Box and Melusine wherever they went, only stronger somehow, blacker. And whatever they touched, they destroyed. The stone slabs of the warehouse floor curled and snapped as they brushed them. The crates nearest them exploded in showers of wood. And still Hettie stood rooted to the spot, a small figure against the woods and snow of the Old Country.

"*Yes.*" Mr. Lickerish's voice came through the milk imp's mouth, soft and sibilant. "Child Number Eleven. You have opened."

The faery butler lurched toward the elevator, but Mr. Jelliby was upon him again, kicking and punching with all his might. Bartholomew started toward Hettie. He felt the wind, smelled the ice and rot of the ancient woods. The door was not very large. Mother always said the one in Bath had been the hugest thing the world had ever seen.

"Go to her, boy," the milk imp said from the ceiling. "Go and get her and bring her home." Its voice held a sly edge now, like silk wrapping a sharp knife. "Don't worry. The sylphs won't hurt you. Not one of their own." The imp leaned down off its hook. "Go on," it coaxed. "Go get her."

Bartholomew did not need to be told twice. He broke into a run, dodging Mr. Jelliby and the faery butler. Then Hettie was in front of him and he was pulling her to him.

Hettie flew out of the black wings of the doorway. Her feet touched the stone floor. Bartholomew had her hand, was already starting to dash for the window, out. Behind them the door gave a horrible jolt. With sickening speed the wings shrieked outward, devouring everything in their path. Bartholomew felt them scrape against his skin, rough feathers and bones. But the imp had not lied. Whatever faery creatures were hidden inside those wings, they did not hurt him now.

"Bartholomew!" Mr. Jelliby screamed, ducking as the faery butler's knife whizzed over his head. "Put her back! Put her back or you'll kill us all!"

In a panic, Bartholomew pushed at Hettie, but the damage was done. The door had almost reached the warehouse roof, a vast tornado of wings swallowing everything in sight. The wind buffeted his face, sharp with snow. The forest seemed to fill the whole space, growing dark out of the crates and the river. Feet pounded the stone floor close by—Mr. Jelliby's or the faery butler's—but he didn't see anyone.

Hettie was trying to reach him again, her hands

grasping for his shirt. On the other side, the forest was no longer empty. Something had emerged from the cottage in the distance. The light was still there, but it blinked on and off as a figure darted in front of it, now hiding behind trees, now rushing forward, coming closer. Behind it, other shapes were approaching through the woods, dark and quick, curious eyes glinting in the moonlight.

The faeries. They were coming.

"Don't you want your sister?" the imp mocked. "Oh, dear little Hettie, do you see? Your brother doesn't like you anymore. He doesn't want to save you."

Bartholomew looked at her desperately. He wanted nothing more than to save her. He had traveled hundreds of miles, braved the Bath police and the Goblin Market and the rat faery to find her. But Hettie was peering at him, eyes round and uncertain.

"You know, if you push her back—if you shove her into the Old Country and that dark winter's wood, with those wicked, wicked faeries approaching from all sides, the door will begin to shrink. Wouldn't that be grand? Wouldn't that be *smashing*? It would become unbalanced. It would implode. I'm not lying. Try it. Abandon your darling sister for a world you don't care a pennyworth for."

The imp's words sparked something in Bartholomew's memory. In a flash, he was back in the greenwitch's clearing, walking away from the painted wagon and the cheery light of its window. *I don't care about the world.* That's what he had said, growling under his breath as they trudged into the night. No one else did either. The faeries didn't care. The people didn't care. They had other things to worry about, like coins, and bread, and themselves. Bartholomew could let them all die. He could pull Hettie away, and the wings would sweep out across that cruel, hateful city. They would destroy everything, topple churches and houses and palaces of government. Mr. Jelliby would turn to dust. And Bartholomew and Hettie would walk away, hand in hand, across the ruins. It would be so easy.

You're no different, that nasty voice had said, and it was saying it again, louder and harsher than ever. *You're no different from the rat faery. No different from Mr. Lickerish, and the greenwitch, and all the other people you thought you hated.*

But Bartholomew *was* different. He knew he was. He was frail and ugly and not very tall, and he didn't care anymore. He didn't care if the faeries hated him, or the people feared him. He was stronger than them. Stronger than the rat faery had been, stronger than Mr. Lickerish ever was. He had gone places and done things, and he had done them not for himself but for Hettie and Mother and Mr. Jelliby, who had taken him with him when Bartholomew was standing alone in the alley. They were what made him belong. Not the faeries, and not the people. He didn't need to be like them.

Bringing his face up to Hettie's ear, he began to whisper, quickly and urgently, his hand tight around her fingers. "Don't listen to him," he said, through the wind and the wings. "He's all lies. Don't be afraid. You're going to have to go in there for a short while, but as soon as the door is as small as it gets, leap back to me. Leap with all your might, do you hear me? It'll work, Het, I know it will."

"Barthy?" Hettie's voice was shaking. And then the wind howled around them and he couldn't hear her anymore. But he knew what she was saying. *Barthy, don't make me go in there. Don't let the faeries get me.*

Bartholomew tried to smile at her. His face wouldn't move. Even the tears were frozen, aching behind his eyes. He hugged Hettie to him, hard and fierce as if he would never let her go.

"It'll work, Het. It'll work."

Very gently, he pushed her through.

Her bare feet sank into snow. Wind whipped through her branches, her clothes. For an instant the wings became still, as if soaring through open sky. Then they seemed to turn, shrieking inward.

"What?" the milk imp spat, clutching at its chain and staring. "What are you doing, you wretched child. Pull her out! Pull her out or you will never see her again!"

I will. But Bartholomew knew there was no point answering. He kept his eyes fixed on Hettie, waiting to shout, to tell her it was time, and she could jump.

The door was shrinking quickly. The smaller it

became the faster the wings spun, until suddenly a pillar of blackness burst upward, screeching along the elevator cable toward the airship. The imp gave a whine and was consumed. From somewhere high above came a deep, rolling boom.

The wings filled the door, blotting out everything. Bartholomew could see only snippets of the woods beyond, little glimpses of Hettie's frightened face, the cottage, the snowbound forest.

"Now!" Bartholomew shouted. "Now, Hettie, get out! *Jump!*"

She wasn't moving. Someone was standing behind her. A tall, thin, shadowy figure, a pale hand resting on her shoulder.

Bartholomew lunged forward. His arm went through. He felt Hettie, her dirty nightgown, her twig hair. He fumbled for her hand, trying to drag her to him, back to London and the warehouse. Home.

"Come on, Hettie, now! Jump!"

But the wings were everywhere, battering him, shutting him out. Hettie's hand was wrenched from his grasp. He was thrown back, flying through the air until he struck a wall of crates. He slid to the floor, head spinning. Something warm trickled across his brow. His tongue tasted blood.

Hettie, he thought blearily. *Hettie needs to jump.* Slowly, painfully, he forced himself up, forced himself to move. "Hettie," he called. "Hettie, you have to—"

Everything was still. The wind had stopped, the noise too. The wings were frozen in midair; splintering crates, hooks and chains all hung suspended. The door was a perfect ring at the center of the warehouse. And framed inside, standing small and lonely among the vaulting trees, was Hettie.

She looked at Bartholomew, her black eyes full of terror. Tears were streaming down from them, dripping over her sharp cheekbones. She raised her hand.

Then there was a sound like a violin string snapping. The spell was broken. Everything was in motion again. Rubble rained down from all sides—wood from the crates, stone from the walls, propellers and burning canvas from the airship. The door vanished.

Bartholomew gave a savage cry. He ran to the place where it had been, clawed at the air, clawed at the stones.

"Jump!" he cried. "Jump, Hettie, jump, jump!"

But it was too late for that.

Above him, there was a tremendous crash. Chunks of roof and burning beams collapsed around him, caging him in. Somewhere in the roiling smoke, an explosion. He fell to the floor, crying and screaming, and blackness enveloped him.

He didn't know how long he lay there. It might have been a year or a day. It would have been all the same to him if he were dead and this were the end of the world. Sounds echoed toward him from far away. Water, icy cold, stung his skin. The black and silver of fire fighters' uniforms glimmered dully through the fog of his vision. Then people were crowding around him, talking all at once.

"A Peculiar," they said. "Half dead. Should we leave him? Leave him here?" And somewhere Mr. Jelliby was being angry, shouting, "You'll get him to the carriages, is what you'll do! You'll rush him to

Harley Street, and if it takes you the rest of your lives, you'll save him! He saved you. He saved all of us."

Go away, Bartholomew thought. *Leave me alone.* He wanted to sleep. The darkness was there again, rolling beneath him and beckoning him. But before he let it take him, he opened his eyes and looked up. He could see the sky through the ruined roof. It was dawn. The sun was just rising over the city, piercing the heavy clouds.

"I'll come find you, Hettie," he whispered as strong hands lifted him onto a stretcher and carried him away. "Wherever you are, I'll bring you home."

THE
PECULIAR

An interview with Stefan Bachmann, a guide to faeries, an illustrated portrait of Melusine, and an excerpt from *The Whatnot*, the book that completes Hettie and Bartholomew's story

An interview with Stefan Bachmann

1. Tell us a bit about your childhood? Where did you grow up?

My childhood was long and uneventful. I was born in Colorado, moved to Switzerland when I was one, and have lived here ever since. I have four siblings—three older and one younger. I started going to the Zurich Conservatory when I was eleven. From then on I was homeschooled for my academic classes. So I feel qualified to wear that awesome T-shirt that says, "I be home-teached." My mom's an artist and my dad's an assassin. Oh wait, no, he's a real estate contractor. I was stung by a jellyfish once. Umm. That's pretty much it.

2. Are you peculiar?

Ha! I laughed really hard at this question. Everybody's peculiar. But yeah, I'm definitely strange-ish. It's what comes from going to an artsy school for too long, I suppose.

3. Are any of your characters' personality traits based on yourself or people you know?

What you guys really want to know is if I live locked up in two rooms and wave at random people through windows. *Rrright?* That would be interesting, but I'm afraid the book isn't very autobiographical. I think aspects of all the characters' personalities are the same as mine, but none of the characters is really me. Bartholomew wants to belong and be accepted by a wider circle than just his family, and I did too at his age. I think just about everybody goes through a stage where they're not quite an awkward teenager yet, but they're starting to be self-aware and are beginning to think they need to be certain things to "belong." I think that's where Bartholomew is in the book. Just much more exaggerated than in middle school.

Aunt Dorcas is very loosely based on my old piano teacher, but that's it. I don't know any faeries, unfortunately.

4. With which character do you most identify?

Ummm, probably Mr Jelliby. He thinks he's cool and important, but he's really just a dork. Ahem. Still, he does the right thing in the end.

5. Where did you write the novel? Did you write the novel in the U.S. or overseas?

Mostly in Switzerland, but I wrote two chapters in America as well. Back in the summer of 2010, I did a road trip with my brother from Oregon to Michigan and then *aaaall* the way back to Colorado (cuz we're such great planners and knew exactly what we were doing), and since the countryside was painfully dull I worked on *The Peculiar* and listened to the *Atonement* sound track on repeat.

The Peculiar

Changeling—The child of a faery and a human, a changeling is small, sharp-faced, and sickly, and is not expected to live past the age of twelve. If his faery blood is particularly strong, he has branches growing out of his head instead of hair. *Don't get yourself noticed and you won't get yourself hanged* is the changeling's most important rule, but he is often not very good at following it. Half-bloods are forever being hung by superstitious peasants or stolen by the faeries, who hate them for their ugliness. They spend most of their short lives locked up and hidden away, and that is how we meet one lonely changeling by the name of Bartholomew Kettle. Bartholomew has not ventured out of doors in years. Until one day . . . one day, he must.

Gnome—The gnome is a sharp-toothed faery with gray-green skin, like a rock in the rain. He is by nature a solitary faery, and distinctly unpleasant, with a foul temper and fouler tongue. He is not well suited to the sooty, stinking streets of London and will do his utmost to be disagreeable to you, no matter what you ask of him.

Sidhe—Sidhe are elegant, spindly, and pale as death. They are also sly and incredibly intelligent, and they hate the English with every bone in their bodies. Once, in the Old Country, these faeries were lords and ladies with great halls of their own. Now, locked in England, they have been stripped of their power and have gone into hiding. But they have never stopped hatching plans and scheming and, slowly, they are reemerging. John Wednesday Lickerish was recently voted into the House of Lords—whether it was by magical deception or because he is so wise, no one knows.

Goblin—Goblins are the bread and butter of English faeries. They are short, brown, and stocky, with rough skin like tree bark. They work hard and have adapted surprisingly well to the old faery slums and fuming factories. They can be kind and generous, more so than most other faery sorts, whose only thought is to play tricks and make mischief.

Lamp Faery—Little glowing faeries are put inside street-lamps to light the way of city dwellers by night. These faeries are often rude and spiteful, but cheaper than oil and lamp wicks.

Spryte—Slender and delicate, sprytes have long pale fingers and antlers like deer. Their quick wits are matched only by their quick hands, and they are infamous throughout England as pickpockets and spies. If you glimpse one during your daily business, you have likely been stolen from without even knowing it.

Fire Spirit—Powerful elemental faeries that have no form but are only invisible essences; they can dart from match to candlestick to fireplace without a sound. A fire spirit was allegedly responsible for the burning of the old Westminster Palace in 1834, though many suspect that story is simply anti-faery propaganda.

Troll—A rare thing indeed in England. No one knows how many trolls came from the Old Country when the door opened in Bath, but they did not adapt well. They are too huge, perpetually angry, and need much space and freedom to live. Eyewitness accounts say there are some far in the north, in the wilds of Scotland, but these accounts have not been substantiated. At one point, one of our heroes, Mr. Jelliby, meets a blue troll with storm-gray eyes that is working as a sort of cab service in the faery city of Bath. Mr. Jelliby rides the palanquin strapped to its back. But Mr. Jelliby is a generally oblivious sort, and he was certainly unaware of the great beast's rarity at the time.

The Lady comes to Old Crow Alley

(Illustration by Sarah Bachmann)

What happened to
Hettie and Bartholomew?
Read on for a glimpse into the world of

CHAPTER I
Snatchers

P IKEY *Thomas dreamed of plums and caramel apples the night the faery-with-the-peeling-face stole his left eye.*

It was a wonderful dream. He wasn't in the bitter chill of his hole under the chemist's shop anymore. The old peeling signboard with its painted hands and hawthorn leaves no longer creaked overhead, and the ice wasn't crusting his face. In his sleep Pikey was warm, curled up by an iron stove, and the plums were drifting out of the dark, and he was eating a caramel apple that never seemed to get any smaller.

He always dreamed of caramel apples when he could help it. And iron stoves, too, in the winter. And plums and pies and loud, happy voices calling his name.

THE WHATNOT

*Tap-tap. Tap-tap. Far, far away on the other side of his
eyelids, a figure entered the frozen alley.*

*Pikey bit down on his apple. He heard the footsteps, but he tried
not to worry. Whoever it was would be gone soon. Folk were always
stumbling into the chemist's alley from Bell Lane, from the gutters
and sluiceways and all the other fissures between the old houses of
Spitalfields. None of them ever stayed for long.*

Tap-tap. Tap-tap.

Pikey squirmed inside his blankets. Go away, *he thought.*
Don't wake me up. *But the footsteps kept coming, limping
slowly across the cobbles.*

*Tap-tap. Tap-tap. Pikey didn't feel warm anymore. The
plums still fell, but they stung now as they touched his skin, spitting,
icy cold. He tried to take another bite of his apple. It turned to wind
and cinders, and blew away.*

Tap-tap. Tap-tap.

*Snow was falling. Not plums. Snow. It gusted into his little hole,
and suddenly Pikey's nose was filled with the stench of old water
and deep and mossy wells. A racket kicked up, old Rinshi straining
against her chain, barking at something and then stopping, sharp-
like. There was a grating, a scrape of metal.*

Pikey saw the blood before he saw the figure, always the blood

trickling toward him between the stones. Then the alley was filled
with screams.

Pikey Thomas was running for his life.

It was a clear day, sharp and cold as a knife, but
he couldn't see a thing. The string that held the
patch over his bad eye was slipping. The square of
ancient leather slapped his face, disorienting him.
He bounced off a drainpipe, did an ungainly whirl,
kept running. Behind him, he heard the sound of a
bell, coming after him, clanging furiously. Ahead
was a gutter. He leaped into it and whistled over the
frozen grime, sliding fast as anything. The gutter
ended in a rusting grate. Pikey hurled himself over
it, struck the cobbles running. His fingers went to
the patch, trying desperately to tighten the string,
but it wouldn't stay, and he couldn't stop. It was only
about to get worse.

The cobble faery tripped him in Bluebottle
Street.

There Pikey was, a knob of black bread clutched
inside his jacket, pounding up a street that was as

empty and icy as any in London. His pursuer was still two or three corners behind him. Pikey was sure he would get away. And then he felt the tremor in the ground beneath him, the rattle of the cobbles as a tiny faery raced through its secret tunnels. It popped up the stone just as Pikey's foot was flying toward it.

Pikey let out a yelp and went careering into the wall of a house. His head knocked against stone. Pain shuddered through him, and he heard a wicked little voice sing, "Clumsy-patty, clumsy-patty, who's a clumsy pitty-patty?"

Pikey spun, pushing himself away from the wall.

The faery was peeking out from under the lifted cobblestone, black-bead eyes glittering. It was a spryte, not three inches from head to toe. Bits of frosty branches grew behind its pointed ears and a dreadful grin was on its face, stretching halfway around. It was a very yellow grin, full of prickly little teeth.

"Shut up," Pikey hissed. He ran at it, determined to smash it into a stringy mess. Too slow. The faery pulled down the cobble like a hat and was gone.

Pikey froze. He glanced back down the street, listening, making sure he still had some seconds to spare. Then he struck his boot heel against the ground three times, getting softer with each strike so that it would sound like he was walking away. The faery shot back up, still grinning. And Pikey leaped, straight onto the cobble. There was a squeak. The cobble smashed back into place. The faery's hand twitched where it was pinched in.

"Serves you right, too," Pikey said, but he had no time to enjoy his little victory. The bell was close now, echoing up between the buildings. An instant later, a huge officer in blue and crimson skidded into the street. A leadface.

"Thief!" the leadface shouted, his voice oddly flat and dull inside his iron half-helmet. *"Thief!"* But before he could see Pikey, Pikey was moving again, slipping under an archway and down a steep flight of steps, heart hammering.